Jeni Finds Safety

THE MAXWELL BRIDES SERIES BOOK 1

KRISSYANN GRANGER

Tug Hill Publishing
Company, LLC

Copyright

To request permissions, contact the publisher at krissyanngranger@google.com

ISBN:9798729714414 (Ebook)
ISBN: 978-1-955609-00-5 (Paperback)
ISBN: 978-1-955609-10-4 (Hardcover)

Second printing edition 2022

Tug Hill Publishing
Company, LLC

Published by:
Tug Hill Publishing Company, LLC.
West Leyden, NY 13489

https://www.facebook.com/KrissyannGranger

Dedication

For my dear friend, Jeni Seavert.
Without your constant support I never could have
finished this series. You were here for me, reading every
word and offering encouragement and insight. No matter
how much you had going on, you always made the time to
read and help.
For my sister, Amanda Dechau. I appreciate the hours of
reading and miles of detailed notes that you provided. You
added color to my series and I couldn't have done it
without you. I love and appreciate you.

Introduction

I wanted to take a moment to tell you a little about Jeni Finds Safety, and the beginning of The Maxwell Brides Series. I had a load of fun writing this collection of stories, and I'm a writer for life after this. The next five books in this series are coming in 2023 and I can not wait to share them with you.

You should know before you begin this journey that The Maxwell Bride Series is meant to be read in order, and completely. Many of the questions remaining at the end of book one are answered in book four, or five. Some people have found that frustrating, so I thought I would let you know up front. If you're not in for an epic saga of love and adventure, turn back now because if you start this series, you won't ever want to stop.

Another thing to know is that there is swearing, and adult situations inside these pages. I didn't drop any big bombs though, the "F" word isn't in here. There is sex on the page, but it is fairly mild, I'd say the spice level is medium at best. And the only other thing you might watch out for is a little violence, including one scene where Jeni is assaulted. I don't write graphic scenes of abuse, but it is there, so I thought you should know.

I try to stay accurate for the time period, but sometimes a more colloquial term just works and I don't kill myself to research a better old-fashioned phrase. There are no "fiddlesticks," in these pages but there might be a "freak out." If I researched the etymology of every word, I'd still be writing the book.

These books are written to be enjoyed. I hope you read them like you're watching a movie. Let them take you away to another time. Escape for a few hours and become someone else.

Books six-ten are on the way for 2023, and as long as I stay on track and don't get distracted by all the other books I want to write, books 11-15 should be coming along in 2024. I'm not ready to promise that yet though, there is an Oregon Trail series doing the woodpecker inside my skull right now.

As always, indie authors need as many reviews as we can get. Reviews sell books as much as the covers, and maybe more than blurbs. If you enjoyed this book please take a moment to leave a brief review, or even a rating. I read and truly appreciate every review.

Chapter One

S eptember 1884

It was time for life to start.

The cross-country trip from Massachusetts to Montana had been grueling, but her destination was worth the agony. Soon, the wretched stagecoach would roll into town, and Jeni MacGregor would get married. Her new husband would take her home from the church, where they would eat a wedding dinner with his family.

Her new family.

He'd outlined the plan in his letter, and having a plan settled her nerves a little. A very little. She needed a hot bath and a hot meal. Maybe not in that order. It would be nice if she could have had them before her wedding, but that was not part of the plan. She brushed the dust from her dingy gray skirt and tried to press out wrinkles that were set in after days of wear. She'd looked cleaner. Lord knows, she'd smelled better.

The matchmaker, Mrs. Phillips, had warned her that this was the way it went for mail-order brides. She'd tie herself to a stranger feeling hungry, dirty, and exhausted.

Her heart squeezed, and a rock formed in the pit of her stomach. This was hardly the wedding day of her dreams.

Jeni wanted to fall into a warm bed and sleep for a week. She wished to awake in a danger-free world. If she could have that wish, she wouldn't be on her way to marry a stranger. If she had that wish, maybe she could have married for love. She sighed. There was no point in painting rainbows when storm clouds followed you. She gazed out the window, sucked in a breath, and rubbed at her eyes. Dust had turned her eyelids to sandpaper, and no tears came to help her out. Months of stress and anxiety had dried them up. Tears might have been better. She ground another layer off her eyeballs.

Exhaustion and anxiety wore on a body. Sleeping on a train or stagecoach was impossible, and she hadn't been sleeping well before beginning her journey. A private sleeping compartment was out of her budget, even though her fiancé had been generous with a travel stipend. She'd been careful with his money, afraid to waste a cent. Instead, she'd slept, sitting on a hard bench on the train for four days, imagining the future and hoping for a miracle.

Jeni's only luck so far had been that the Northern Pacific Railroad could bring her within two hours of her destination. Thank goodness it was almost over.

The carriage jolted, and Jeni struck her head

against the window frame. Again. Crashing around inside the coach for two hours had bruised her elbow and given her a terrible headache. The driver didn't seem to avoid the holes at all. She narrowed her eyes; he was aiming for them.

At twenty-four years old, she shouldn't be so worn down, but Jeni MacGregor was at the end of her rope and nearing her destination. Exhaustion-fueled anxiety had her writhing in her seat. The thumping of her heart matched the smashing hooves eating up the open road. Mr. Maxwell would be at the station waiting to meet the stage. Her groom, a man she'd never seen, would take her to meet the reverend. She nibbled her lip as she tried to brush the wrinkles away again.

Jeni had received only one long letter from Mr. Maxwell. In it, he described himself as tall and wide, with shoulder-length black hair and dark skin. He was half Indian. It was important to him she know before accepting his proposal. There was a stigma involved with marrying across races, and she appreciated he gave her a choice. Race was the least of Jeni's worries. She had enough of her own problems. People often judged her by her appearance, so she'd learned not to do the same to others.

What did he mean by 'wide,' though?

The image of their rotund baker back home startled a nervous giggle out of Jeni. Mr. Potter was the tallest, fattest man she'd ever seen. When Jeni first read Mr. Maxwell's letter, she'd pictured Mr. Potter meeting the stage to take her to the church. Jeni hoped her mental image was incorrect, but no matter what she did, she couldn't shake it. She'd marry him, though, no matter what he looked like.

She slumped in the seat. Beggars couldn't be choosy.

Mr. Maxwell's letter was forthcoming and gave the sense of a man of honor. She'd reread his letter many times before she left Boston. She'd studied it even more while she traveled. He was direct and straightforward about his life and what he wanted.

The scenery around her changed once again. Small purple mountains appeared in the distance. They didn't have mountains like that in Boston, and certainly not from the windows of the Merciful Hearts Orphanage, where she grew up. Mr. Maxwell's ranch was near them, but not in them. The faint scent of crushed grass mingled with the dust from the road. A lovely piney scent of early autumn drifted in. Even with the dust, the air was cleaner than she'd left behind. The air was cleaner than any she'd ever breathed before and she was happy to live the rest of her life in the wide open air. She'd be excited if she weren't so anxious.

Mr. Maxwell had built a house on the ranch that he worked with his cousins and close friends. He needed a wife who would cook for him. Jeni was an excellent cook, and she couldn't wait to prove her value in the kitchen. She could clean and do laundry, make his clothes, and raise his children, too. She'd be his friend.

His letter said nothing of love.

He'd said he didn't realize how much their housekeepers cared for him until he moved out of the main house. The housekeepers, he'd said, were more like mothers than employees. He missed the chatter of Rose and the quiet comfort of her twin sister, Iris. It was nice that he'd taken the time to describe his home and family. Having other women nearby would make her more comfortable.

She'd never been part of a family before.

Mr. Maxwell wanted children. Jeni always paused at reading that part. She wanted children too, but children with this stranger she'd imagined looking like Mr. Potter made her pulse jump and her skin crawl. Living in the orphanage wasn't like having a family of her own, and she'd always wanted one. So, no matter what, she wasn't turning back. She'd do whatever she needed to do.

He'd promised security, and she needed that more than she needed an attractive husband. She figured it was unlikely she'd get a handsome husband as a mail-order bride, anyway. Mr. Potter's image popped into her head again. She sighed, folded the letter, and returned it to her reticule.

She had to admit Mr. Maxwell had courage. His letter hid nothing. Jeni expected the possibility of anger with the townspeople over the mixed marriage. He'd warned her about the stigma over mail-order brides. The women in town had not received others with kindness. He'd also described long and brutal winters, being stuck on the ranch for months on end.

She could trust him. Everything in her heart told her she could. He would take care of her. His detailed letter was fair, and she believed he wasn't luring her into a situation under false pretenses. That had given her the confidence to accept him without further correspondence.

Of course, she battled with fear and anxiety. She'd be a fool if she didn't. Jeni pictured every way that their meeting could go wrong. She would deal with whatever came up.

THE COACH ROUNDED THE CORNER INTO TOWN AND stopped in front of the depot. It was a small building, little more than a shed at the far end of town. A hitching rail in front and stable behind was all the station boasted.

Jeni gulped back fear. She'd never seen such a small town. A single street of false-fronted businesses and two side streets were the entirety of Hope.

Jeni waited for the driver, fidgeting with the wrinkles on her dress and nibbling her lips until she tasted blood. She forced herself to still and followed the progress of the driver. The stage dipped to the side as he climbed down. A thump told her he'd placed a step for her. Then he opened the door and offered his hand.

Her eyes blinked in the afternoon sun. She searched for her groom until she had to drop her gaze to watch her feet. Stumbling into the dirt was not how she wanted to introduce herself.

After so many days of anxious travel, Jeni's gaze

landed on the most beautiful man she'd ever seen. Maybe not the most handsome, but his intriguing features held her spellbound. Mr. Maxwell was not at all what she'd imagined. When he'd described himself as wide in his letter, he should've said broad.

He was no Mr. Potter!

She delighted in her good luck and beamed at him, hoping this was the man she'd marry.

"You're not Miss MacGregor, are you?" He asked as he glanced over her shoulder at the stage.

"I am. You're Mr. Maxwell?" She raised her eyebrows and cocked to the side.

He didn't reply. Just watched her swipe at the front of her dress and nibble away at her lip. He looked like he wanted to run.

She forced herself to stop fidgeting.

He finally nodded, then sighed and stared. His jaw muscles twitched as he ground his teeth, and his eyes narrowed. Why was he angry? What did he expect? She was a mail-order bride.

He could have received worse.

"I'm happy to meet you." She held her hand out to him. "I'm your bride."

He groaned. He actually groaned.

Of all the reactions she'd prepared for, this was not one.

Jeni was unsure how to progress. This couldn't be her Mr. Maxwell. She experienced a momentary disappointment at the loss of such an attractive groom, but instead of dwelling on it, she scanned the vicinity for another man waiting on the stage.

"What are you doing?" his voice was deep and smooth.

"Looking for the Mr. Maxwell who sent for me."

"That's me."

Yet he'd taken one look at her and groaned out loud. It couldn't be.

Jeni was horrified. She was offended.

His refusal was a punch in the gut. It stayed with her long after the initial paralysis of shock wore off. Surprise faded to panic. She was destitute. She was in Montana with a groom who was repulsed by her. What if he refused to marry her? Jeni couldn't afford to go home and even if she could, she had no home to go back to. She needed him to marry her. She had to force him to honor his proposal.

How humiliating.

Jeni's appearance often inspired powerful reactions from people, but this was extreme. There was nothing she could do. Jeni held her head high, straightened her spine, and looked up into his inky eyes. She wouldn't back down. She came here to marry him, and she was going to marry him.

"This won't work," he said.

"What?" She couldn't puzzle why he stood in front of her, opening and closing his fist, as if she'd somehow lied to him. What could he have expected?

Jeni wasn't afraid of her hesitant fiancé. Even simmering with anger, he remained calm. The tick in his jaw and tension in his hands were the only outward evidence of his feelings. She felt safe, insecure, but safe.

The butterflies in her belly robbed her of the

ability to think. He looked like he wanted to punch a wall. The longer he stared at her in mute frustration, the more wildly the butterflies flapped.

What is his problem? His letter had included train fare and requested that she telegram the date of her arrival. She'd followed his instructions. He hadn't asked for a physical description, and she hadn't provided one.

His rejection broke her heart. He was everything she needed. He was big and strong, and he would protect her if she were his wife. She craned her neck to make eye contact with him and held it.

"I'll take your things to the boarding house and get you a room." The growl in his voice, and his movements showed impatience. He did not take her outstretched hand, and he didn't offer his arm when he turned and walked away.

Jeni half-ran to keep up with his long strides. He didn't slow to accommodate her. "Why the boarding house? Your letter said we'd meet the reverend as soon as the stage arrived, then head to your ranch for dinner." When he didn't answer, panic mounted in the pit of her stomach, and Jeni could not let him dump her in the middle of this town by herself.

How could she be so stupid?

How did she get herself into these messes?

She had no luck at all.

"We're not getting married. I'll get a room for you at the boarding house and a return ticket on the next stage."

Defeated, Jeni pulled her composure around her like a cloak and followed along beside him.

Just hold it together.

People stared, following her and Mr. Maxwell with their curious eyes as they marched down the street.

Nothing ever changed.

"I can't go back to Boston. I have no home there now. I'm here to marry you. Don't you think I deserve an explanation?"

Mr. Maxwell looked down at her, then glanced away. He acted like he didn't want to look at her at all. Why would it bother him to look at her?

"You ain't for me."

"What does that mean? You are Scott Maxwell, aren't you? I came here to marry you. You sent for me!" She tipped her head to the side and stared at his profile. His features were bold. Chiseled. That's how they would describe him in her cherished dime novels. She watched the tick in his jaw and the tension in his neck and shoulders. He stared hard, straight ahead, avoiding the gaze of every person in town, and everybody in town watched with interest.

"I mean what I said." He grumbled without looking at her.

Jeni wanted to reason with him. She'd always enjoyed taking care of people, bringing joy or peace to people who needed it. Her biggest desires in life were to be needed and loved for herself. She wanted to have that with him. It's what she'd placed all her faith in as she'd traveled across the country. She could not let him do this to her.

Backed into a corner, though, she had a ferocity that surprised even herself. She was a fighter when push came to shove. He was pushing. The tightness in her chest was suffocating. She could not let him out of his promise.

The only thing guaranteed for a mail-order bride was a groom, and she was going to have hers.

Stopping in the middle of the sidewalk, Jeni turned on the giant man. They were halfway down the main street of town, standing in front of the large mercantile window, in sight of just about the entire community. People stared, not wanting to miss the scene.

She hated attention, and she was drawing a lot. Too angry and desperate to back down, she faced him and planted her feet on the wooden sidewalk, on full display. If she read him right, he didn't want attention any more than she did. She'd use his discomfort against him if she had to.

This was a heck of a way to start a marriage.

Jeni stepped in front of him and pulled her spine as tight as she could. She wouldn't let him treat her like this. He'd made her an offer of marriage, and he would not reject her, especially without reason. At least if she knew why, she had something to work with.

With one hand held up in front of her, fingers splayed, she stopped him in his tracks. One more step, and her palm would rest dead center of his abdomen. For an instant, she imagined she could feel the heat from him on the palm of her outstretched hand.

"What changed your mind?"

———

THE LONE PASSENGER CLIMBED OUT OF THE STAGECOACH and approached him. Scott groaned out loud; this could not be Jeni MacGregor.

What was he going to do with a woman like this?

There was one thing he would not do. Marry her.

He should've asked her to write back and describe herself. Or he should've been more specific on his specifications regarding his bride's appearance. He had a picture in his mind of a mail-order bride, and it was not this.

He looked over her shoulder, into the stage, hoping to find another woman, but he knew there was none. She'd looked up at him with shining eyes and a bright smile. She'd looked so hopeful and relieved to see him. Scott wished his feelings could match hers. He hated to let her down, but he had to do it. He couldn't take this woman home; he couldn't marry a woman like her.

When he sent away for a mail-order bride, Scott expected a nice, plain woman to arrive. She could be short or tall, fat or thin. He didn't care; he'd only written about the qualifications he needed in a wife. He should've realized that pretty and ugly were things to be specified.

Scott ran his hand through his overgrown hair and shoved his hat back down on his head.

Love was never his goal in marriage. Scott needed a woman to take care of the house and feed him while he was working on the ranch. He wanted children, sure, but he didn't think that he'd need a lot of attraction to manage that. He'd expected a plain desperate woman, or a spinster to arrive, needing security and a home.

What would he do with a woman like this?

Jeni MacGregor was more than gorgeous. She was stunning!

She caught the eye of everyone. They'd drawn a crowd because small towns liked a dramatic scene, and because of curiosity over the new woman on the street.

Miss MacGregor was about average at five feet five, but was still short compared to his six feet one. Her hair, hidden under a big gray bonnet, showed bright auburn red curls that peeked out around her face and at her nape. He'd never seen such bold red, even the fake red hair he'd seen at the saloon.

If her hair weren't enough to turn a man to mush, the rest of her would do the job. Her eyes were mesmerizing, and he couldn't look for fear of staring. They were bright and clear and some sort of color between green and blue, with tiny golden flecks playing around the edges of her pupils. Long, dark eyelashes rested against her ivory cheeks when she lowered her gaze.

She had the loveliest complexion, pale with a delicate blush that made him want to protect her. He wished he could run his fingertip down her cheek. He bet her skin was silk. She also possessed the most kissable rose-colored lips he'd ever seen. Her bottom lip was fuller than the top, which had a perfect dip in the center.

For crying out loud. This woman was stealing his wits.

The instant his eyes lowered to her mouth, he'd imagined her taste. He needed to get her off the street and into the boarding house so he could get away from her. He needed to get her back on a stage to Boston.

She was a temptation he could not afford.

He'd kick his own ass for his thoughtlessness.

He'd send her back home right now, but there wasn't another stage until next week, so he'd put her in the boarding house until then. One of his brothers, well, they were like brothers to him, would have to ensure her safety until he could get her out of town.

God damn, he was a selfish son of a bitch. He wished he could take her to the church and then home, as he'd planned.

She couldn't be his, though. It wouldn't work.

She didn't know what she was getting herself into.

He snatched her bags from the driver and turned toward the boarding house. She skipped and hopped, trying to keep up with his long stride, but he didn't slow. He could only think of getting her out of sight.

Her eyes shifted from side to side in panic as they strode down the Main Street. If only there was a way to help her. A way that didn't involve marrying her. He racked his brain, feeling terrible for bringing her to the territory. If only he'd considered the possibility that someone like her might arrive, he could've avoided all of this.

Damn it. He kept his eyes forward, avoiding the hurt in her face.

He needed to talk to his brothers. Scott mentally groaned but held back any further outward displeasure. He already knew what they would say. They would tell him to marry her.

They didn't understand.

Caine would tell him to screw everyone, take the pretty girl and run. Caleb would just go on and on about his right to be happy whenever he could. Will wouldn't care, as long as he wasn't being tied down. Hank would get hung up on her feelings and Scott's duty to the girl he'd sent for. Daniel was the only one who might see his side, but even he would want to fix it without sending the girl away.

Scott cursed his circumstances.

In a perfect world, he'd have won the jackpot with this treasure. This wasn't a perfect world, though. This was Montana Territory, and there was no lottery his brown skin would let him win.

She sure didn't win any lottery.

He was so caught up, brooding over his dilemma, she shocked the hell out of him when she spun and planted her feet in front of him.

Chapter Two

W ith her dander up, Jeni lost all sense of self-preservation.

Knowing that about herself didn't make a difference.

She blocked a man who towered over her from three feet away. He could have brushed her aside, but he stopped. She held her hand steady between them and stood her ground.

Something in his nearly black eyes gave the impression that she was safe. He was disappointed, but he wouldn't hurt her, and that gave her the courage to confront this giant.

"I'm not taking another step without an answer. Why are you rejecting me?" She pulled her spine even tighter and added, "I deserve an explanation." She forced her hand not to shake as she held steady. Her heart knocked against her rib cage, and she was sure everyone for a mile could hear it. She wanted to be strong.

She was determined to be strong.

He stared at her.

"We can stand here all day if you'd like, Mr. Maxwell, but I will have my answer. I've traveled almost a week to get here. If you're abandoning me now, I should know why. I have no friends here. This is cruel and I deserve an explanation." She fought tears. It figures, after being like sandpaper for the last four days, now her lids wanted to water and add to her public embarrassment. She held her breath and willed the tears away. Crying on the street in front of strangers was out of the question, but she couldn't get control over her emotions after the exhausting trip and bitter surprise.

"You alright, ma'am?" A man called over her hesitant groom's shoulder. The man's eyes ogled her body. She should be used to leering men by now, but she wasn't. A shudder shot through her. When Mr. Maxwell shifted his weight to the left and blocked the man, Jeni was encouraged.

He cared.

"I'm fine, thank you." She replied, not looking his way. She kept her eyes locked on Mr. Maxwell's, hoping her voice was strong. His eyes narrowed, but he didn't speak.

People drew closer, wanting as much fuel for the gossip mill as possible. This kind of attention would hurt her, but she needed to see it through. Let the people say what they wanted. They would talk no matter what.

Jeni had taken a stand, and she couldn't bring herself to budge one inch until she got what she wanted. An explanation. She'd rather turn and run, hide in the boarding house, and never come out again, but her pride rooted her to the spot.

Jeni had never reacted to a man like she reacted to him. It was like magnets pushing and pulling at her. Most men made her nervous, mistrusting, afraid. He made her feel safe. She couldn't let that go. Why was he fighting it? She couldn't figure it out, and she wasn't letting him off the hook.

She wanted him to marry her, and not only because she was his mail-order bride.

The only thing anyone ever noticed was her appearance, and she wanted to be wanted for more than that.

Jeni considered all men threatening, because even the nice ones could be dangerous. Men changed from sweethearts to monsters in the blink of an eye. Rejecting them was dangerous. Her instincts had saved her more than once.

Those instincts told her Mr. Maxwell was trustworthy.

Jeni had never felt safe in Boston, and the last few months were the worst. She'd rejected a mighty man, Roger Benson, but he wouldn't take no for an answer. He began a campaign of stalking and threatening her. He had the muscle to back his threats up. Hired muscle. Mr. Benson didn't care about her; he just wanted a pretty wife. There were plenty of lovely women in Boston. Why'd he set his cap for her? Mr. Benson frightened her more than all the other men in Boston combined.

He would terrorize her for the rest of her life, and she refused to live in fear forever.

If Mr. Maxwell didn't marry her, she wouldn't feel safe here, either. If Mr. Benson didn't get her, someone else would. Looking around, she didn't like that idea either. The men were a lot rougher than she'd expected. They were mostly dirty cowboys and farmers, and most of them had sauntered out of the saloon at the end of the street. She didn't see a single acceptable alternative husband in the crowd.

What she'd give for Mr. Potter to step forward now.

The people in the town stared, not even feigning innocence. She doubted anyone remained inside the saloon. They'd wandered out, one by one, for a smoke on the porch after she'd rounded on Mr. Maxwell. Groups formed around the shops, and she could feel eyes burning into her from inside the mercantile. People in the street gathered closer, watching the scene play out. They had no shame as they closed in.

The only comfort she felt in the entire situation was in the way Mr. Maxwell shifted to block as many eyes as possible.

She should back down, get out of sight, and talk to him in privacy, but anger and hurt kept her in place. Jeni couldn't break eye contact with him. She was determined to know why he wanted to break their engagement..

"What's going on here?" a raspy male voice demanded.

Jeni turned to see a pot-bellied man waddling her way. He was sweating and winded, as if he'd been running, but he didn't look like he could actually run if he tried. His smell had reached her before she'd turned to look at him. The star pinned to his vest and guns slung under his overhanging belly said he was the sheriff. He displayed the red-faced appearance of a man more likely to be found in the saloon than at work. His beady eyes scanned her body with unhidden lust.

He was not to be trusted. She stepped closer to Mr. Maxwell and lowered her hand to her side, clutching her skirt.

"You holdin' up this woman, injun?" He asked before he spat on the ground in front of Mr. Maxwell's feet. Turning to Jeni, he sneered, "I'm Sherriff Danes." He puffed himself up. "I'll help ya." His chapped lips stretched to reveal corroded yellow and brown teeth. The sight and smell of him tied her stomach in a nauseous knot. She slid a little further away. One more step and she would fall off the sidewalk.

He was still too close.

"I'm holding him up." She stated matter-of-factly. "I have business with Mr. Maxwell. If I need any help, I'll surely call on you." Jeni hoped he would move away, but instead, he wrapped his beefy, clammy hand on her elbow and pulled her away from her protector.

She felt violated and couldn't stop a flinch.

He didn't notice. "A sweet little thing like you

don't have no business with no injun." He jerked her arm to punctuate his comment.

"I appreciate your concern, but I am fine. I will be out of the street as soon as I finish my conversation with my fiancé." She emphasized the last word, hoping Mr. Maxwell's imposing figure would entice the revolting sheriff to release her.

"The hell you say?" The sheriff demanded. "No injun in this town is marryin' no white woman."

"I came to town as his mail-order bride. We have an agreement, and I intend to hold him to it." She tried to remove her arm from his grip, but his fingers were a vice, pressing on the bruises she'd collected on the stagecoach.

"A mail-order bride, you say? I'll have ya instead. I was thinkin' on gettin' me a wife, and you're a real pretty one. You need a white man, anyway." He tugged on her arm again. She resisted, leaned as far away as possible and silently pleaded with Mr. Maxwell to step in and end the abuse.

In the crowd, someone whispered loud enough for everyone to hear, "I think it's Cooper's new girl."

The sign announcing Cooper's Saloon at the end of the street hadn't escaped her attention, and neither did the gasp from the ladies closest to the loud-whispering drunkard leaning against the hitching rail.

"Sheriff! You wouldn't marry a whore, would ya?" A woman called with absolute shock in her voice. She pressed a handkerchief to her heart, faking a flutter.

"Cooper's been talkin' up his new girl all

month," the same stumbling man announced. He lost his balance and had to grab onto the hitching rail to keep from falling. Jeni wished his hat had landed in the nasty water trough. It would serve him right for starting such a rumor.

"Someone should shut old Cooper down." Another woman said as she consoled the mock-fainting nitwit.

Jeni flinched, tried not to roll her eyes, and didn't bother to defend herself.

The crowd closed in, shouting opinions.

"I'll take ya, whore or not," a filthy mongrel in front of the hitching rail shouted with a laugh.

"It ain't right to have a thing like that living among decent people," the supportive friend said, bolstered by the other woman's antics.

"Bring her down to the saloon; we'll her. Coop did good this time."

"Ne'er saw such a purty woman in m'life. I'd pay to look at 'er."

"I'll tell yer wife ya said so." That got a laugh out of the group.

"I'd put money down for a ride." Jeni flinched.

"Your wife'd skin ya alive for even thinkin' it."

That last one snapped her out of her silence. Jeni was used to these types of comments, but she wasn't used to having them shouted in the middle of the street. She pulled as much courage as she could from Mr. Maxwell's gaze and stiffened her spine. She'd picked this fight, and she was going to hold up her end. "Whom I choose to marry is none of your concern. Remove your hand from my arm. You're hurting me. I made my choice before leaving Boston, and I will marry Mr. Maxwell. I will only marry Mr. Maxwell."

Instead of releasing her, the sheriff squeezed harder. His fingers cut into her tender flesh. She wanted to be strong, to stand tall, but when those meaty fingers dug into her arm, she cried out.

The anger rolling off Mr. Maxwell became palpable. "If you want to keep that hand, you'd better take it off Miss MacGregor's arm." His voice remained calm, but there was no mistaking the threat.

"You ain't gonna marry this woman."

"No, but I won't watch you abuse her in the street, either."

The crowd gave the sheriff courage. He didn't let her go. Instead, he tugged hard enough that she fell against him. Her stomach rebelled, and if she'd had anything to vomit, she would've unloaded all over him. Instead, she heaved and choked on nothing.

"I won't tell you again," Mr. Maxwell said.

The sheriff reached for his gun, and Jeni froze. Her wide eyes clung to her intended. He tried to send some silent message with a shake of his head, but she sprang into action.

She had to protect him. He was her fiancé, and she'd put him in danger. She couldn't let the sheriff shoot him when she needed him so badly. He was her safety, the only safety she'd ever felt.

She wrenched her arm and dislodged the sheriff's grip, and then she threw herself at her reluctant fiancé. He had no choice but to catch her as she wrapped her arms as far around his body and held on. Her hands burned where they touched the solid planes of his back. It was obscene, but she couldn't let anyone hurt him. Jeni tried to cover as much of him as she could. The crowd hummed with her brazen behavior.

Mr. Maxwell pried her arms from his body and shifted her behind him. He stood between her and the blustering sheriff.

The whispers increased.

Instead of her saving him, he was protecting her. She couldn't get back around him. Every time she tried to move in front of him, he blocked her. He faced off with the sheriff and hid her.

"You'll be sorry for that, injun," the sheriff cursed and spat.

Jeni placed her hand in the middle of Scott's back and held her breath. She didn't know how else to support him. It was a simple gesture, but she hoped he could read the apology in her palm. The touch was inappropriate.

The ladies would think her dirty for sure.

HER HAND PRESSED INTO THE CENTER OF HIS BACK. Warm and sweet, giving him back the patience that had only moments before escaped his control. He settled back into the heels of his boots and stared the sheriff down.

Scott fought to maintain a surface calm while his blood boiled and his muscles twitched. It was a skill developed over years of need, but it came at a cost. He locked his eyes on the sheriff, ready to rip the bastard to shreds.

She was his responsibility, even if it could never become forever.

Danes was either too stupid to take the warning, or too bold from the effects of drink and the energy from the crowd. He pranced like a peacock. He'd offered to marry Jeni. It would be over his dead body before that ever happened. Scott came danger-ously close to agreeing to marriage, just to save her from that terrible fate.

Scott had waited to see how Jeni would handle everything before swooping in and taking over. She was a tough little thing, standing up to him like that, and he wanted to see how she would manage Danes. Few men possessed the courage to stand toe to toe with a Maxwell man. Between his size, heritage, and reputation, he got by without needing to fight. A threatening look, or sharp word, was all the fight he needed to cow most men.

Not Jeni MacGregor, though. It was impossible not to respect a spirit like that. If he could choose a wife, she was just the kind he'd want. There was more to her than beauty. It'd only taken minutes to see that. She was so easy to respect.

Once she'd thrown herself at him, he had no choice but to take over. He was glad to have her away from Danes. One more squeeze on her arm and he would have fed the asshole his teeth. It felt better with her behind him, but now he had to face down the ego-bruised sheriff.

He wished he could just throw her into the wagon and drive her right out of town.

He resisted a sigh.

Vulnerability was not something he liked to show on the street. His disappointment would have to wait for another time.

When his sister-in-law Amy had died, he'd watched his brother grieve, and he'd vowed never to love a woman like that. He never wanted to feel pain that deep, even if love was worth it. And Jeni was a woman he'd love if he spent enough time with her.

"I'll have that woman," Danes growled.

Scott's face heated, and his muscles coiled, ready to strike. He was about to pound the sheriff when he saw movement in his periphery.

He suppressed a smile as Danes' glare turned into a sneer. Then Scott's brothers flanked him on either side, and Danes nearly shit his pants. His hand dropped from his gun, and he took a stumbling step back. Scott rarely found a man willing to face him down, and he'd never met one willing to face down The Maxwell Group.

THE NEXT THING JENI KNEW, MEN SURROUNDED HER from every side.

Big men.

Strong, dangerous men.

The crowd closed in, and Jeni hid behind Scott.

Scott, she thought, not Mr. Maxwell. They were in this together now: he was hers.

One hand splayed across his back and the other twisted wrinkles into her skirt. She said a prayer for his safety and tasted blood as she nibbled her lip.

Vulnerability was getting old. She wished she could protect herself.

Jeni sighed, accepting reality. She needed a man to protect her, and she wanted this man.

Jeni glimpsed the sheriff through the gap between Scott and another man. His courage was failing him. He held both hands up, and when he sputtered and backtracked, Jeni realized that these new men were Scott's friends, probably the brothers he's written about.

Realizing that they weren't there to hurt her squashed some of her anxiety, her hand steadied, and she released the lip she'd been about to bite clean off. They were there to protect her, and they would defend Scott, too. He didn't deserve the trouble that followed her, even if he had determined to reject her.

Without concern for her reputation, Jeni released the breath she had been holding and let her forehead rest against Scott's back. Her skirts swirled around his calves, and she breathed his scent. He smelled like horse and leather and pine. She closed her eyes and inhaled deeply.

For the moment, at least, she was safe.

Without lifting her head, Jeni glanced around. The crowd was on top of them, but less threatening. With another breath, she relaxed more against Scott's back. She held tight to the sides of his body and hoped he would accept her.

The strength of muscle under her fingertips made her more determined to marry him, and every moment of safety behind the wall of his brothers fortified her determination further. Although he stood in front of her, his support wrapped around her.

That was silly, as he wasn't even touching her.

She sensed it just the same.

He didn't stop her from touching him. She rested against his back while he dealt with the sheriff, and he didn't step out of her reach. It gave her a measure of hope.

Jeni couldn't see the sheriff. She tried to look around Scott's shoulder, but he moved to block her. Another man shifted, and they trapped her behind them. Two men shielded her from behind. They were so close that her skirts pressed against her legs as they boxed her in. One more man stood close to her side. Jeni tipped her head to see his face. He was beautiful, too. They all were. Maybe she thought so because she was protected from every side. It wasn't that, though. They each had more than just a physical presence.

They were a very handsome group.

The anger that had sustained her for so long abandoned her. The only thing Jeni had left in her was weakness and rejection. She was more vulnerable now than she'd ever been in her life. Losing her anger ushered the return of desperation.

She wilted.

The sheriff grunted and then his heavy boots banged down the sidewalk.

Was it over?

They hadn't even said a word. Their presence was enough to drive him back. Theirs was the protection she'd come to the West hoping to find. She needed to get Scott to marry her. Nobody else would protect her as he would. Nobody else could.

The tears her windburned eyes had longed for finally fell.

Scott turned to her and drew her into his chest, holding her as she wept. She lost herself in his embrace, wondering how he could hold her so tenderly and reject her so completely at the same time. His big hand cradled the back of her head in such a comforting way. Jeni had never held her in like that before. She sank into his embrace and took all the support she could from him.

The other men did not leave. They gave her time to get her feelings under control. None spoke, but silent communication was obviously going on over her head. Their giant bodies shielded Jeni until the crowd dispersed and she could breathe again.

With a final sniff, Jeni straightened. Without opening her eyes, she breathed deeply to calm herself. Once. Twice. The gentlest touch brought her back to reality. Scott's thumb wiped a tear from her cheek and nearly started the whole outburst over again. His eyes softened and his jaw unclenched as his anger dissipated. He looked almost as defeated as she felt. For the briefest moment, she thought he would give her what she needed. Nobody had ever touched her so tenderly before, and she never wanted him to stop. He released her, though, and she missed him instantly.

He said, "Do you see now why I can't marry you?"

"No."

"You must know you're beautiful."

Seriously? How could that be his problem?

"Bullshit" was cursed by at least two of his brothers.

Scott jerked his head up and glared at them.

"I don't understand." Jeni was out of steam. She needed to get through to this stubborn man, but she didn't understand his refusal at all.

"You'd be in danger."

"Why? Because a few people in town are against a white woman marrying someone like you?" Jeni's skirt would never recover from the twisting.

He didn't answer, but the fight had gone out of her. "It doesn't matter. I'm in danger either way."

She turned, picked up her carpetbag and walked in the direction they'd been going before she'd spun on him. He wouldn't change his mind today. She'd rest and try again. She wasn't used to crying in the street, and the embarrassment of their little show compounded with the stress of everything that had driven her out West in the first place. She was at the end of her rope, and needed to have a long private cry.

Scott picked up her other bag and followed. His brothers murmured, but she didn't turn. They walked as a group to the end of the sidewalk, where his brothers broke off and headed toward the saloon.

Scott called to her and motioned a large white house with a new white picket fence and immaculate gardens. The little sign above the door said, "Bix's Boarding House."

With a sigh, as all of her hopes crashed around her, Jeni approached the gate and entered the yard.

He wasn't going to marry her.

She was truly destitute. At least in the city, she'd had her two best friends, Denise and Sarah. Here she had nobody.

Not even the man she'd come to marry.

Chapter Three

J eni had said, "I'm in danger either way."

What did that mean?

Scott followed her down the street and then called to her and indicated the boarding house. Her sagging shoulders and slow pace ate at him. He didn't want to let her down, but the best he could do was protect her while she was in town and try to get her back on the next stage.

"What's wrong with you? Take her to the church, and let's get her home." Caine shoved Scott hard enough to make him stumble. Caine and his twin brother Caleb were Scott's cousins on his mother's side. They were closer than cousins though, they had long considered each other brothers. Daniel, Hank, and Will had been with them since they were all teenagers, and the group ran the Maxwell Ranch together. They had created a successful and respected organization with over a decade of hard work. The Maxwell Group was known far and wide; their network spread from coast to coast.

"You know better."

Caine shook his head. "Live your life, man. You can't let what happened to Amy stop you from being happy forever. Hell, I'm thinking about writing for a mail-order bride. It's time for us to move on." Caine didn't speak about Amy often, and hearing him say Amy's name caused a fist to close around Scott's throat as her image flashed in his mind. This was more than Caine had said about Amy in more than three years. Scott choked up, but it didn't change the situation with Jeni. Scott clapped him on the back and watched the sway of Jeni's figure as she walked up the street ahead of them.

He just couldn't do it.

It wasn't Amy holding him back, and they knew it.

Behind him, Hank and Will talked between themselves about the sheriff. To Scott, Hank said, "We need to do something about him soon."

Scott nodded.

Jeni continued on ahead, shoulders slumped and head bowed.

He hated to hurt her.

His attention returned to the conversation behind him. Sheriff Danes had been a problem from the first day he stepped foot in Hope. The town had taken him on without an election. Without so much as an interview, they had established him as the new sheriff. They soon found that he was lazy, mean, and drunk most of the time. He did nothing to ensure the town's safety. Whenever an incident occurred, it was one of The Maxwell Group that settled it. There was a theory around town that he had blackmailed old Sheriff Jackson into giving him the job.

"You should take Danes' job, Daniel," Caine said.

Daniel nodded. "Been thinking about it lately. I might just have to do that."

"He won't go easy," Hank said.

"Doesn't matter," Caine said. "He's just got to go."

"I'll catch up with you as soon as I get her settled in here," Scott said with a half-shrug and nod towards the boarding house.

With a final "I think you should just take her over to the Rev and head home," Caine left him and walked away with the others.

Caine knew better.

They all knew better.

WITH A FEW GROUND-EATING STRIDES, SCOTT CAUGHT up and reached around Jeni to open the front door without knocking. He let her inside and closed the door behind himself.

The parlor was comfortable, cheery even. Tiny yellow flowers decorated the wallpaper, and the sunny color was scattered around the room in a way that made one think of sunshine. There were shelves full of books flanking the fireplace. A pair of comfortable armchairs sat between two long settees with an oval topped coffee table in the center. Embroidered pillows and lace doilies gave a homey feel to the room. It created a cozy place for people to congregate and enjoy each other's company.

Everything sparkled. If a speck of dust was so bold as to settle on any surface in this room, Jeni was sure someone would immediately banish it. The stairway leading to the second floor stood to the left of the entry. A doorway leading into another room stood opposite. Jeni assumed it led into the dining room or kitchen, based on the delicious smells released when the door opened and a large woman with jet black hair burst into the room.

"Scotty, it's good to see you, boy." The hostess gave Scott a hearty thump on the shoulder and a smile.

"Elenor Bix, this is Jeni MacGregor. She needs a room for a few days. Not sure how long."

"My, but you're a beauty, aren't you?" the woman admired. "You're going to cause a lot of trouble around here." She turned to Scott and added, "I'm not so sure it's a good idea for her to stay here at the moment."

Jeni dipped her head as the tears ran anew.

"Oh dear, you poor thing. I didn't mean to upset you. It's just that the house is full of men right now. There is only one room open, and you would be the only woman besides me. I'm safe enough," patting her big belly with a chuckle, "but you're pretty as a picture, and I hate to be responsible if anything happened to you in my care."

The tears wouldn't stop; Jeni couldn't do

anything about them. She stood in the middle of the room, looking pathetic, while Scott and Elenor talked over her head. Her voice wouldn't work. Jeni had no fight left. For the moment, she didn't care what happened. As long as she could get food in her and a warm bed, she could figure things out once she was rested.

Surely Scott would sleep on it and decide to do the honorable thing. All her instincts told her he was the answer, and she couldn't give up on him. He'd come around. She just needed a bed to crawl into until he did.

"The Maxwell Group will provide a guard for her."

"Well…"

A man descending the stairs stopped dead in his tracks, with his eyes glued to Jeni. She was looking dejected, barely holding back tears, and the man had the gall to look interested. His eyes scanned her from top to toe in an assessing manner.

He smiled at her.

Jeni shrank.

Scott stepped closer.

Elenor noticed. "This is why I can't have the girl in my house," she stated.

"Jeni has the protection of The Maxwell Group." Scott said, eyes locking with the stranger on the stairs. "Nobody will be stupid enough to cause trouble."

The man ducked his head and exited through the front door.

"I don't like it," Elenor groused. "A woman

needs a husband. What's your story?" She demanded of Jeni. "Why are you here, and why is Scotty following you around?"

Elenor waved Scott away when he began to answer. She obviously wanted Jeni to speak for herself.

It took half a minute for Jeni to get her voice to work. She opened and closed her mouth several times, swallowing past the lump in her throat before she figured out how to word her response. "I'm a mail-order bride. My groom has rejected me, and now I'm at your mercy." She straightened her spine as an idea occurred to her. "I'll work to earn my keep and find a job as soon as possible. I'm an excellent cook and can sew and do laundry. With so many men and so few women in this town, I imagine I should be able to take in laundry and mending and support myself."

Elenor took her measure and looked at Scott. "You rejecting this woman?" She sniffed.

"Who said I was the groom?"

"I ain't stupid."

"You know it wouldn't be safe," he said.

Elenor sniffed again. "Safer with you than without. Not all women will end up like Amy, you know."

"It's not about Amy."

Jeni wished she had enough energy to ask who Amy was, but she just wanted to sit down.

"Sure." Elenor turned her attention back to Jeni. "Follow me. The last open room is next to mine, so at least I'll hear if anyone tries to get in during the night. If I hear of you inviting any man into your room, I'll boot you out the door lickety-split. There'll be no shenanigans in my house." With a quick nod, Elenor walked away.

Jeni's head dropped.

Jeni turned to face Scott, her gaze not making it higher than his chest. She didn't speak. She took her bag from his hand, picked up her other bag from the floor where she'd all but dropped it, and left him there.

SCOTT WAS READY TO KICK HIS OWN ASS. HE COULDN'T marry this woman, but she was his responsibility, and as long as she was here, he'd take care of her. He couldn't deny that he was attracted to her, and the more he learned about her character, the more he liked her, which made the whole situation worse. When she'd offered to work, he'd nearly scooped her up and taken her home. Why couldn't she have been less appealing?

The unfairness burned in his gut.

He'd offered the protection of The Maxwell Group twice, even though everyone was needed at the ranch. He'd ask Caleb to stay at the boarding house with her until they could send her home. As a white man, it would be easier for Caleb to stay in town than it would be for him. He needed to stay away from her, anyway. When she'd offered to work, he'd nearly scooped her up and taken her home.

Of course, Caleb would give him a shit wagon full of grief over it, he would accept the assignment. He couldn't ask Will to go instead. No one would trust him to guard Jeni after what had happened to Amy. No, it had to be Caleb. He'd bitch about it, but he'd stay with her. That's how things worked in the Maxwell Group.

When Caine, Hank, Will, Caleb, and Daniel backed him up, he'd felt relief in the pressure of her hand on the back of his shirt. He wished he could have told Jeni who they were, but the situation on the street had been too intense for introductions. But whether she was aware or not, he'd looked over her head and made eye contact with each of his brothers. One by one, they'd nodded. She had their protection.

Scott stood in Elenor's parlor, staring at Jeni's closed door. The memory of her tiny hand on his back burned a hole straight through to his heart. When they'd surrounded her, her breath hitched, and she froze. Tension had vibrated through her and into him. The moment she realized they were friendly, the tension left.

When her head rested against his back, he nearly groaned for a different reason. He itched to hold her and tell her it would be ok. It took every ounce of his focus to keep his attention on the sheriff and the crowd. All he could feel was her warm breath and the tears that soaked his shirt.

The intimacy of her head pressed into his back haunted him. Her warm hands were on the sides of his body and her breath shot chills up his spine.

When he'd pulled her into his arms, it felt right. She fit him perfectly, and her rose scent filled a hole in his soul.

If she stayed, he would love her.

He needed to stay away.

He was helpless against those tears, and he needed to hold her, as much for himself as for her. He shouldn't have invited such intimacy with a woman he was trying to reject.

It wasn't fair to her.

Damn, he was a selfish bastard.

Did he kiss her forehead?

What was he thinking?

When his thoughts shifted to Amy, he shook his head and left. He hadn't thought about her so much in years. She chose a hell of a day to haunt his ass.

With one long breath, Scott turned and left Jeni to Elenor's care.

He'd known Elenor for most of his life. She was a few years older than him and nearly as tall. Nobody messed with Elenor. She'd run the boarding house by herself for almost ten years and had earned herself a reputation for being tough. She had a sense of humor, though, and enjoyed the company. Jeni would be safe with The Maxwell Group and Elenor for protection.

At least for a little while.

Scott headed to the saloon. Just as he knew they would be, all five men were waiting at a table with a bottle. Scott grabbed a chair, turned it around, and straddled it. He rested his head in his hands on the back of the chair and took a deep breath. They all knew how he was feeling and what he was thinking. It didn't look like they agreed with him, though.

It was rare for all six of them to be in town together. They rotated trips to make sure someone was always at the ranch. They owned the most extensive spread in Montana, and protecting it was as much a job as breeding and training horses. Today, they'd ridden to town en masse to attend Scott's wedding.

What a nightmare.

Scott shook his head.

His letter had been honest about the hardships. Why would a woman like her agree to the rough life that he'd described? He kicked himself for not being more specific.

What was he thinking?

And what was he was going to do now?

He couldn't marry Jeni. But he didn't feel right about leaving her, either. Scott stared into his shot glass, foolishly wishing it had the answer to his dilemma.

Long minutes later, the hairs on his skin tingled. He was being watched.

He lifted his head.

Every single one of his brothers was looking at him. But they seemed to know he was dealing with a lot, so they gave him a few more minutes to collect his thoughts before getting down to business.

Caine spoke first. "We've arranged a watch. Caleb can get away easier than any of the rest of us, so he'll stay in town with Miss MacGregor. He'll go over to the boarding house tonight. If Elenor doesn't have a room, she'll let him bunk in the barn until one opens up." Caine and Caleb were almost identical. As children, they could fool people by changing names. But then Caleb had been cut, stopping a brawl several years earlier and a scar on his chin put an end to that.

"I should've foreseen this. I never meant to send away for this kind of trouble. I'm not sure how to deal with her now."

"You sent for a bride. A bride arrived," Hank said. "What do you plan to do? Marrying her is what you should do." Hank had a sense of right and wrong that went bone-deep, and he couldn't stand to see a woman or child hurt. This abandonment would not sit well with him, and Scott knew it. It wouldn't sit well with any of them.

It didn't sit well with him.

"I never expected a woman like her to show up." Scott explained. "Why would a woman as beautiful as that want to be a mail-order bride? I expected a homely spinster and hoped for a pleasant personality. I'll get her a ticket on the first train back east where she belongs."

Caleb frowned and raked his blonde hair back from his face. "She must've left for a reason. Did you talk to her at all? Do you know what she wants?"

Will held up his glass for another round, and Caine reached over with the bottle and poured.

Caine held the bottle up to the others in silent question, then set it down. "She doesn't seem willing to do anything but marry you."

"She can do better'n me." Scott sipped his

whisky and wrinkled his nose. He hated the stale air in the saloon. They should've gone home and had a drink on the porch to discuss this. The stink of dirty cowboys and smoke suffocated him.

"Bullshit," Caleb said.

"You think she's safe?" Daniel pulled his jacket off and tossed it over the back of his chair. Scott sat up straighter. If Daniel was frustrated enough to wrinkle his jacket, Scott wasn't going to piss him off further by ignoring him. Daniel may look like a pretty boy with his neat clothes and clean boots, but nobody wanted to see him lose his shit. "Even with the protection of our name, she won't be for long." He picked up his jacket, folded it, and laid it back over the chair again. "These guys will not let this go." He swung his arm to indicate the men around them, half-watching the group.

"Of course not. But in town, she'll meet local men, and maybe she'll choose one to marry." The thought of Jeni with another man made Scott's blood boil, but the thought of loving her scared the shit out of him.

"You're not ok with that," Caine said. It wasn't a question.

"You were there. Of all people, you know how dangerous it is."

"Don't use my wife as an excuse for your cowardice." Caine took a drag from his cigarette and flicked the butt toward the spittoon in the corner. "What happened, happened. None of us could've changed it." All eyes darted to Will and the front legs of his chair hit the floor with a bang. For a second nobody said anything, but then Caine sighed and continued, "Amy deserves better than to be used like this."

A round of guilt went down before another shot of whisky.

"He's right," Caleb said. Caleb's attention focused across the room, where the sheriff huddled with a group of men at the bar. Tipping his head toward the group, he said, "That's going to be a problem."

In a move choreographed over years of working together, each man looked toward the bar without drawing attention. One at a time, they assessed the situation and nodded as they came to the same conclusion that Caleb had.

The sheriff and his friends were planning something, and after what happened in the street, it was pretty easy to conclude that Miss MacGregor was the person they had set their sights on.

"We got us some new meat in town!" Scott glared at Clint Baker as he tripped toward the sheriff. He'd been leaning against the horse trough during their little street performance earlier. "Coop's new girl arrived today. She's the purtiest girl anyone's 'er saw, too." He was already drunk, and it was just mid-afternoon. He went straight for the bar and swung to the left to throw an arm over the sheriff's shoulder. "If Conner gits her in here like they say, I'm gonna take me the first go on 'er. Pay extry for it."

He was flat on the floor before he'd taken

another breath. Knocked out cold. Scott stood over him and glared.

Men across the room took a step away from the menace in Scott's expression. Everybody but the sheriff.

In a loud, clear voice, Caine called out. "Miss MacGregor is under the protection of The Maxwell Group. We will be watching her, and if she is bothered, the consequences will be severe."

The sheriff spoke up. "If'n I go a courtin' I ain't askin' your permission."

From somewhere in the back, someone laughed. "You ain't courtin' with a beautiful woman like that sheriff. She can do better'n you."

The sheriff blustered. "We'll jus' see about that." He choked when he realized that Scott was standing at his elbow.

Scott stared down into the sheriff's face and didn't say a word.

The sheriff cowered, but didn't admit defeat. "I have as much a right as anybody."

"Just see that you respect her when she says no."

With that, the sheriff ran away again.

Coward.

The Maxwell Group each nodded in turn. Again, in silent communication and understanding. This sheriff had to go. They'd see to it. Daniel would be installed in that position before long. Daniel already spent half of his time in town doing the sheriff's job, anyway.

Elenor showed Jeni to a nice room near the back of the house. She nodded to the door across the hall and said, "That's mine. You need help, just shout. I'm a light sleeper. I'll hear if there is a commotion."

The room was furnished with a bed, a small arm chair and table. In the corner was a chest of drawers. A small wardrobe and wash stand stood against the wall. It was another cheerful room with yellow scattered playfully around. If she hadn't been so disappointed, Jeni would have been delighted. She had never had a room this nice to herself before. The warmth and colors were homey and comforting.

"What are you going to do?" Elenor asked. "Go back?"

"I have no home to go back to." Jeni admitted, plopping down onto the side of the bed. "I came here to marry, so I could finally feel safe. Right now, my plan is to recover from my journey and get my feet back under me. I will figure it all out when I'm rested. I just can't understand why he would reject me for being pretty. Usually it's the only thing men like about me."

"Scotty has his reasons. He'll have to tell you his own story. I'm no gossip. I will tell you, though, he was hurt badly a few years ago. All the Maxwell men were, I don't think any of them have really recovered." She waved Jeni off when she looked like she would ask for more details. "I won't tell another person's private stories. When he wrote for a bride, I think he was hoping for more of a housekeeper. He probably would have been happier if I'd stepped off the stage than you," she chuckled and patted her generous middle.

"I certainly didn't expect to step off the stage and look into the eyes of an angel, either, but I did. I didn't try to back out of it when I saw the danger in his eyes or the anger in his gaze. I was ready to fulfill my end of the bargain." She was starting to feel angry again. Anger was so much better than depression. She wanted to hold on to that.

"What made you decide to be a mail-order bride? You could have any man you wanted looking like that. A snap of your little fingers, and they would probably fall right into line for you." Elenor was trying to figure her out. She understood that.

Jeni rearranged her skirts while she tried to rearrange her thoughts. Elenor settled into the arm chair to hear the story.

"I thought that if I went as a mail-order bride, the groom would accept me before he saw what I looked like. I had expected him to be relieved not to get an ogre. I never even considered that he might reject me. I guess what it boils down to is that I wanted to be accepted for who I am." Jeni frowned. "I don't know if I'm explaining well. I'm tired and hungry."

"I think I understand. It can't be easy to feel like you're not seen as a person." Some of the hardness had left Elenor. "Do you still want to get married?"

"I want to marry Mr. Maxwell. I know he's rejecting me, but I'm not ready to give up on him.

"Back home there is a dear old woman whom I used to visit with. She's the neighborhood midwife. Even now that she's in her seventies she still works as she always did. Miss Samantha likes to talk about her husband and how their marriage came to pass. She loved him and she knew he loved her, but he would not marry her because he felt that she deserved someone better.

"To Miss Samantha, though, nothing was better than her Harry. She never gave up on him. She wore him down, and they had 40 happy years together." Jeni giggled thinking about that beautiful old woman telling the shocking tale of compromising her lover. It was her favorite memory of having tea with Sarah, Denise, and Miss Samantha. "Scott will eventually come around."

Elenor eyed her sideways. "What's so funny?"

Jeni held her tongue, and Elenor finally let it drop.

"Scotty's a good man. All the Maxwell Group are. They have done a lot to keep this community safe over the years. I don't want to see any trouble come their way, and it sounds like you come with a fair amount of trouble. I know it's not your fault, and there is nothing you can do about it, but I hope for Scotty's sake you know for sure what you want."

"I'm not going to bring him any trouble if I can help it. I want to marry him. I don't want to hurt him." She considered her next words carefully. "I promise to give him time to come around. I won't do anything to put him in danger. And I won't compromise him. I will give him a choice."

"I think I'm going to like you, Miss MacGregor."

"I'm going to like you, too. Please call me Jeni."

"Elenor."

Elenor rose from her chair. "Take a little rest there, and I'll heat water for a bath. I don't suppose it'll be hard to find people to carry water for you. You'll have to eat in the dining room. I have to keep strict rules or there will be food all over my house. I'm sure it will be a little awkward, but we will just have to get used to it."

Chapter Four

E lenor was right; supper was awkward. But the food was delicious.

Elenor made the best flaky biscuits Jeni'd ever tasted, and the stew she'd made to go with it reminded Jeni of better times. She ate heartily. After eating lightly while traveling, she was starving.

Sitting at the table beside Elenor, Jeni felt like she was on display for the men in the house, and they didn't hesitate to gawk. She kept her eyes down and a steady stream of chatter between herself and Elenor, hoping it would stop the men from speaking to her.

She knew better.

The ladies chatted as Jeni filled the hollow canyon of her belly and tried not to allow gaps to form in the conversation. To say Elenor was astute was an understatement. She filled in while Jeni chewed, telling stories and laughing, drawing as much attention to herself as possible.

Jeni's heart warmed to her new landlord.

Elenor had the most beautiful laugh. It was rich and came all the way up from the soles of her feet. It was a laugh that eased Jeni's anxiety and filled her with peace and hope, like the unselfconscious laugh of a child. She was grateful for everything Elenor had done.

The men around the table made constant efforts to draw Jeni out with questions. They tried to outshine each other and thought nothing of inter-rupting the conversation. There was no polite way to ignore them, and Jeni couldn't refuse to acknowl-edge them after a while.

She was used to avoiding men. After practicing it for so many years, she was an expert. As long as she could remember, she'd been trying not to make eye contact and doing her best to keep out of situa-tions where she would have to talk to them. Mostly, she'd evaded men, and that made it even more uncomfortable to be in such an intimate setting with so many.

Jeni kept her eyes fastened on her bowl and answered their questions with as few words as possible. Some of their questions she chose not to answer at all. She swirled a biscuit in her gravy and wished for dinner to end.

"Where are you from?"

"Boston."

"How long are you staying in town?"

"I'm moving here."

"Are you married?"

"Engaged."

These questions were simple enough to answer. Others were more difficult.

"What made you want to be a mail-order bride?"

"Will you be looking for another husband if Mr. Maxwell doesn't take you?"

"Will you go back to Boston if he doesn't marry you?"

She didn't answer these. After a while, the questions became more aggressive, and Elenor stopped them before Jeni lost her patience.

"Let the poor girl eat! She's been traveling all week, and she's had a long day. She don't need no interrogation from the likes of you. I'll be sleeping with my shotgun beside me and one ear open. If I hear so much as a footstep in the hallway, I'll shoot first and ask questions later." She glared around the table. "Am I clear?"

With a nod from all the men at the table, the interview ended.

Jeni helped Elenor clean up. She needed to feel useful, and since the men had all gone in their own directions, she could relax. Elenor didn't hover, which was nice. She was easy to converse with, and when she wanted information, she asked for it, but she didn't need to fill every minute with chatter. The two women worked quickly to put the kitchen to rights.

With the work done, Elenor and Jeni decided to get the bath set up in Jeni's room. They carried pot after pot of water from the stove. Before she left, Elenor added a few drops of rose oil. The scent wafted up from the rippling surface and filled the room, turning it into a relaxing oasis, a safe place. Sinking into the warm water was decadent after such a tough week.

Jeni took her time in the bath. She scrubbed away a week of dust and grime while she contemplated her situation. As she washed and soaked, she wished she could lie back and enjoy the bath without the weight of Scott's rejection on her shoulders. Jeni couldn't think of a time in her life that wasn't filled with worry. She couldn't think of a time in her life when she'd felt safe.

When she settled into the big, soft bed, she prayed for Mr. Maxwell to change his mind and then cried herself to sleep. Being rejected and abandoned haunted her dreams. Sleep did not relieve her from the horror or shame. All night long, she relived the scene on the street. Each time the sheriff got bigger, stinkier, and more aggressive; and each time, she grew smaller and more helpless. In every version, though, Scott Maxwell was there to protect her.

He took care of her.

There was no other man for her.

He had to see that.

THE FOLLOWING DAY, JENI AWOKE REFRESHED AND determined to make the most of her day.

The morning was her favorite part of the day. Anything was possible in the morning.

She wouldn't wallow in self-pity and doubt forever. Scott Maxwell had another think coming if he thought she'd give up. Jeni needed to make a plan and put it into action.

There would be no planning before coffee, though.

Jeni washed in frigid water at the pitcher in her room and dressed for the day. She piled her hair on top of her head and stuffed pins into it to keep it tamed.

She checked the hallway for lurkers, then headed toward the kitchen, where she could already hear Elenor working. The breakfast scents drifting down the hall made her walk a little faster.

She found Elenor looking cheerful in a bright yellow work dress, singing to herself.

"Can I help?" Jeni asked brightly.

"We could use some more coffee. You any good with biscuits?"

"I can handle both, though those biscuits last night were better than any I've ever made." The two women worked together as if they had been doing it for years. Moving around each other and passing things back and forth like a choreographed dance. They nursed their coffee as they worked quietly, and the quiet companionship was just what Jeni needed.

Elenor had a soothing effect.

At the breakfast table, the questions began again. Jeni stifled a sigh and kept her eyes on her breakfast. These meals would be tedious. She tried to think of a way to stop the conversation, but came up blank.

Would they force her to suffer this interrogation at every meal?

She took a big bite of pancake and washed it

down with coffee. Everything Elenor made was delicious.

"What brought you to town?" The man from the stairs yesterday asked. He'd missed dinner.

"My fiancé is here." She responded in as cheerful an attitude as she could manage.

Elenor's right eyebrow rose, but she didn't say a word. She wondered if Elenor approved of her using Mr. Maxwell in this way. Since she still planned to marry him, she didn't consider it a lie to call him her fiancé.

"Who's your fiancé, then?" The same man asked.

"Scott Maxwell. You saw him with me yesterday when we arrived." His head shot up, and his eyebrows snapped together.

"Not the Indian fellow?"

"That's the one." She'd take the protection of his name, whether he planned to marry her or not.

"Did that Indian lure you here under false pretenses?" Another man asked. "That ain't right."

"You don't have to marry him," a third man said.

She held her hand up. "There were no false pretenses. He wrote to the mail-order bride agency, and I responded to his letter."

"He should'a told you he was injun before you came all the way out here." Someone said.

Jeni's throat tightened, her hands shook, and she gripped her fork and knife. They would not drag his name through the mud like this. Mr. Maxwell might reject her, but she didn't doubt that, in his mind, he was doing it to protect her. "He was very clear about everything I needed to know."

Every man at the table stared as if she'd lost her mind.

"You came here on purpose to marry an Indian?"

"I came here to marry Mr. Maxwell. His heritage didn't affect my decision. I'm happy with my choice." She couldn't take any more. These men had no right to judge her. They had no right to judge Mr. Maxwell. Who were they to set themselves above anyone else?

Before anyone could speak, she said, "I do not have to defend myself, and I do not have to explain my decisions. I am here with The Maxwell Group's protection, and until my fiancé is ready to be married, I will remain here. I will stay out of your way, and I hope you will all show me the same courtesy."

"It ain't right." The man next to her said, more to himself than anyone else.

"I never asked for your approval."

"That's enough," Elenor barked in a way that brooked no disagreement.

A big man at the end of the table silently watched Jeni. He hadn't been there the night before. The way he watched her didn't make her nervous like the other men did; something was almost familiar about him. Something was safe about him. His posture remained relaxed, but he paid close attention to the conversation as he ate breakfast. Jeni had watched him from the corner of her eye as he followed the question-and-answer session.

Jeni couldn't help wondering about him and watching him, and she knew he was as aware of her.

Her curiosity was piqued. There was something familiar about him, but she just couldn't place him.

Elenor noticed the direction of Jeni's attention. "Jeni, this here's Caleb Maxwell, Scott's cousin. He's here for The Maxwell Group." She looked pointedly around the table. "He'll be staying as long as Miss MacGregor does."

Jeni looked more closely at Mr. Maxwell. He was beautiful, like Scott, but fair skinned. He didn't look to have any of Scott's Indian heritage. Scott was only half Indian, so she assumed Caleb was a relation from his Caucasian side. His black hair and dark brown eyes gave him a dangerous air, but there was something playful around his eyes and mouth. Crinkles that suggested he was more likely to smile than frown. She hoped that was true.

Caleb inclined his head to her. "Miss MacGregor."

Jeni nodded back. "Please, call me Jeni, Mr. Maxwell. It's very nice to meet you. You're here to babysit me, are you? Did you lose a bet?" She fought a small smile when she saw him do the same.

Caleb nodded. "Something like that. Call me Caleb." And then he tucked back into his breakfast, the tiny wrinkles around his eyes and mouth still giving his amusement away.

Jeni liked him.

Maybe he could help her change Scott's mind.

There sure were some handsome men in the West.

If she could get Scott to marry her, maybe she could get some of his brothers to marry her best friends, Sarah and Denise, and they could all be together. She needed to get her groom on board first.

A babysitter, though?

Why would he send his cousin to watch her instead of coming himself?

At least if he were here, they could get to know each other. If he didn't want to marry her now, maybe he could warm up to the idea. That was probably the exact reason he hadn't come himself — he didn't want to get to know her too well.

Jeni helped wash the dishes and watched Caleb chop wood in the backyard. She liked that instead of sitting around and staring at her, he'd found something helpful to do.

As Elenor didn't serve lunch at the boarding house, Jeni returned to her room until it was time to begin supper preparations. Jeni figured it was wise for her to remain in her room as much as possible. Maybe, after a day or two, Scott would realize that he was wrong and do the right thing.

Jeni grabbed a book from the sitting room and escaped into some much-needed solitude. She didn't know what Caleb did with himself while she holed up in her cell, but whenever she emerged, he was there. His presence gave her a sense of security.

Jeni wasn't used to being shut up all day, though, and after an hour, she was going crazy. She sought Elenor and asked for supplies to write a letter, then returned to her room and settled into the chair at the table. She wrote to her friends asking for their advice. Whenever any of them had a problem, the three girls had always come together to solve it.

Not having them to talk to right now was killing her.

My Dearest Friends,

I am saving myself from writing two letters by simply writing to both of you together. Please, share it with Miss Samantha if you see her; she always has the best advice.

I'm afraid I have bad news! I am not writing my first letter as Mrs. Scott Maxwell as I had expected to be. Instead, I remain Miss MacGregor!

Mr. Maxwell has rejected me. Boldly rejected me in the middle of the street! Would you like to know why I was thusly rejected? Well, I would too! He's given no acceptable excuse for his behavior. I'm to believe that I'm too beautiful for him or some other nonsense like that.

He said I'm so beautiful that it would be dangerous for me to marry him. I see his worry though, because it appalled the men here that I would consider marrying a man with Indian blood, which is silly. I can feel that there is a more solid reason, but he won't give it to me.

So, instead of putting me in danger by marrying me, he has thrown me to the wolves. He brought me from the stage office straight to the boarding house, and then he was off, and here I sit.

He wants me to accept a ticket to return to Boston, but you both know I cannot go back there. If Mr. Benson finds me unmarried, I have no hope.

I will be fair and say that I have not been left me wholly unprotected. Mr. Maxwell's family has formed some sort of (for lack of a better word) gang. They call *themselves The Maxwell Group, and from what I can tell, that has significance here. Twice yesterday, he declared me under the protection of The Maxwell Group. This morning at breakfast, there was a new face at the table — Caleb Maxwell, Scott's cousin. Elenor, the lady who runs the boarding house, informed the tenants (who are all men) again that I am under the protection of The Maxwell Group.*

I'll have to write another time to describe Elenor. I like her very much. She's an incredible western woman, and you would both enjoy her as much as I do.

I'll take a minute to describe Scott Maxwell to you both. He's nothing short of magnificent. Girls, he is like every beautiful boy we've ever dreamed about multiplied a hundred times. He's tall and broad and dark in a dangerous way, but with gentleness hiding underneath. His eyes are almost black, they are so dark brown, and his hair is black and down past his shoulders. His face has sharp, chiseled features with high cheekbones, and his mouth is full. I can't think of a more beautiful man in our acquaintance. I could look at him all day and never tire of the view.

No Mr. Potter for me. HA!

The townspeople seem to think they have a say in the matter, and I'm sure this is why he thinks marrying me is dangerous. It would be better if he would talk to me about it, but he just won't.

I got off the stagecoach and walked right into a very embarrassing scene on the sidewalk. As I said, Mr. Maxwell rejected me in public. People from all over the town came out to watch my utter humiliation. When the sheriff showed up to come to my rescue, he only bruised my arm and caused more commotion. The disgusting lawman was truly repulsive and I nearly wretched when he offered to marry me, like he was doing me a favor. He kept saying it was out of the question for me to marry an 'injun'. Such ignorance!

The incident yesterday left me feeling weak. After the already arduous journey and embarrassing public rejection, it reduced me to tears in the middle of the street.

Another shocking thing about the situation is that at least half of the town took me to be the new (apparently much anticipated) whore and expect me to begin work at the saloon. They stood there and shouted filth at me while my fiancé refused to marry me. I've never been more mortified.

When the dust had settled, and the sheriff walked away, Mr. Maxwell held me in his arms so gently and soothed my distress. He wiped a tear from my face with his big, work-roughened finger, and I knew he was the only man I could ever marry. Even in his ferocious anger, the gentleness with which he handled me has convinced me he is not immune to me any more than I am to him. I've never been held so sweetly. It went straight to my heart.

I was sure that he had changed his mind and would marry me, but I was wrong. It was like being rejected all over again. Even now, sitting in my room alone, I feel his arms around me.

I just don't think he understands how dangerous it is for me to be left out here without marriage protection. If it's possible to imagine, the men out here in the West are worse than in Boston. They aren't held back by the social graces of the city. In the city, men lay in wait and assault without a witness. Here, a big sheriff put his hands on me in the middle of the sidewalk, standing in front of my fiancé, with a crowd watching. He nearly pulled me off my feet!

The protection of The Maxwell Group will only last so long. I need a plan. I need to figure out how to make Mr. Maxwell overlook my beauty and marry me after all.

I wish I had Sarah's skill with a blade or a gun! Maybe I could have forced him to marry me yesterday.

I miss both of you so very much. I wish we were together drinking tea and working this out.

There are loads of beautiful men out here. If I get settled, maybe you two can join me and have husbands of your own.

Your Faithful Friend,
Jeni MacGregor

JENI SIGHED AS SHE FINISHED HER LETTER AND WAITED for it to dry. She tapped the paper gently and then blew the last remnants of sand off before she tucked it into the envelope. She could make her way to the post office and back without incident, so she didn't bother to seek out Elenor or Caleb. The post office sign was clearly visible from the front window of the boarding house.

Jeni snagged her shawl from the peg by her door and threw it around herself. Hiding as much as possible under it, she left the house.

"Going somewhere?" A deep voice asked from the side of the porch.

Caleb was sitting in a chair with one boot cocked on the railing and the two front chair legs lifted off the floor. Like the rest of the men of The Maxwell Group she had seen the day before, he exuded confidence. He emanated strength.

She studied him for a moment. He had dark brown eyes, and his hair was a little longer than usual. It's funny that she considered cutting his hair. She didn't even know him.

She must've seen him the day before on the sidewalk, because the feeling that he was familiar hit her again. She'd been too distressed to have gotten a good look at any of Scott's brothers the day before.

Holding up her envelope, she said, "I want to run over and post a letter."

He nodded.

Chapter Five

To get to the post office from the boarding house, one had to pass an alley between the saloon and a business with no sign. Jeni didn't know what was in that building, but it got little traffic, and she avoided it.

Caleb rose to walk with her, but Jeni waved for him to sit down. There was no reason for him to bother himself. He could watch her from where he was.

As Jeni approached the sidewalk, a young woman, probably only a year or two younger than herself, pulled her skirts aside to evade having them brush against Jeni's skirts. She was an interesting little woman. Her dark blonde hair was barely constrained in a bun and a long lock had escaped entirely and hung down her back.

"Everyone says you belong at the saloon instead of walking around town?"

"Why do you think I belong in the saloon?"

"That's where whores belong."

"Why do you think I'm a whore?" Jeni had done nothing to deserve such a title.

"I have ears."

As simple as that, she'd heard rumors and believed them. "Let me show you something. Do you have a moment?"

The other woman looked skeptical, but after studying Jeni's face for a moment, she asked, "What do you want to show me?"

The woman bounced on her toes as she thought and she carried two heavy looking ledgers under one arm. Her quizzical expression gave Jeni hope that she might have an open mind. Her look was judgmental, but in a way that suggested she was judging for the truth. It was a look her friend Sarah would give. She cared about what was true and not what was popular.

"Would you please walk across to the post office and wait for me there?"

The other woman's brows knitted, but she turned and half-skipped over to the post office. She was cute, average height, but she had a sweet bounce in her step and moved like she owned the town. People nodded to her as she went, and she returned their greetings. When she reached the other side of the street, she turned and shifted her books in front of her body and shrugged. Then she watched Jeni cross to meet her. Jeni held eye contact and watched the new woman's reaction as she made her way across the street.

"Hey pretty, when you gonna start workin'?"

"We got a room ready for ya, and we all want the first ride."

Someone reached out to grab her arm. She side-stepped in a well-practiced move. Jeni continued walking, matching the course and speed that the other woman had taken, not breaking eye contact as she went.

"Filth."

"Whore."

"The sheriff shouldn't allow these types among decent folk." One woman said to another as she shielded her child from seeing Jeni. "That saloon needs to be shut down. It brings in the wrong sort."

"Com'ere, baby. I'll marry ya."

"I'll marry you."

Jeni stepped up on the sidewalk next to the young woman, who had watched the entire scene with narrowed eyes and pursed lips.

"Look at me. Look at my dress. Look at my hair. Look at my shoes. Look at me. What is it about me that screams to these people that I am a whore?"

The other woman stopped and actually looked at Jeni, who stood at the end of the sidewalk and let her take in her measure. It was a surprise when the other woman relaxed.

"You're not the girl Cooper's been talking about for the last two months, then?"

"Cooper?" Then it dawned on her. It was hard not to see the giant sign right in front of her that said Cooper's Saloon.

"No, I'm not. I came as a mail-order bride." At

least now she understood why the town thought her a whore. What a mess.

"Well, this is quite a situation to be in." She shoved her books under one arm and stuck out her hand. "I'm Opal Whitfield."

"Jeni MacGregor."

"Are you really a mail-order bride? What an adventure. Is that why you were with Scott Maxwell, then? Are you going to marry him?"

"I don't know anymore. I came here to marry him, but he says he won't have me because he didn't want a beautiful wife, whatever that means. He's determined that it isn't safe, and from the reactions of the townspeople, I'm beginning to wonder if he might be right."

"He is right, but that can't be his real reason. Do you want to marry him?"

"I do. I traveled all this way to marry him. I don't know what I'll do if he really refuses me."

"I'm going to help you."

"Why?"

"Because I like something about you and I want to be your friend. I'm sorry for judging you; sometimes the gossip is hard to ignore."

Jeni reached out and embraced her new friend with hope in her heart that she could trust this odd girl. "I need a friend more than you can know."

Opal indicated the letter, still clutched in Jeni's hand and smiled. "Post your letter and let's go get a cup of tea at the bakery."

"Ok, but let's go back to the boarding house for

the tea instead. If I stay out like this, the horrible comments will never stop."

"Deal. I'll meet you out here in a few minutes." Opal bounced twice and then darted into the Mercantile next door to the Post Office.

A KNOCK AT HER BEDROOM DOOR THE NEXT DAY startled Jeni. Opal hadn't planned to visit, and she didn't know anyone else. Before opening the door, she asked, "Who's there?"

"You have visitors. I'll make tea. Caleb's in the sitting room with them."

Visitors?

Jeni checked herself in the mirror before going out.

Two middle-aged women sat in the living room, side by side, on one of the two settees. They had to be identical twins. They were exactly the same. Their dresses were the same pattern — different fabrics, but otherwise, they matched. Their strawberry blonde hair, streaked with gray, was pinned into a neat bun at the back of each head.

Caleb patted the settee next to him and made the introductions. "Jeni, this is Rose and Iris Dunn. They have been part of our household since before Caine and I were born. Iris, Rose, this is Jeni MacGregor, Scott's would-be bride."

"We're so sorry for what has happened to you," Rose blurted. "You poor thing. We wanted to meet you at the stage, but there was too much to do with preparing a wedding feast and all. We were sad not to share that with you, I promise you that." She scrunched up her lips as if she'd eaten something sour, and her eyes burned with utter vexation. "Gave that boy a piece of my mind, I did. After hearing about how he treated you, we're glad we weren't there." Rose glared at Caleb as if it Scott's bad behavior was somehow his fault. "I would've snatched that kid bald right there in the street. We're horrified. We raised him better than to treat a girl like that."

From the corner of her eye, Jeni watched Caleb struggle not to laugh at Rose as she rattled on in a mixture of sympathy and frustration. Jeni was particularly tickled by how Rose spoke about these men as if they were still little boys.

"He has his reasons and a good heart," she conceded, "but it's not right. You really are as pretty as they say you are, aren't you? Can you believe how pretty she is, Iris? We're so frustrated with Scott. I nearly boxed his ears, and Iris here gave him quite a talking to, I promise you. We had to get one of the boys to bring us right to town this morning to check on you. You poor thing. We hope the boy comes around and brings you home. You poor thing."

She rambled on in a friendly way, speaking for both herself and her sister for quite some time.

There was something irresistibly likable about Rose, the talker.

Iris sat quietly beside her sister, nodding as she sipped her tea and studied Jeni. Iris was peaceful, like Elenor, but without the energy. Jeni would've loved to spend an entire day with Iris; her silent support was a deep breath after being underwater for too long.

"I'm so happy to meet you both," Jeni said. "Mr. Maxwell told me about you in his letter. I know you're very special to him. I'm sorry to have caused any distress. I'm sure we'll figure this all out in time." She nibbled at a cookie and sipped her tea, enjoying the meeting. These women were like mothers to Scott, and it sounded like they were on her side.

Caleb refilled her cup and smiled at the two women.

Rose swallowed the sip of tea she'd taken. "Oh, it's no fault of yours, we know. You can't help it that you're beautiful. As if that was even a good enough reason to reject a woman you've sent all the way across the country for. Paid a lot of money to the agency and tickets and stipends and boarding house and all of that. There is a better reason than 'too beautiful' and I'm going to find it out. I have my suspicions, but I don't talk, you know. Secrets are secrets, but I'll find out. You poor thing. It's just that the boy has had some hurt in the past and is afraid that you could be in danger and…"

Caleb cleared his throat at the same time that Iris elbowed Rose, and Rose shut up. She took a sip of tea, and her eyes shifted around the room.

Iris broke the uncomfortable silence. "The boy has his reasons. He isn't trying to hurt you." The voice was the same as Rose's, but softer and gentle.

Jeni's shoulders slumped. "I know. I'm still hoping I can change his mind, though."

Rose mumbled again behind her teacup, "you poor thing," and made Jeni smile.

They all had a pleasant visit after that, and when the sisters went away, Jeni felt like she had two new friends. They doted on Caleb. It was adorable how he let them do it, too.

During their visit, Jeni learned that Iris and Rose had been housekeepers in the Maxwell family home since before Caine and Caleb were born. Scott had come to live in the house with the boys when they were thirteen years old and Scott was twelve. The sisters had adopted him into their hearts right away. Because of Rose's predilection for rambling, Jeni learned that neither sister had ever married. She said that they'd been happy to raise the boys after their parents had passed away. The other three had come along as teenagers, and the sisters had taken them on as well.

Jeni struggled to keep the names straight as Rose spewed personal details about each man that Jeni was sure they wouldn't like shared. This was quite apparent by Caleb's behavior. He couldn't keep a smile from his face as she shared embarrassing stories about his brothers. When she came to him, though, he seemed to have quite a tickle in his throat, which Rose successfully managed to ignore.

After Caine, Caleb and Scott, there was Will, Hank and Daniel. She struggled to remember which wanted to be the sheriff, who wanted to have an adventure, and which was the caretaker. She'd get them straight in time. They would be her brothers when Scott agreed to do the right thing.

Rose said the boys took care of her and Iris, but it was clear from the way they coddled Caleb, and from the letter that Scott had sent, that the sisters still took care of their boys.

———————

THREE WEEKS DRIFTED BY IN A MONOTONY OF EATING and pacing in her tiny room. Jeni was about ready to die of boredom, and she did not know how Caleb could stand to babysit her all the time.

She spent most of the first week in her room, only coming out to help Elenor with chores or to choose a new book from the sitting room.

The second week, she started spending time with Caleb during the middle part of the day. They didn't talk about anything personal. Mostly they spoke of the town or the weather or made silly jokes about people walking by. When she was with Caleb, she could walk around town without the crass insults or threats that pelted her when she was alone. All it took was a look from him, and the abuses stopped.

Jeni asked daily about Scott, but Caleb would not answer her questions. She knew he talked to Scott, though.

Jeni wished it was possible to understand what Scott was thinking; she just wanted to talk to him. He wouldn't come to see her, no matter how many times she pressed Caleb to ask.

Three weeks was a long time, and she thought

she'd be forced to look for another husband. She didn't want another though, she only wanted Scott.

Caleb and Jeni killed time in the evenings playing board games or sitting on the porch. She wanted to be spending this time with his cousin, whom he called his brother. Caleb was patient and kind, but he wasn't her fiancé, and it wasn't the same.

Jeni was grateful for the nonjudgemental way Elenor treated her situation. Elenor didn't complain or advise. She didn't scheme or dictate. She accepted the company of her border and minded her own business.

Elenor enjoyed a joke, and after a week or two, she was pranking Jeni in little ways. One morning when Jeni grabbed the bag of flour, it flew off the shelf. The bag was enormous and looked heavy with its puffed-up sides. It wasn't though, it was full of air and tied closed to keep the shape. When Jeni hefted with all her strength, the bag flew. White powder rained down from holes in the sack's bottom. Elenor had to cross her legs as the laughter shook her entire body. The little humorous surprises always shocked Jeni, but she enjoyed them. Before long, she and Caleb were thinking up little surprises for Elenor, too.

Jeni had never been around someone so full of humor. She wanted to be like that. She tried to think of a way to get Elenor back. Still, her mind wouldn't come up with anything. Playing tricks had been a common occurrence in the orphanage, but Jeni had never partic-ipated. Caleb, on the other hand, was an experienced prankster, and he helped her hone her skill. Before long, Jeni hid a frog in the empty breadbox and packed flour into the pockets of Elenor's apron. This was a mistake, though, because when Elenor snapped her apron, as was her habit before putting it on, the mess was an enormous amount of work to clean. It was funny, though, and they all had a laugh as they cleaned up, even Caleb grabbing a rag and helping to wash the walls and cupboards above their heads.

Visits with Opal were the best part of Jeni's week. Opal was an interesting and funny woman, and it felt good to have a friend her age again. Opal gave her camaraderie, sisterhood like she had at home with Sarah and Denise.

Unlike Elenor, Opal always had ideas and wanted to share. She liked to gossip and soon had informed Jeni about everyone in town. Opal enjoyed brainstorming ways to get Scott's attention and always mentioned it to Jeni if she spotted him in town. She had limitless energy, and her mind worked a mile a minute. Jeni was jealous of Opal's intelligence and confidence. She was so easy to admire.

"Come to work with me today," Opal said.

"I'm supposed to follow you around and watch you add sums in a ledger all day?" Jeni appreciated the mornings when Opal stopped by before making her rounds to the businesses around town.

"I only have to go to the Mercantile and Cooper's today, then we can go to my house and fix lunch. Or we can go to the dress shop and visit my mom and

Millie. Millie's been asking to meet you and I know mamma wants to see you too. You spend too much time in this house." Opal scooted over to the stove and grabbed the coffee pot. After filling both cups, she resumed her seat.

"You think I'm going with you to the saloon?"

Opal laughed. "Ok, I see your point. Why don't I stop after work and then we can go to my house for lunch?" Opal blew over the top of her coffee. "I shouldn't be more than a few hours. The Mercantile's in good shape, and I got Cooper's books sorted out last week. He's a mess with numbers. You know, when I started doing his books, they were such a mess I couldn't even use them. I had to make him buy new ledgers and start over from the beginning. The man can't add two and two."

"Ok." Jeni couldn't help laughing. "I'll go with you if you promise not to tell me any more about Cooper's books."

"Deal."

Opal skipped off to do what needed to be done, but was back earlier than expected and the girls had a nice visit at Opal's house. It was nice to see a different place. Jeni was tired of yellow. Opal's house was neat, but her room was a disaster.

How did she live like that?

The change to her daily pattern was refreshing, and Jeni and Opal started spending more time together at Opal's house. They lunched together nearly every day. Caleb walked Jeni to Opal's house each day and returned to escort her back to the boarding house a few hours later. Sometimes he stayed, and they had a great time together.

Jeni didn't see Scott during that first few weeks, and it hurt that he hadn't come to check on her. It was frustrating when Opal or Elenor mentioned seeing him, because she knew he was avoiding her. She didn't know how she would convince him to marry her if he wouldn't talk to her.

Jeni could have moved on to another man. There were plenty willing, but Scott was the only man she could imagine being married to. One of the primary reasons she had for being a mail-order bride in the first place was that he wouldn't see her before she married him. The men in this town didn't care about her, they just wanted a pretty wife. She reread Scott's letter to herself every night, and all the reasons for choosing him in the first place remained.

Jeni considered writing to a man in another town to go as a mail-order bride again, but she wasn't ready to give up The courage had been hard enough to muster the first time. Who knows that a second groom would be like. Her new fear was that he'd be like the sheriff, and that image was a million times worse than the fear she'd traveled with. She'd take ten Mr. Potters before she'd marry a man like the sheriff.

The memory of Scott's muscular arms stayed with her. When he'd cradled her against his hard chest, she was safe for the first time in her life. Jeni wanted that feeling back. She wanted his body wrapped around hers again, with his hand supporting the back of her head as his warmth sucked her in. She couldn't give that up. His embrace was everything she needed.

One familiar topic tended to be the theme of their lunch conversations. With so little going on, Jeni obsessed over Scott's neglect.

"He doesn't care how I'm doing here, does he?" No matter how determined she was, melancholy swallowed her up.

"He knows how you're doing. You know he's keeping track of you," Opal said. But Jeni didn't want her friend to be reasonable. She wanted to pout, and she wanted Opal to commiserate with her.

The two had already repeated this conversation several times, but Opal never seemed to tire in her efforts to reassure Jeni.

"Do you think he will ever come to see me?" She asked.

"Do you want him to?"

"You know I do."

"It's a small town; you'll run into him. Scott must have a good reason for doing this. Not doing the honorable thing is probably killing him."

"They've only offered me the protection of their name because Scott feels responsible for bringing me here. I'm sure that is their way of maintaining honor when I'm sitting here destitute, with no future."

"I don't think that's all there is to it, though," Opal did a little wriggle that meant she was about to share some juicy tidbit of information she'd gathered. "I don't think his hesitation is about you. There was some kind of situation a few years ago, and a woman died, Caine's wife, Amy. Nobody really knows what happened. The whole thing was hush-hush. The town would have a fit if he was to marry you, but I think he'd do it if something else wasn't holding him back. I think he's trying to protect you, but I think he'll come around, and the town will accept it in time."

"Were you there when the sheriff grabbed me in the street the day I arrived?"

"I was, but the Maxwell men surrounded you when I came up, and I couldn't see you.

"I could see that Scott was interested. When he held me, his heart was pounding, but his hands were tender. He kissed my head as if he cherished me. I thought he'd changed his mind, but he didn't."

Opal nodded. "I heard you were beautiful, and the rumor was that you were the new girl that Cooper sent for. They said that you were trying to trick Scott into marrying you so you wouldn't have to go work in the saloon."

Jeni sighed, shook her head, and shrugged.

"After the sheriff walked away, Scott held me in his arms. I've never felt comfort like that, and all I want is to crawl back into his embrace and feel that protection again." Jeni wrapped her arms around herself for a moment, then dropped them with a sigh,

"Like I said, it's a small town. He can't avoid you forever."

"I think the town is just big enough for him to manage it."

"It's not."

Jeni wanted to believe that, but she grew more

desperate every day. Scott was the only man she was willing to marry. But she couldn't tell him if he wouldn't come and check on her, and it was making her crazy. Scott was an infuriating puzzle. Her mail-order husband had proven mere minutes after she'd gotten off the stage that he would die for her, but he wouldn't make her his wife.

Caleb was a good man, but he was no help. He'd become Jeni's best friend, and it frustrated her he still took his brother's side and didn't convince him to do the right thing. Caleb would die for her, but he wouldn't fight for her with his brother.

———

OCTOBER SPRUNG, CRISP AND COOL, OVER THE TOWN. Jeni enjoyed morning walks through town with Caleb, and they took their explorations further and further into the countryside. He knew all the local plant life names and pointed out animals and land-marks as they strolled. The exercise was wonderful, but nothing would get Scott off her mind.

"Have you talked to Scott lately?" She hated to bring it up because sometimes speaking of Scott would really upset Caleb.

"Uh-huh."

"Is he ever coming to see me?"

"The train ticket wasn't enough to tell you how he feels?"

Jeni bristled. It was the most he'd said on the matter, and it hurt.

"Do you want me to leave?"

He didn't reply.

She stopped and turned to him, craning her neck to look up into his face. "You don't have to stay with me if you don't want to."

He nodded but wouldn't respond. He just turned and started the slow walk back toward town. Caleb never walked too fast for Jeni to keep up with, even when he was irritated with her. She glanced up at his profile. He had the same tick in his jaw when he was angry as Scott did.

Caleb had grown distant and a little sullen over time, and no matter how Jeni tried to bring him out of it, he resisted. He wouldn't talk about Scott, and he wouldn't talk about himself. Even their walks stopped, and he avoided her. He kept the town's men away, but he wouldn't spend time with her anymore.

She missed him.

She considered using the train ticket and taking her chances back in Boston. When she got news from home, she'd decide. She couldn't go on like this forever.

Chapter Six

A nother month had passed, and Jeni was on edge. She haunted the Post Office, but no word from home had arrived.

Caleb was showing restlessness, and she knew he wanted to be rid of her. Jeni could see it in the way he looked at her and the clipped way he spoke to her now. He always seemed irritated with her now, no longer patient and understanding.

Losing his friendship hurt, but it was a surprise that he'd lasted so long.

Jeni was crawling out of her own skin. It was time for her to make a plan and do something. She couldn't wait around forever.

Any hope the townspeople would get used to her and settle down had disappeared. Opal had spread the word that she wasn't the soiled dove they thought she was, but since that woman never arrived, they didn't believe her. The town's men grew more frustrated with waiting for her to give up on Scott. They either expected her to head over to the saloon and work on her back, or choose another groom. Every day there was a knock at the door, with someone asking if he could escort her on a walk.

At first, Caleb had been the one to dismiss the suitors, but he seemed tired of the task, and it had forced her to stroll with several men, feeling dirty every time. Every day, the townsmen grew less patient with her refusals. Jeni feared that she'd have to accept one of them.

WHEN JENI HAD BEEN IN TOWN FOR EIGHT WEEKS, SHE finally had a return letter from her friends. Jeni couldn't believe the time it'd taken for mail to travel between them. She'd already written another letter to Sarah and Denise, telling them about Opal, Eleanor, Rose, Iris, and the town. How could her communication with them be this slow?

On her way back from the post office with her letter, a hard hand shot out of the alley and yanked her off her feet and out of sight. Sheriff Danes jerked her into the shadows and slammed her hard against the side of the building. She cursed herself as her head connected with the siding.

The alley was the only place between the Post Office and the boarding house that provided cover for an attack. Hadn't Caleb warned her a million times, she thought, as her shoulders hit the wall? Jeni was diligent about keeping her eyes open and giving the area a wide berth. Today, she was simply too excited about her letter and had walked close enough for him to reach out and pull her in.

Jeni let out a scream that was silenced when he slammed his beefy hand over her mouth. She tasted blood and filth and saw stars when her head crashed back against the wall a second time. He cursed at her and gave her a few hard shakes, which threw her head into the wall two more times. She thought she might be sick when he leered at her. His fingers drilled holes through her arms as he battered her against the side of the building. His body odor overwhelmed her senses when he pulled her close. She gagged. His crusty lips came down over hers. Jeni gagged again. She tried to punch, but he pinned her arms to her sides. She tried to kick, but her efforts didn't land. His hand grabbed her breast and squeezed so painfully that she cried out, but his mouth was on hers, silencing her again. Her heart pounded and her body trembled. Terror shot through her. This was worse than what she'd left behind in Boston.

His mouth was only on hers for a moment before his head jerked backward and she was thrown to the ground.

She turned and emptied the contents of her stomach into the dirt. For a minute, she could do nothing but heave and gasp for breath. Her head pounded and her vision blurred with tears. She could not stop the shaking in her arms and legs. She could not get herself off the ground.

Her whole body rejected the assault of those

hands and horrible mouth on her, making her shake violently even though she was free. She lay on the ground for several minutes, trying to control her thoughts and muscles.

The unmistakable sound of blows on a body brought her back to reality. Caleb must've been watching after all.

Jeni scooted back away from the scuffle and lifted her head.

Oh, no.

Caleb hadn't come to her defense. It was Scott.

What would he think of her?

It must have looked like she was sparking in the alley with sheriff Danes. Would he know she was being assaulted, or would he think she was loose? Her heart broke.

Her mind snapped back into focus as quickly as it had been muddled. Scott was still beating the sheriff hard enough to kill him. She would lose him for sure if he did. Her body sprang into action. She jumped on Scott's back and wrapped herself around his neck. She didn't know how else to get his attention, so she pressed her lips to the warm flesh under his ear and whispered, "Scott, please. I need you."

Scott spun so fast and glared at her with such a harsh expression Jeni thought she'd angered him, but he pulled her into his arms and held her the way she'd been dreaming he would. It was the same way he'd held her after the first time she'd been assaulted by this beastly sheriff. Scott pressed a kiss to the top of Jeni's head and rocked her in his arms.

Scott turned Jeni's face up to his, surveyed the damage, and cursed. Her lip was cut, and a bruise was blooming at the side of her mouth. She had blood in her hair. Scott tried to dig through her hair to see the damage, but he made no progress amidst the hairpins that secured her thick bun. He knew her arms must be bruised from the way she'd been grabbed and held against the wall, and he feared he might have injured her when he knocked her out of Danes' reach.

"Did I hurt you?"

"You saved me."

"I tossed you harder than I meant to."

She reached up and touched the muscle working in his jaw, obviously trying to soothe him as he comforted her. Damn, she'd take this wrong, but he needed to hold her and make sure she was ok. He was responsible for her, and every drop of her blood wrecked him.

"You didn't hurt me."

Caleb ran up, and Scott practically growled at him.

Caleb threw both of his hands in the air in self-defense and said, "I was in the outhouse. What happened?"

Caleb looked at Jeni, and what she saw was guilt and fear in his eyes. There was something else, too.

Disgust?

Anger?

His hands opened and closed in tight fists as he took in the sheriff, beaten to a pulp.

What was he thinking?

Scott scowled at Caleb. "I saw her get jerked off the street and into the alley." He turned to Jeni. "You're lucky I was looking out at just that moment." It had become his habit to sit in the saloon window where he could see the boarding house porch. When Jeni had stepped out without Caleb, he'd followed her with his eyes. It wasn't like Caleb to let her go to the post office alone, at least not without him watching from the porch.

Thankfully, Scott had been watching when she disappeared so quickly from the sidewalk. She'd had the most angelic look as she walked back to the house with her letter. When he saw her disappear into the dark alley, his heart slammed into his rib cage, and he bolted. Holding her now, he wanted to drag her off to the church. He had to steel himself again, though. Scott couldn't put her in that sort of danger. He'd already caused her enough grief. Amy's face flashed in front of him, but he shook his head. He had enough to deal with without ghosts chasing him.

"Why did you go there alone?" Scott hadn't meant to use a demanding tone, but damnit, the thought of what could have happened turned him inside out.

"I wanted to check the post office. I was so excited about my letter that I forgot to watch out for the alley, and I knew better. Caleb has warned me at least a hundred times." She looked at Caleb, hoping he would soften, and she might see her friend return.

Caleb stepped up to Jeni and gently took her face into his hand, as Scott had just done. Surveying the damage, he cursed before he let her go. "Go get her cleaned up." He looked angry rather than relieved.

"You got this?"

"I've got this."

Scott scooped Jeni into his arms and carried her back to the boarding house. The trust that she showed when she rested against him cut off his air. He didn't deserve it. Not one bit.

Still, he held her tighter when she wrapped her arms around him and pressed her face into his neck. She smelled like roses. She breathed him in, just as deeply, and his heart clenched. His lips on the top of her head trembled with the thought of what could've been.

IN THE KITCHEN, HE LOWERED HER INTO A CHAIR. Scott grabbed a bowl and filled it with warm water from the stove, then found a clean towel in the stack over the sink and took the chair beside her. Tenderly, he cleaned the cut on her lip and washed away the sheriff's touch.

"I don't feel like that kiss will ever wash away," she said, tears forming in her eyes again.

"That wasn't a kiss. It was an assault."

Why was it that every time she was around this

man, all she wanted to do was cry and crawl into his arms for support?

This man was her comfort.

This man was her safety.

He was her future.

He should be her husband.

"Are you ready to talk to me yet?" she asked.

"No."

Jeni took his hand in both of hers. "Scott, you're the man I came here to marry. You're the only man I want to marry. If the protection that I need is in a man's name, you'll have to give me yours."

"Nothing has changed."

That would have been a better argument if he weren't removing pins from her hair to get to the wound on her head. His fingers were careful when he touched her.

"What are you doing?"

"Your head is bleeding. I'm checking to see if you're going to need stitches."

When he set the last pin on the table and unwound the coil of her bun. He took his time. He didn't just let the bun unwind and fall onto her back. Scott untwisted the rope and spread it out across her shoulders. He ran his fingers through it several times, massaging her scalp before running them down the length.

Her hair was her best feature. At least she thought so. It was long and thick and soft and Scott was not immune to the charm of it. She would have sat there for hours and let him run his fingers through the length of it. She sighed and relaxed her sore muscles.

He probed the edges of the wound. He picked up the cloth from the bowl on the table and cleaned it. "It could use a few stitches."

"Is that really necessary?"

"I'm afraid so. It's going to scar."

"Who cares about a scar under my hair? A scar on my face might do me good, though." Her eyes were closed to hold back more falling tears.

He ran his finger down her face. Such a simple touch, but it packed so much emotion.

"Let me get something to stitch this with. I saw Elenor out back by the hen house a minute ago." His voice had softened and choked with emotion. This was as hard for him as it was for her. She wanted to hold him.

Scott didn't move right away. He stood there with her head cradled in the palm of his big hand. Scott relaxed. Still wound up from his fight, her nearness soothed him. She turned and pressed a kiss to his palm and noticed the blood on his hand.

"Let me clean that up."

"I'll get it after I stitch you."

"Please, let me take care of you."

"It's fine. This won't work, you know. I think it's time for you to make a new plan."

"I came here to marry you." She'd decided to stick to her plan to marry him. The last few minutes had confirmed that he was the right man for her. As long as she never deviated from her goal, she would succeed. She needed him.

He turned away from her. "It's just not possible."

"Because it's too dangerous?"

"Yes."

"Do you think I'm safer somewhere else? Where is this magical place that will keep me safe all the time? Or is it just easier for you if I'm unsafe out of your sight?"

He snapped his head up to look at her. "You need a husband to protect you."

"I thought so, too. In fact, that's why I came here."

"You need someone else."

"Being here like this puts me in as much danger as marrying you would." She was frustrated. She never thought she would be in the position to force a man to marry her. "Your ranch out of town seems like the safest option to me."

"There are other men you could marry." He stood and began to pace.

"Like the sheriff?" she scoffed.

"Not hardly. He won't be around here again, anyway. We're making Daniel the Sheriff."

"You think you can just do that?"

"It's done. We were already planning on it. This will push up the schedule. He was already doing the job more than Danes ever did."

"Let's get back on topic." He grunted, and she knew that was what he was hoping to avoid. "You're the man I came to marry. You're the only man I want. It's your arms that comfort me. It's with you I feel safe. I want you." Her words were getting through to him about as well as a piece of goose down trying to bore into a rock.

Jeni stood and planted her hands on her hips. "Who do you suggest I marry, Mr. Maxwell? Who would you like to see me with — his side pressed to mine and his arm around my waist?" His jaw ticked. She was getting somewhere now. "Who would you like to see me kiss at the alter? Which man would you like to father my children? You name the man, and I'll marry him today."

Scott stared at her as if he wanted to pound her hypothetical fiancé into the dirt.

Her anger drained away, leaving frustrated pragmatism. "I know you feel the same attraction for me I feel for you. I know you want me as much as I want you."

Desperation had driven her to go too far, but she was exasperated, and her head was pounding. Why not tell him how she felt? She had no idea when she would see him again. Until he married her, nothing she could do would settle her nerves.

Angry tears flowed, and the more she tried to stop them, the harder they came. Angry crying was the worst.

He reached for her, cursed, and stormed out the back door.

She ran to the back door and shouted after him, "Name the man, and I'll let him court me right away." She slammed the door and returned to her bedroom to fume and fret in peace. As soon as she relaxed, every muscle in her body reminded her of the assault. She was sore, and she was sad. She couldn't believe he was rejecting her after all of that.

Caleb tapped on her door and asked her to join him in the kitchen. He came in with supplies to stitch her head and laid them out on the table. He handed her a cup of willow bark tea to ease her pain. Caleb's hands shook and every time she winced, he stopped, but he closed up the gash in her head and washed the blood away. It didn't take long, and then he cleaned up after himself.

He didn't try to talk to her, but before he walked out the door, he whispered, "I'm so sorry."

Thank goodness she didn't have to explain what had happened between her and Scott.

She could hardly process it herself.

OPAL SUGGESTED SHE USE HIS JEALOUSY AGAINST HIM. It hadn't felt right to do, but he was so stubborn, and the look he'd given her when she'd threatened to wed another man lent merit to Opal's plan. She had to get through to this man. Jeni had a moment of panic every time she wondered if he might show up with a substitute groom. But, no. He wouldn't. The look on his possessive, conflicted face told her this was the way to go.

Jeni wondered if she should tell him about Mr. Benson, the suitor she'd run away from. She'd worried more and more over the last week or two. If Mr. Benson found her still unmarried, she would have no hope. Jeni sighed. Thinking of ways to convince Scott had become her hobby. Still, she couldn't figure out how to get through to him.

Maybe Denise and Sarah had some idea of how to help her. Oh, how she missed her friends.

Jeni pulled their letter from her pocket. Den's perfect handwriting on the envelope had new tears stinging her eyes. She wished she could see their faces and hear their voices. Sarah would've had this problem solved on the day of her arrival. She would've drawn her gun on him and marched him straight to the church. Smooth, irresistible Denise would've charmed him with sweet and willowy grace.

Jeni sighed again as the scent of Denise wafted to her when she opened the envelope. The smell of lavender would always make her think of Denise. Jeni was homesick.

Several greenbacks fell out as she unfolded the pages.

Dearest Jeni,

We're shocked. We both feel a mixture of sadness and anger. Sarah has said several times she wishes she could be there with her gun on that Scott and force him to marry you. It took quite a while to stop her ranting just to finish your letter.

I get a feeling from your letter that you like him, though, that you trust him. I've always respected your instincts for people, so I think you should stick with Mr. Maxwell. Give him time, but don't stop reminding him that you are waiting. My heart hurts that you don't have the safety you sought in the West.

I fear for you, and I worry about you constantly. Sarah does too, but you know her worry looks like anger, and her rage leans toward violence. Every time she thinks about you, I can tell, because she fiddles with the edge of the knife in her pocket.

In case he hasn't come around yet, we have some ideas for you.

First off, Sarah wants you to get yourself a gun and insist on him teaching you how to use it. It would be good for him to have to stand close to you, wrap his arms around you, and spend some time with you. If he won't, maybe jealousy of the man teaching you would inspire him. Sarah said that once you're good with a gun, point it at him and take him to the church. She will never change.

Next, we're worried about you, so we sent you some money. It isn't much, but it is what we could scrape together. Miss Samantha even contributed. She came for tea yesterday, and we discussed your situation. We'd just read your letter before she arrived, not expecting it to provoke such anxiety. We really couldn't think of anything else. Please hide the money away in case of an emergency. I just can't stop worrying that Mr. Benson will find you. This way, if he does, you can get a ticket and find somewhere else to hide.

No matter what you do, do not let that man send you back to Boston. Mr. Benson is looking for you, and Sarah heard a rumor that he has sent scouts out around the country to find you. We don't want to upset you or make you afraid, but you must be on the lookout. He even came here to my house and threatened me. I'm fine. I told him that if I heard from you, I would send him a message. He blustered, but then he left.

We hope you've had some luck in convincing your man to do the right thing by now. It took a terribly long time to receive your letter. Much longer than it should have, and when it arrived, it had been opened. We're afraid that it was opened at the post office here, and your whereabouts could be known. I hope this letter and warning finds you much more quickly than your letter found us.

Do not come home. If you haven't told your Mr. Maxwell about Mr. Benson, you must tell him now. We are convinced he would marry you if he knew such a monster was chasing you across the country.

We have discussed this in depth, and both think that you have a right to demand that Scott Maxwell marry you. Since he brought you out there, he should do what he promised. We have other ideas about how you can get him to marry you. You know how Miss Samantha is with a problem to solve. It will take courage, but I think you should take her advice.

THE LETTER CONTINUED WITH DETAILS OF THEIR IDEA TO help Jeni trap Scott into marriage. It was a crazy plan, and she didn't know if she was brave enough to do it.

Jeni frowned to herself and considered her options. She didn't want to trap Scott — she wanted him to choose to marry her. Jeni hadn't come to Montana for a love match, but she'd secretly hoped for one. And she could love Scott.

That she was so desperate that she needed to trap a man hurt.

Jeni wallowed in self-pity for a moment, then started reading the last page.

She gasped, "Oh, my!"

And now, before I say goodbye, I have a surprise of my own! I am engaged to Mr. Dylan Johnson. I'm beside myself with joy. He is devoted to me, and I know we will be happy together. It has taken two years to get him to propose, but I'm so excited. He says the engagement will have to be at least another year, until his parents are ready to approve, but what's a year when we're already engaged? I'm planning my wedding in my head every day.

Sarah is fine. She is tired of finishing school. She is still the wild beast that she always was, only now she looks like a refined lady. You should see her. You've only been gone for two months, but she has already changed so much. Only her appearance, mind you. She's finally finished the custom holster she was making and altered her dresses to wear with it. She's very proud of that holster and the fact that she can pull a blade or a gun faster than any gunslinger in the West. The real Sarah will never change.

Sarah and I love you dearly, and we wish you the best.

Please write again soon.

All our love,

Denise and Sarah

Denise deserved all the happiness in the world.

Her friend had been talking about Mr. Johnson for a couple of years now, and it was wonderful that he had finally made her an offer of marriage. A moment of sadness overcame Jeni when she realized that meant that Denise wouldn't be traveling to Montana to marry one of her future brothers.

The money was a blessing. It must have been hard for any of them to part with. It touched her to know how much they loved her. She hid it away under the bottom of her carpetbag in the wardrobe.

Jeni had a laugh at Sarah's expense. She could not picture Sarah as any sort of lady, refined or otherwise. Sarah had been raised by her father after her mother had passed, and she grew up working on her father's ranch as if she were a son and not a daughter. She'd always worn denims and boots, and she wore a knife before any of the boys in school did. Jeni pictured Sarah with her hair coming out in every direction, her half-washed face, and brilliant eyes shining brightly. Jeni could not wrest the image of Sarah from the girl wearing her favorite Stetson and racing her huge buckskin into any prim and proper lady.

Denise and Sarah had both suggested that she use jealousy to trap Scott, as Opal had. The thought of trapping him into marriage hurt, but what other choice did she have? Maybe in time, he would grow to love her. Maybe the end would eventually justify the means.

Jeni set the letter aside and left the room to go help Elenor with supper. There was a lot to think about, but having something to keep her hands busy would be welcome. Even with her head pounding, she needed to feel useful. She could think better when she was working.

Fear of Mr. Benson finding her would overwhelm her if she didn't find something else to do. What if he had read her letter and followed her? How stupid could she be? She should have at least changed her name. She should have suspected that the post was being watched.

At supper, Caleb watched her. They all watched her. The black eye and split lip did nothing to help her be invisible, and the men at the table were unusually silent when they glanced her way. Caleb was especially attentive, though, and Jeni felt like she had her friend back again.

Man, she'd missed him.

Chapter Seven

A few weeks later, Jeni put her friends' plan into action. Jeni and Opal spent time working together as much as possible. She stopped going to the post office and only ventured out of her room to help prepare meals or use the necessary.

Caleb had taken to avoiding her again. She didn't know what she'd done to upset him, but the friendship that they had enjoyed was gone. He slept at the boarding house and took all of his meals there, but he kept busy and didn't seek her company during the day. Jeni missed him. The days were long when she worked in her room by herself.

When she left her room, she searched for Mr. Benson constantly, imagining him around every corner. Each time she entered the dining room, she feared that he'd be sitting at the table waiting for her. It was a never-ending torment to her.

She should talk to Caleb about Mr. Benson so he could tell Scott, but she didn't know how to start

99

that conversation. She had not seen Scott since the day he rescued her from the sheriff, but she knew he kept track of her as he always had.

Her conversations with Caleb had become strained even more since the attack. There was anger beneath his calm that she couldn't figure out. He looked relaxed, as always, but the muscles in his jaw worked overtime, and his patience appeared to have run out. His post as a babysitter bored him, and he wanted to be somewhere else.

Who could blame him?

It had been almost three months.

If she asked what was wrong, he brushed her off. She couldn't ask him to leave because she needed him, but a part of her wished he would take his attitude and go. He was the only person protecting her while she rejected marriage offers from the men in town, and she didn't want to face that alone. She wasn't only turning down the men from Hope now; men had traveled into town from all over to propose to her. The story of Scott's rejection had spread to the outlying communities and neighboring villages, and suitors were coming in to try their luck. The boarding house never had an empty room, and the suppertime interrogation became a nightly routine. She maintained her position as Scott's fiancé and dodged as many questions as possible. If any man got too pushy, her reluctant protector was there to set him in his place.

She wasn't sitting on her hands every minute of the day, though. Jeni was busy designing and sewing a dress for the community Christmas party.

It was a dress meant to knock everyone's socks off, especially Scott's. With every tiny stitch, she thanked her lucky stars that the nuns at the Merciful Hearts Orphanage in Boston had taught her a skill. She could stitch a gown as well as any modiste, and this was her very best work.

The Christmas party was the last social event before winter hit hard, according to Opal. After that, travel back and forth from town to the outlying areas would become much more difficult, sometimes impossible. It could be months before she would see the men from the ranch again.

This was her last chance.

Jeni could not risk Scott being stuck at the ranch if she needed him. With the threat of Mr. Benson looming, she would feel safer if she was married and out of town when travel stopped. If Scott had visited, she might've confessed, but he hadn't, and now she was done waiting.

As Sarah and Denise had suggested, Jeni played up her womanly assets for the first time in her life. She had shared the letter from her friends with Opal, and her new friend had jumped at the chance to help. Opal had ordered the most luxurious emerald green silk from New York, and she insisted Jeni take it. Jeni had never touched such extravagance in her life and tried to refuse the offer. The green silk was expensive, and Jeni could not pay Opal back. In the end, Opal won, and the two women designed a gown — each adding her own personal touches until they had a one-of-a-kind masterpiece.

Mrs. Whitfield, Opal's mother, worked at the

dressmaker's shop. Opal had learned the trade from her mother and was every bit as good at sewing as she was at passing gossip, even if she did sometimes forget she was supposed to help and just disappeared. Other times, she stitched all night long and fell asleep on Jeni's floor in a pile of silks and ribbons.

Jeni had always used drab colors and plain patterns to camouflage herself, but this new gown put all her best attributes on display. Opal loaned Jeni a corset and a little bustle to wear under the dress and showed her a fresh way to wear her hair. The skirt was decked out in layers of ruffles. A swag of fabric at the waist swept back and connected to a small bustle. The fitted bodice of the dress had vertical panels running up to a lace collar and tapering at the waist, emphasizing the narrowness of her middle. A row of tiny pearl buttons ran down the back. Jeni would need help to get into and out of this outfit.

Under the shimmering green gown, Jeni wore a corset that cinched her waist from small to tiny. The added bustle maximized her hourglass figure and created an extreme silhouette. She put on her drop pearl earrings. The beautiful white beads looked delicate hanging from her ears, and she felt special wearing the only real jewelry she owned. She'd worked hard and saved to buy the earrings for herself, and she was proud of them; somehow, the little drops gave her courage.

Jeni's hair, which she always wore on top of her head, hung down her back tonight. She remembered

Scott's hands running down the length of her hair and decided that leaving it down would capture his attention more than curls and tucks. She pulled the front of her hair back and pinned it to frame her face. Her natural, wavy curls were vibrant and shiny. Highlights of blonde and lowlights of auburn mixed with the bright red to create a cascade that never failed to draw the eye.

As she studied her reflection, she felt beautiful. She rarely felt good about being attractive. Something was empowering about how she looked tonight, though. She felt bold looking in that mirror. All her life, people had said she was beautiful, but she rarely felt it.

Tonight she did.

The feeling frightened her, though. This was a dangerous game she was playing. If this plan backfired, she was out of options.

Out of time.

Out of luck.

She wrapped herself in a cloak, drew up her courage, and exited her room.

Caleb waited in the sitting room. His eyes widened when he saw her, but he didn't say a word. He picked up the basket Elenor had put together for the party and held out his arm to her.

AT THE CHURCH, EVERY EYE IN THE ROOM TURNED TO take her in. For a moment, Jeni's tenacity faltered.

Ignoring the butterflies and tingling limbs, she pasted a smile on her face and glanced around.

The town residents had decorated the church for the Christmas party and it was lovely. They'd moved the pews to the sides to make room for dancing, and everywhere she looked, there were boughs of pine. The women had done miracles with the simple space.

Jeni spied the tables of food along the far wall. Perfect. Having something to do would make it a lot easier to join the party. The first step was the hardest.

Here goes nothing, she told herself as she removed her cloak.

Conversations close to her faltered.

Her courage briefly faltered along with them.

She'd expected attention, but this was ridiculous. Jeni tried to look as casual as possible, maintaining that pasted-on smile and holding her head high. She knew the heat she felt rising in her cheeks could be seen in a rosy blush on her face. She wanted to run away, but she'd come with a plan, and she'd see it through.

When she turned to Caleb, she saw an admiration in his eyes that had never been there before. Her friends were right. For this to work, she had to accept the attention of every man in the room. Tonight, she would dance and smile at all of them.

She had to.

She smiled at Caleb and took the large basket from his awe-weakened grasp. Jeni skirted around the crowded room toward the food tables.

As she made her way, people cleared a path in front of her that fell closed again as she passed. The chatter stopped as she approached and began anew as she moved away. Jeni smiled at everyone and kept walking. She hoped she didn't look as afraid as she felt.

Opal, wearing a lovely deep blue and silver gown, caught her eye from the end of the dessert table and smiled. With a not-so-subtle wink, she let Jeni know she was doing fine.

Jeni smiled and nodded at her; she appreciated the solidarity.

Elenor was directing the women at the food tables, so Jeni headed toward her. Elenor looked cheerful in a bright red dress with white lace trim. Jeni knew she was particularly proud of that lace collar and remembered to compliment her friend on it. Elenor beamed.

Elenor looked Jeni over and whistled. "You look like the queen of Christmas!" She whistled again. There was admiration in Elenor's voice, but no jealousy.

Jeni plucked at a ruffle on her skirt and swished her skirts around her legs. "I thought I would try something a little different tonight."

"If that doesn't get you what you want, nothing will." Elenor chuckled. "Ya got a plan?"

"I'm going to have fun."

Elenor let go one of her wonderful belly laughs and slapped her hands on her skirt. "That'll do him in for sure." Elenor enjoyed this far too much. Jeni took courage from the other woman's humor and smiled even brighter. She lifted a roll out of the basket and threw it at Elenor. It bounced off her apron, and Elenor caught it with a laugh.

Jeni spotted Rose and Iris at the other end of the table. She stopped to visit with them for a few minutes and then chatted with any of the ladies present who would speak to her. She kept the bright smile pasted on her face the entire time, then she turned and surveyed the room, looking for Scott in the crowd.

Tonight she wouldn't hide her light under a basket. Tonight she wouldn't make herself small so that other people could feel better about themselves.

She was going to torture a good man.

* * *

The music played, and Scott watched as three men asked Jeni to dance. She smiled and took the hand of the man who was closest to her. Scott wanted to punch him.

"She made that dress special for you," Caleb said as he reached the punch bowl where Scott and Caine were standing.

"I know," Scott said. "She hasn't exactly been keeping her intentions a secret."

"What are you going to do about it?" Caine asked, holding up his flask and offering to top off their cups of punch.

All three men sipped their spirits and watched Jeni move around the floor, smiling up at a cowboy and allowing him to hold her much closer than she should.

"Not a damn thing." Scott threw back his whisky and held his cup for another.

"Oh no you don't," Caine said. "It's not going to be that kind of night. This is the Christmas party. We're not leaving here early to carry your ass home." He pocketed the flask.

They watched her float as man after man cut in. One after another, dance partners approached. She said yes to all of them. Whirling and smiling, she never looked in Scott's direction after the first time she'd seen him standing there. He couldn't take his eyes off of her.

His mouth watered just looking at her.

After several songs, she excused herself from the dance floor and walked toward the reverend, who was standing to the side of the room with his wife. Scott watched as she stood, back straight and head high, talking to Reverend Simon for a few minutes.

Her hair was long, and Scott remembered the feel in his hands. It bounced when she tossed her head. He wanted to have his hands in her hair again. He kicked himself for taking the liberty in the first place. He wasn't trying to send her mixed signals, but he knew that's what he was doing. The gown drew his eyes to her lush curves, and he had to shift his position to hide his reaction.

He shouldn't have touched her, because now that he had, it was all he wanted to do. He couldn't be what she wanted. He'd learned from Amy's death, and Jeni deserved better.

He needed to learn how to keep his hands off of her when she was near.

She should've just accepted his ticket back to Boston.

The Reverend agreed with whatever she said, nodding and smiling and shaking her hand. After a moment, she turned and walked away with a small, satisfied smile playing across her lips. There was still sadness and stress in the lines around her eyes, though. He wondered what she would look like if she were ever completely happy.

He'd probably never know.

It was hard rejecting this woman. Doing it repeatedly was worse. Every time she tried to make him see reason, it was harder to tell her no.

When she approached The Maxwell Group standing together, she held her hand out to Caleb. "After all of this time together, I wondered if you would do me the honor of a dance."

"Who could say no to that?" He took the hand she held out for him, shrugged at his brother, and followed her to the floor. She smiled warmly up at him and stepped into his arms for a slow waltz.

Caine could not suppress a laugh. "She's really coming for you tonight, cous."

"Uh-huh."

ENOUGH WAS ENOUGH.

She had no more time to play games with him. Scott was going to marry her. Right now.

She never wanted to do this, but he gave her no choice.

The hour was getting late, and Scott had not asked her to dance. She'd danced with just about every other man in town. She was at the end of her rope, exhausted and out of time.

It was now or never.

"Reverend Simon," she called over the din. All eyes turned to her, and voices stopped. The musicians had taken a break to get some food before the women were to pack up what was left over, and the room was relatively quiet. "Please do me the honor of performing my wedding now?" she sweetly asked.

"I'm ready." He responded. He walked toward her slowly, holding his bible, with his wife by his side. "Do you have a groom?"

She turned, "Scott Maxwell. This is the last time I'm going to propose to you." A din of laughter went around the room. "If you don't marry me now, I will marry another." She stared right at him, trying to read his reaction. Everyone in the room did the same. There were a few chuckles, followed by intense silence.

You could hear a pin drop.

Nobody in the room even breathed.

"Shit," he cursed. "We've been over this."

She didn't break eye contact as she walked straight up to him, pulled him down to her height, and whispered into his ear.

He stood and cursed again.

Scott kept his gaze directed over her head. He looked anywhere but into her eyes.

"I told you before, I'm not asking again, and I'm

not waiting any longer. If you won't marry me tonight, then point out a man you trust, and I will marry him right now." She was serious. "I'm not leaving this room an unmarried woman. Make a choice!"

Every person in the room waited for his answer.

He made them wait, too.

He stood there, face to face with Jeni, and stared at the wall behind her head. She didn't move a muscle; she stood straight as an arrow, hands on her hips, and waited him out. Behind her, the Reverend waited, and around them, so did everyone else.

Scott sighed.

He shook his head.

Jeni smiled.

There was no doubt left when he cursed again — he was hers.

Releasing a breath, Jeni grabbed his hand and walked him to the Reverend.

A few people chuckled, a few groaned, but most of them looked like they enjoyed the show.

Caleb slipped out of the room with Will right behind him. Why would they want to miss their brother's wedding? She shifted and looked up into Scott's eyes and forgot about everyone else. Opal pressed a bouquet of silk flowers into her hands and kissed her cheek.

She expected to meet anger or frustration in Scott's expression, but she found humor and desire. "You're going to pay for that little whisper tonight." He threatened quietly. Not quietly enough. A few chuckles told her that at least a few people had heard him. By the end of the ceremony, everyone would know what he had said. Jeni was grateful that only Scott knew what she'd whispered.

She couldn't stop the blush from spreading up her chest and covering her face. She could feel the path of heat riding up her skin. She was sure she must be red as a beet, but she didn't care, and Scott seemed to enjoy her situation.

Jeni was getting the security that she'd been searching for. She was finally getting married. Before the end of the night, she would be his. She could take a little laugh at her expense.

When all the vows were said and the 'I dos' finished, the Reverend announced, "You may kiss the bride," and boy did he ever! Scott drew Jeni into his arms, pulled her tight against his rock-hard chest, and pressed his mouth to hers. With the whole town watching, he branded her as his own.

If it were possible, Jeni's blush deepened, and the assembly laughed when she gasped.

She probably deserved that after putting him on the spot.

Jeni's knees went rubbery. If he hadn't been holding her so tightly against his body, she would've dropped to the floor.

He whispered into her ear, "Time for us to go." And he swept her into his arms and carried her out of the church while everyone tittered.

His brothers were all waiting outside, mounted and holding Scott's horse. Caleb had Jeni's carpet bags. He nodded when she noticed them, but he didn't look happy for her.

He looked disappointed, and Jeni wondered, not for the first time, if he agreed with the town that she was not suitable for Scott. It made her sad that the man she considered a good friend was not happy.

Caine held out her cloak and said, "Welcome to the family."

Without another word from any of them, they moved in unison. Scott mounted his horse, and Caine lifted Jeni up into his arms. It was an odd feeling to sit in his lap — an even stranger feeling to be on his lap, riding his horse. Jeni had never ridden a horse before and clung to her new husband.

His arms around her supported and thrilled her. His scent surrounded her, and she breathed deeply, filling up every square inch of her lungs with him. This had been her favorite scent since the first time he had pulled her into his arms. The smell of leather, and horses, and Scott.

She noticed the same scent of leather, and horse, and man when Caleb had been close to her sometimes, but it was different. Scott's scent was pure Scott. She nuzzled close and drank him in as they rode slowly out of town.

He leaned over, pressed another kiss to her mouth, and rested his forehead on hers. For two beats of her heart, he didn't move. It was the most intimate touch Jeni had ever experienced in her life, and she melted into him. He was everything she'd ever hoped he'd be, and she couldn't get enough.

She was going to love him so much.

He would be so easy to love.

"Time to go!" Caleb announced as the church started emptying with people headed for home.

"Is everything ok?" Jeni noticed the stress on the faces of the men. It wasn't only Caleb who didn't like this.

Was the whole Maxwell Group upset about this marriage?

That was going to be hard to live with. Jeni knew how important these men were to each other. She hoped she had caused no sort of rift.

"Wait, what about Rose and Iris?" She hadn't noticed until now that the two women weren't with the group before.

"They'll be along later. They have farmhands to escort them." Scott said.

"Are we ok?"

"As long as nobody follows us. We're going to head right on home, and not leaving until spring. You make a supply list, and I'll send someone into town in a few days, but after that, everyone is staying home." Scott told her. "I told you marrying me would be dangerous, and now you're going to find out what that means."

She reached up and touched his cheek. When he looked down at her, she said, "I'm sorry."

He turned his head and kissed her palm, as she had done to him in Elenor's kitchen. "I'm not."

Chapter Eight

S cott cradled Jeni in front of him and kissed the top of her head but but there was tension in the air that was impossible to ignore. His hold was gentle, as she knew it always would be, but he was anything but relaxed. She couldn't see Caleb or Hank, but his other brothers watched the horizon as anxiously as Scott did. Caine turned to scan behind then and the moonlight revealed the same tense jaw that she saw when she tipped her head back to stare at Scott.

Testing her courage, Jeni placed her palm against Scott's chest through the open front of his jacket. His breath hitched. His muscles twitched. Jeni ran her fingertip over his stubbly throat.

"Are you angry with me?" she asked.

"I'm afraid for you." Scott shook his head and cuddled Jeni close for a second. Jeni's heart overflowed, it was the most cherished she'd ever felt. His tenderness didn't last, though, because as soon as he settled into her, his muscles bunched again.

"You said you weren't sorry."

"I'm not." He pressed a kiss to the top of her head and let his cheek rest against the spot for a second.

"What *are* you feeling?"

"I wish I knew." He shook his head again. "It's like all of my dreams came true, and I'm afraid I could lose them. I don't know. Right now I just want to get you home and out of the open. There's still danger out here for us."

"Do you wish you'd named another man?" Jeni's heart was in her throat waiting for him to answer.

"I never could have done such a thing. You've been mine since the day you arrived, I just wanted to protect you." He ran his warm hand down her arm and squeezed her close. "I do wish I understood your rush."

"What were my options?" she hoped he didn't hear the whine in her voice, she was desperate but she didn't want to seem whiny. "Were you planning to pay for the boarding house forever?"

His mouth didn't react, but his body did.

Jeni tensed. She gnawed on her lip. As his tension grew, hers did too. "It's been months, Scott. I'm out of time. I need to be married, and you are the only one I want."

Whenever she mentioned that she wanted him, his heart skipped faster under her hand. They needed to talk, but she sensed that they would be great together. He held her like she was the most important thing in the world. Jeni pressed her face into his neck and tried to soothe him as well as she could.

After a few minutes he relaxed again and responded. "How long I pay for your board is my business. And why are you out of time?" Scott wrapped his arm around her waist and pulled her up tighter to his body. When she winced, he ran a finger over the edge of her corset, and then read-justed to make her more comfortable.

She didn't want to tell him about Mr. Benson like this, so she gave another truth. "Opal said that this event signals the coming of winter, and travel back and forth to the ranch would become impossible. I couldn't stay in town until spring."

"Why?"

"I told you. It's not safe."

"And I told you *this* wasn't safe." He tensed and half-stood in his stirrups. Jeni clung to him and waited for him to sit back down. He was strung too tight to have this discussion.

"Let's talk about it when we get inside." Scott's hand was warm through the cloak and corset.

"You read my mind," she said.

She prayed that they would be safe. Now that she had him, she would let him go. She was ready to be all of the things he'd asked for in his letter, and more.

He didn't press for more information, and it relieved her to let it go. He softened a very little bit, and Jeni focused on his warm hand as it traveled up and down her arm. She petted his chest in the same way, offering any comfort she could.

For the next half hour, Jeni let her mind wander to more pleasant topics. Scott's body tensed and relaxed periodically as his attention was drawn and released from various spots on the horizon. With the six strong men to protect her, she allowed herself to focus on her new husband.

Husband. She liked that.

She'd been told what to expect on her wedding night, and as nervous as she was, her excitement overrode all other emotions. When she'd whispered into his ear at the party, his reaction was unmistakable, as was the way he'd shifted to hide it. Jeni hoped tonight he'd be able to let all the worry go. She let him be, deciding to wait until they were alone to try talking again.

THE ONLY THING THAT SCOTT COULD THINK ABOUT AS he nestled Jeni close was that he could lose her like Caine had lost Amy three years ago, and he'd never survive. He braced himself against the pain that Amy's memory always ushered in.

He tried to push away the memories and fear and be in the moment with his wife, but then some movement on the horizon would catch his eye, or a sound would pull his attention away. When he tensed, she did too. He struggled to keep her comfortable, but her corset dug into her ribs every time he had to adjust her, and every little wince made him cringe, too.

It was a long ride, and he was glad when he could see the lights of home. He'd get her inside and they would be fine.

He hoped.

His brothers would protect the house. They'd give Scott privacy and protection on his wedding night. It's what he would do for any of them.

He couldn't wrap his mind around the fact that he was married, and to such a special woman. Jeni wasn't just his mail-order bride, she was a mail-order dream come true. She was everything, strong, smart, funny and beautiful.

Caleb had talked about her non-stop, and Scott felt like he knew her intimately. It was probably the reason Caleb never stopped telling stories of Jeni's best friends, of her usefulness to Elenor, her pranks and jokes, and about how warm she was to Rose and Iris. With every story, Scott had grown closer to her. It choked him up to think of sending her away, or of pushing her to marry anyone else.

Now she was his, forever.

If overwhelming fear didn't have him by the balls, he'd be on top of the world.

The cabin glowed in the distance, and Scott pointed it out to Jeni. Someone, probably Hank, had ridden ahead and stoked the fire and lit a lantern in the front room. The smoke rising from the chimney lit up in the moonlight, and the windows glowed gold in the darkness.

The curve of Jeni's waist in his hand kept his

mind wandering forward a few hours into the night. He wanted to explore these curves. He wanted to explore every square inch of her soft body.

As soon as he became too comfortable in his romantic thoughts, fear pushed in again. He couldn't help but wonder if he should have pointed her toward a different man. He could have taken the pain of losing her, to protect her. He wouldn't have had her, but at least he'd have been able to watch her from afar. It was foolish to even consider, nobody else would love her like he would. His fear was useless. He kept pushing it away, and it kept pushing back in.

If he lost her like they'd lost Amy — he couldn't even think about it.

They were wed now, and they'd face whatever might come together.

When they rode up to the front of the house, Caine was waiting for them. He helped Jeni to the ground and waited for Scott to dismount, then led the horse away and left the newlyweds alone in the yard.

IT WAS TOO DARK FOR JENI TO SEE MUCH AROUND HER. The cabin was small but sturdy, and everything she could see in the moonlight looked well-tended. Scott opened the door and, in the most romantic gesture possible, he scooped her up and carried her inside.

He gently set her back on her feet and pressed a

quick kiss to the top of her head. She could get used to that.

Scott closed the door, removed his boots, dropped them on a mat, and hung his coat on a peg above them. He motioned toward her feet as he took her cloak and hung it beside his jacket. She assumed he wanted her to do the same but that was not as easy as it sounded, and self-consciousness suddenly had her by the throat.

"Iris never let us wear shoes in the house. It's a pretty ingrained habit, and I'd like to keep it up," he explained.

She nodded, but blushed and didn't move. She couldn't speak.

His eyebrows came together in a quizzical expression that made her laugh.

"I can't reach my boots with the corset," she finally admitted.

He did laugh at that.

He kneeled in front of her and picked up one foot. She wobbled and had to place her hands on his shoulders to keep from falling over. He made quick work of removing the buttons from their holes and slipped her foot out of the boot. He held it up and looked at it with some wonder in his eyes. It was easy to understand his fascination when he placed it on the floor beside his own huge boot. He repeated the process with her other foot.

His hands burned where he held her ankle and when he ran his hand up her calf, sparks flew to her center. Her hands were hot against his broad shoulders. His muscle rippled under her fingers as he worked on her shoes. Heat rose to her face, but she forced herself to stand still and let him lead.

If he touched any more skin, he would burn her alive.

Scott rose and finally looked at her. "Coffee?"

"Do you have tea?"

"No, but you can add it to your supply list, and we'll get it in a few days."

"Coffee is fine. Thank you."

He moved to the kitchen. She followed, looking around as she went. The kitchen was neat, clean, and well organized. There was a sink with a pump to one side and a large stove on the other. He hadn't known he'd be attending his own wedding. He must be naturally neat. That would be nice.

Jeni determined that tomorrow she would take the time to familiarize herself with where everything was.

"Are you hungry? You didn't eat at the dance."

He *had* been watching her. His thoughtfulness was touching.

"I'm not hungry, thank you. I ate before Opal helped me into this contraption." She tapped the stay on the corset and blushed again.

It was cute when something she said startled him. But he said nothing. He poured coffee into two mugs and brought them to the table between the sitting room and the kitchen. He held a chair for her before he lowered himself into another.

His anger and worry faded away with his first sip. He looked wrung out and tired. He looked like she felt. She reached for his hand, and when he ran his thumb over her knuckles, the butterflies in her belly went wild.

———————

THEY TALKED ABOUT SMALL THINGS AS THEY DRANK their coffee. Jeni looked like she was wrestling nerves as much as he was, but he imagined hers was a different sort of anxiety.

After a while, she rose from her chair and approached him. Anticipation already had his stomach in knots, and every move she made twisted him up more. He thought she'd kiss him when her eyes darted from his eyes to his mouth.

She didn't, though.

With a breath as deep as the corset would allow, she turned her back to him. She reached one hand back and drew all of her hair over her shoulder, and with her other hand, she tapped the top button on the dress. She didn't need to speak.

Several times he had to reposition himself in his chair as his fingers skimmed her soft skin. He forced his hands to stay steady as he worked his way down the long pearly row. Her skin was warm where the back of his fingers touched the nape of her long neck.

As he approached the bottom of the gown, the top opened and slipped prettily forward off her shoulders. She caught it and held the front, protecting her modesty.

She wouldn't have much of that left by the end of the night.

After the last button was free, she stepped away. Still holding her bodice with one hand, she flicked her hair back with her other. The way the lantern light played off the colors in her hair made him stifle a groan. He wanted to run his hands through the shiny curls. He wanted to feel all of that softness against his body.

Patience would kill him.

Jeni's voice shook when she asked for a moment to get ready for bed.

All he could see was innocence in her furrowed brow and pleading eyes. Scott stood from the table and pulled his wife into his arms. He rocked her from side to side. She still clutched the dress to her chest and the pounding of her heart was so rapid he feared she'd pass out.

They swayed in the night for several minutes before her breathing became almost normal and her heart slowed to a less concerning pace. Scott tipped her face up to his and pressed his lips to hers. Every so gently, he probed the crease with his tongue, and she opened to let him in.

She warmed with his kiss. One hand released her gown and grasped the back of his neck. She rose to her toes and pulled him down for a more solid connection.

Her passion matched his.

They stood like that for a while, coming up for air and then diving back into the coffee flavored depths. Scott stopped the kiss and pressed his forehead to hers, catching his breath. A moment later, he lifted his face to look into her eyes.

"I'll give you a minute."

Jeni's eyelashes fluttered over her cheeks when she nodded and stepped back. She held the bodice with one hand and gathered the skirt with the other. Then she made her way to the bedroom. Their eyes locked until the door was closed behind her.

Scott washed up at the pump in the kitchen. He rinsed the coffee from his mouth and then dried his face with a clean towel.

He'd just finished stoking the fire when a muffled sob brought him up quick. He crossed the room in three long strides and entered the bedroom.

———

THE MATTRESS DIPPED AS SCOTT SLIPPED INTO THE BED beside Jeni, and it startled her. She hadn't heard the door open or close. When he slid his arm under her and rolled her into him, she went.

She curled herself into his side with her face pressed against his chest and let the tears fall.

Months of stress had built up so much pressure and she hadn't seen it coming. She'd pulled the covers over her and one tear had trickled out. When she tried to stop it, the floodgates had opened.

Scott held her for a long time and Jeni's body racked.

As her tears slowed, his hands moved. He rubbed up and down the arm she had thrown across his abdomen. His other hand alternated between rubbing her back and toying with her hair. They lay together on the bed for a while before either spoke.

When she had caught her breath, and her body was relaxed against him, he asked. "Are you ok now?"

"This is the best I've ever been in my life."

"What brought that on?" Scott twisted her hair around his fingertip.

"I guess it was just the release of finally being safe." Jeni admitted.

It was strange to be lying in bed with a man, intimate and surprising. It was nice, but also still felt a little wrong. He was her husband; she had to get that thought through her head. She circled his chest with her hand, catching the cuff of her nightgown on the buttons of his shirt.

"You know Caleb would have stayed with you as long as you needed. All winter if it was necessary. We never would have left you unprotected."

"It's not the men in town that I fear, and Caleb was growing wearier and wearier of watching me. I could tell." She paused, trying to figure out how to go on. His hand in her hair was something to focus on, helping her organize her thoughts. He was so warm. She snuggled a little closer, but it didn't feel close enough. Nothing would be close enough.

"Caleb thinks there's something you haven't told us. It would be easier if you'd just spit it out so we could deal with it. Are you running from the law?"

She drew back. "Running from the law?"

"It's obvious you have a secret."

She giggled a little at the thought of herself as a criminal. If one of them were running from the law, it would be her friend Sarah. That gave her a laugh because, as hard as it was for her to think of herself as an outlaw, she could see Sarah as one with no problem.

"What's so funny?"

"I was picturing myself as an outlaw."

He chuckled, too. Then studied a lock of her hair. Twisting it around his fingers absentmindedly. "What's the secret, then?"

Lying in his arms in the dark room, whispering, gave her courage to confess. If he had waited until tomorrow to have this conversation, she probably couldn't have managed.

"I never wanted to be married to a man who only liked the way I looked. I want to be seen as a person, not just a pretty face. One of my suitors, Mr. Benson, didn't like to take no for an answer."

He continued to stroke her hair, arm, and back. Giving encouragement through his gentle touch. His heart rate increased under her ear, and she had a feeling he sensed where this was going.

"I discussed it with an older woman who lives in our neighborhood. Miss Samantha suggested the mail-order bride agency. It made sense. I could correspond with a groom and have acceptance without him having ever set eyes on me."

"I know that part. I want to know the other reasons."

"Men were getting forceful, impatient. You saw how it was in town here; add a year or two to that. My only friends were Sarah and Denise and Miss Samantha, and they couldn't protect me for long, though they tried."

She closed her eyes and plunged into the heart of the issue. "Mr. Benson is a rich, powerful man. At first, he was a gentleman. He brought flowers and asked me to dine with him. I refused as delicately as I could. Even in the beginning, when he was trying to be sweet, I could sense that he was dangerous. It wasn't just his reputation for being ruthless or the thugs that always surrounded him. There was something about him that felt particularly threatening."

His chin bumped her forehead as he nodded against the top of her head, and he pressed a kiss to the part in her hair. It was the sweetest thing, and for a moment, she didn't want to go on. She didn't want to talk about her fear. She wanted to sink into her husband and take the comfort that he was so generously giving.

"Let's have it all, so we don't have to do this again."

"Every time I rejected Mr. Benson, his pursuit became increasingly aggressive. One day I was on my way to the mercantile, and one of his goons stopped me in the street. He said Mr. Benson was becoming impatient with my nonsense, and that if I didn't take him up on his offer, I would be sorry. That day, Denise, Sarah, and I decided it was time for me to leave town. The mail-order bride agency was my only option."

"What about your family?"

The question surprised Jeni. Surprised her, because it reminded her of how little they knew about each other. He'd never asked her about herself before. She'd assumed that Caleb had told Scott about their conversations. For a moment she mused on how strange it was that her husband's brother knew her better than her husband did.

"I grew up in an orphanage until I turned seventeen. After that, I took an apartment near my friends. As a dressmaker, I could make ends meet. I still had to take in mending, but after a few years, I stopped doing wash."

"So, you were pretty much on your own?"

"Yes."

"Leaving as a mail-order bride isn't the end of the story, though, is it?"

"No."

Jeni relayed the contents of Denise's last letter, at least the parts concerning Mr. Benson, and shared her fears with him.

"I should've known not to write using my name. I'm afraid I've led him straight to me." She rubbed her hand back and forth across Scott's chest, absently running a finger around the outside of one button before moving to the next. "I would've given you as much time as you needed if I could. Putting you on the spot like that was a desperate move, and I'm sorry to have done it that way. The only time I've felt safe in the last few years is when you've been holding me. I couldn't even bear the thought of another man."

He tilted his head and looked into her eyes. "What would you have done if I'd named another man tonight?"

"I would've married him. My heart would've broken, but nothing could be worse than Mr. Benson finding me. Marriage was the only way I could guarantee my safety from him."

He looked a little taken aback. Maybe he really had thought she was bluffing. "Are you sure he'll give up just because you're married?"

"I can't imagine why he would want me now. I still don't know why he wanted me so badly before. There are plenty of beautiful women in Boston who would have him."

"I'm afraid you made this cat-and-mouse game more exciting with your rejection. A hunter wants to catch his prey. He might not be willing to let his trophy go just because you're married."

They lay silent for a while. Scott rubbed her back, and she explored the planes of his chest through his shirt.

His heart no longer raced beneath her ear, and she was relaxed and warm against him. When she turned her face up to look into his eyes, he lowered his mouth to hers.

The kiss was long and lazy. Her lips moved with his, soft and unhurried. His lips grew bolder and more assertive as his hands roamed more of her body. She'd never been kissed like this, but she followed his lead. The feelings his hands and mouth sparked were mesmerizing. Pleasure and anticipation took over.

She forgot everything outside and focused on her husband.

Her husband.

This man with the magical hands made her feel things she'd never imagined. Everywhere he touched, fire ignited and radiated to her center. None of her imaginings could measure up to the feel of his solidness against her.

He raised himself over her as he moved his mouth from hers. He licked the corner of her mouth, then nibbled his way along her jaw to the side of her neck, burning a track into her skin and stoking the fire he was building.

Scott kissed his way up her neck, and his hand slid up the front of her nightgown. He cupped her breast through the sheer fabric. So many feelings shot through her at once. She didn't know where to focus when he nipped at her ear and squeezed the hard tip of her breast. She stopped breathing entirely.

Jeni moaned and arched up into him. She clung to his arms, not knowing what she should do, not able to devote much thought to figure it out.

Scott growled in her ear. "I like that."

"Oh my goodness, me too."

He chuckled and did it again.

He worked his hands expertly over her body. She let herself feel and not think.

When Scott removed her gown, she fought a brief panic. He was her husband. It was ok for him to see her like this. No matter how she tried to convince herself, modesty was not easy to overcome. The anxiety growing inside of her wasn't entirely nerves, though. Something exciting grew inside of her, and she wanted to feel it through to the end.

Scott removed his clothes and slowly returned to the bed. The candlelight allowed her to see the ridges and valleys of his abdomen that she'd been memorizing with her fingertips. She couldn't bring herself to follow his body downward, though he took the opportunity to study her.

He took his time slipping back into the bed, and Jeni was ready to crawl out of her skin by the time his mouth returned to hers.

Sweet anticipation took her breath away.

When she was writhing beneath him and nearly senseless, Scott positioned himself to press into her. He paused and stared deep into her eyes. Jeni pulled his mouth down to hers and pressed up toward him. The next moment, Jeni welcomed a painful pressure at her core. A feeling of indescribable fullness replaced a quick burst of pain as he thrust inside of her in one smooth motion. He stopped moving and let her get used to him, but she needed relief from the delicious ache that ran deep.

She needed to move.

Jeni rose to meet him and hungrily pulled his mouth to hers again. Instinct took over, and she moaned and rocked her hips.

His lovemaking was gentle at first but became flurried as the storm inside of them grew. He clung to her hips and she could do nothing but ride the electric wave that flowed between them until it came crashing around her. Every nerve in her body exploded in one sublime bolt of lightning.

As the storm eased, Jeni found herself resting against his body again. Both of them were sated and trying to catch their breath. His heart raced under her ear again.

Jeni was happy.

Blissful

Scott was hers, forever.

As she drifted off to sleep, Jeni painted dreams of their future. He would love her, and she was ready to love him. She imagined their children playing in the yard, a sweet kiss for her husband on his return from the fields, evening meals and bedtime stories. Then she let her mind wander to more nights like this, tumbling into the circle of his arms.

Chapter Nine

"Now you have to keep me" She snuggled deeper into his embrace, once again feeling like she couldn't get close enough.

Before he could reply, there was a knock at the front door — series of knocks, clearly a signal. The Maxwell Group had various forms of nonverbal communication, and she recognized it for what it was.

If she hadn't already guessed, Scott's reaction would have clued her in.

He leapt from bed and shoved her dress at her. He snatched his pants on and strapped his guns around his hips. After he shoved his arms into a shirt, he grabbed both of their boots from the front door. When Jeni fiddled with the buttons on her shoe, he shook his head, grabbed her hand, and moved toward the kitchen.

Jeni feared she would lose a shoe with every step. The tops flopped open against her ankles, and the heels slipped up and down as she trod. She curled her toes and hoped she could keep them on.

Scott made no sound when he moved, which was impressive for such a big man. Jeni tried to follow suit and kept as quiet as she could. It was impossible with her shoes scuffing across the floor, but she did her best.

Jeni couldn't hear anything outside, but the air crackled with energy that shot straight to her spine. The hair on the back of her neck prickled, and Scott's hand was stiff in hers.

In the kitchen, he opened the trapdoor into the root cellar and tossed his boots down. He took both of her hands in his and lowered her into the hole. Using the ladder, he followed and locked the door above them. It took him a minute to pull his boots on, and Jeni followed his progress by the sounds he made.

In the pitch black, Jeni was blind. She felt Scott, though, and the connection to him was all she needed. Still not speaking, he reached for her hand and turned her to him. He held her for a second and brushed his lips across hers.

"I'm sorry, Scott." Jeni whispered.

His lips brushed over hers as he shook his head. "Shh. It's going to be ok."

He turned and let go of her hand. Jeni couldn't stand to lose connection with him, so she reached out and placed her hand against the middle of his back. He was feeling along the wall for something. A chill waft of stale air reached her, and she heard the soft scrape of a door opening.

She wished she could see.

They were underground. Where could the door possibly lead?

Jeni trusted Scott, though, and when he took her hand, she followed. They felt their way, shuffling, and when she was through the doorway, he reached back. The scrape of the door sliding back into place grated on her nerves. Metal scraping across rock made goosebumps race up her spine. The lock clicked as he secured their hiding place. Jeni expected them to hunker down and wait. But a gunshot from above and Scott's urgent pulling on her hand sent her floppy boots into motion again.

They crept down the dark tunnel, each with one hand on the wall and the other clinging to each other. The dark overwhelmed.. It pressed down on her from all sides, and the smell of mildew saturated her nose. When she tripped on her unbuttoned shoes, Scott caught her. Battling through the dark tunnel with her shoes constantly tripping her made the anxiety double. The gunshots weren't repeated, or they couldn't hear them, and Jeni wished to know what was happening above ground. Guilt at what could happen tripped her like her boots, and she was once again fighting tears.

A faint light ahead signaled that they were coming to the end of the tunnel, and instead of calming her, it boosted her fear.

They exited the tunnel out of the mouth of a cave. He must've found the cave and extended it to his house. She couldn't imagine the amount of work that would've gone into a project like that. She didn't have time to consider it, though, because Scott pressed her down behind several large rocks. He whispered to her as he placed a gun in her hands.

"Stay here."

"Don't leave me."

"My family is up there; I have to go."

She knew he had to go, but it didn't make it any easier to let him. In a move that shocked them both, she placed her hands along the sides of his face and pulled him into a searing kiss. "Come back to me."

He pressed 1 quick kiss to her lips and left.

FIVE MEN HAD TRAVELED FROM TOWN AND SAT ON horses in front of his cabin.

It was a pretty sad posse. They were drunk, though, and that made stupid men brave. It disappointed them that Jeni wouldn't be working at the saloon. They shouted that—repeatedly—and that it wasn't right for an "injun" to marry a white woman. They kept confusing their motivation for chasing Jeni out to the ranch.

Clint Baker's voice was among them, the one he'd heard in the crowd the day Jeni arrived. His voice was unmistakable with its higher-than-usual pitch. When he said he would take a ride on Jeni, Scott could've ripped his throat out.

Jed and Matt Peterson were there, too. The brothers worked a farm on the opposite side of town. Jed and Matt had also been vocal in their hope that the beautiful Miss MacGregor would give up the act and go to work at the saloon.

The other two men were strangers. Scott had seen them in the saloon, but didn't know their names.

Scott waited to reveal himself. He needed to return to Jeni if things got out of control. His brothers could handle the locals easy enough. The other two had his attention. Clint did the talking for the posse, but from Scott's perspective, he could tell that both Caine and Caleb focused on the strangers.

A hoot-owl sound to his left meant that Will had a bead on one. Another hoot signaled Hank had the other. If this exploded, the two strangers would go down first. He didn't have to be psychic to know what each man in the group was thinking. They'd lived, worked, and ridden together for so long that they were of one mind. It was a dance choreographed over years of experience. Scott gave another hoot to let everyone know he was there.

If this escalated, Caine and Caleb would handle the townies. He hoped this wouldn't come down to a shootout, though. Drunken ignorance did not go well with loaded revolvers.

The earlier gunshots might have been warnings. None of The Maxwell Group had been injured, and the five trespassers on horseback were fine. He didn't see anyone down or any horses without riders.

"Just bring out the woman," Clint said in his girly voice, "and we'll take her back to town, where she belongs."

"She belongs here with her husband," Caleb said.

Jed Peterson spat on the ground. "She don't belong with no injun."

"You saying she belongs at the saloon rather than at home with her husband?" Caleb was getting riled up. He was too close to Jeni, and he had a short temper. Scott hoped he could keep it together, but Caine took a half-step forward and Caleb took a breath. Good. He didn't need Caleb escalating the situation.

Jed just couldn't let go. "Ain't right, a white woman with no injun."

Caleb bristled. "Ain't right carting a woman away from her home and husband to work in a saloon."

Caine shifted slightly to keep Caleb from responding again.

"We aren't taking her back to the saloon." One stranger stated. His accent said he was from the East.

"Wha'd'ya mean we ain't takin' 'er back ta the saloon? We rid out here ta git 'er and take 'er back." Clint jerked to look at the men he'd ridden out with.

"She's engaged to be married in Boston. This marriage is being annulled, we'll take her to her fiancé."

"Sorry friend, she's married. Any prior engagements are void."

"She's coming with us, one way or another," the easterner insisted. "Her intended has gone to great lengths to get her back home where she belongs, and we're not leaving without her. The marriage can be annulled, or she can be widowed, but she will marry Roger Benson before another month has passed. Let's not make this harder than it needs to be."

That's what you think, Scott grumbled in his thoughts. The unmistakable click of a hammer next to his ear made his heart pound and his spine go stiff. Nobody had gotten the drop on him in years.

"Move out, slowly," a male voice said, deadly calm.

Scott stood and walked through the yard toward the front of the house with his hands spread wide, palms out.

The chatty easterner nudged his horse forward. "Where's the woman?"

"My wife is safe."

"We don't want trouble; we just want the woman. Looks like she's going to be more trouble than she's worth to you, and her fiancé wants her back."

"My wife has no interest in Mr. Benson. I'm her husband. She has no fiancé. Ah!"

A deafening blast sounded, and a bullet ripped through his gut. He went down as all hell broke loose around him.. Instant reports from Hank's, Daniel's, and Caleb's guns precipitated the three strangers dropping to the ground. The entire battle ended before Scott's body hit the ground.

Yet the two-second battle felt like hours.

His mind raced. There were real monsters after his wife, and he wasn't going to be there to take care of her. It was one thing to take down a man amid battle, but it was a different thing altogether to shoot an unarmed man in his own yard.

This was not a shot he would come back from. He'd been shot before, more than once, and this was different. He needed to protect Jeni, but he was going to die before he could reach her.

He felt the life leaving him.

Gutshot.

He was going out gut shot.

She'd be a widow after only a few hours of marriage.

He watched Caleb bolt toward the cave while Daniel dashed to his horse and raced for town. Going to get the doctor. He doubted he'd last that long. Hank removed the weapons from the dead men and gave the townies hell.

Caine was there. His cousin. His best friend.

He coughed and Caine supported his head. The pain choked him. His head and heart squeezed, but it was worry for Jeni that had him grasping Caine's hand and pleading with God for more time.

"Just breathe." Caine pressed his handkerchief into the wound, buying time. They both knew it couldn't stop the inevitable.

"Jeni."

"She's coming. Hold on."

"They'll keep coming for her. Get her married… tonight… She has to pick one of you… Caleb… They know where she is." He sputtered and gasped, "They'll keep coming."

He gasped between sentences. Blackness crowded the edges of his vision.

"We'll take care of her."

"She's not safe."

"I promise. We'll keep her safe."

He shook his head and forced Caine to understand. "Not safe… We don't know all… Get her married."

The sound of Caleb's heavy boots came from behind them. Hopefully, he was bringing Jeni. Scott wanted to see her one more time. He needed to tell her to be happy. To live her life. He wanted to tell her he was sorry for leaving her.

Caleb ran towards him with Jeni in his arms.

It was too late. A deep rattle in Scott's chest signaled his last breath, and the blackness that had been crowding his vision took over.

"No!" Jeni screamed, trying to fight her way out of Caleb's arms. "No! No! No! No! No!"

As they bolted across the yard, Jeni watched in horror as Scott trembled all over and went limp in Caine's lap.

She wouldn't get to tell him goodbye—wouldn't get to tell him she was sorry. Her selfishness had gotten him killed. How could she live with herself?

Grief overcame her, and she let out a keening wail.

When Caleb set her down, she threw herself onto Scott's still-warm body and sobbed. There was no escape from her grief or guilt.

Nobody touched her. They didn't remove her

from Scott. They didn't hold her. Her grief, her keening, reflected their feelings, and they let her weep for herself and for them.

When Caleb, not Scott, had come crashing through the forest to get her, she'd known the worst had happened. She'd felt it deep in her heart. He'd said nothing, just grabbed her hand and started running back toward the house. She hadn't asked. She didn't want to know that her instinct was right. Jeni wanted a few more minutes of hope before her world shattered. She'd known her heart would break wide open.

Jeni couldn't breathe. The blood staining his shirt was proof that his fear had been justified, and she'd been wrong.

Dead wrong.

She'd gotten a good man killed. "I'm sorry, Scott. I'm so sorry. What have I done?" She sobbed into his chest and begged for him to live. All she could do was apologize and wrestle with the guilt and sorrow that she knew she deserved.

When she saw the tears in Caine's eyes, she wept harder. She apologized to Caine and Caleb, and when Hank came over, she apologized to him. She begged, again and again, to trade her life for his. She pleaded so fervently she lost track of how long she lay on the ground, bargaining with God to bring Scott back.

The grief was crippling.

It was unlike the worst feeling she could have imagined. She could do nothing to ease the suffering that she felt or saw reflected in the eyes of the men who loved Scott most.

He was her husband for a few hours, and now he was dead.

It was her fault.

Her hand roamed his body in search of signs of life and found none. "I'm sorry," was all she could say, and she said it over and over as she continued to beg him to take a breath.

Caleb finally dragged her to her feet and crushed her to his body. The force squeezed her breath out of her. His rough grip was almost painful, but she welcomed it.

She deserved it.

The pain in his grip was a relief that she centered on. His fingers bruised her tender flesh, but she welcomed the pain that the bruises would bring. She needed the pain. She was unredeemable.

She crumbled, and Caleb held her tight.

He crushed her to his chest and didn't let go. It wasn't the same as being held by Scott, but there was comfort in Caleb's arms, and she let him hold her. She pushed away and sank back to the ground next to Scott, and choked on sobs again.

Caine said. "We've got you, Jeni." Then he chucked Caleb on the shoulder and went off to speak with Hank.

Jeni could barely choke the words out, but she couldn't keep silent. "Look at what I've done. I- I can't live with this — he was more important than I will ever be. He was needed so much more than anyone will ever need me." Guilt crashed over her again, and she swallowed back a sob. "I trapped him. He told me so many times that it was too dangerous, and I didn't listen. This is my fault. My selfishness killed him." She gave in to a fit of rib-cracking sobs. Her mind was a labyrinth of pain and regret that she couldn't navigate. She couldn't think straight, and yet she couldn't stop thinking about everything.

Caleb gently rubbed her shoulder. "You didn't force Scott to do anything he didn't want to do. If he had wanted you to marry another man, he would have named one. Think about what you could have done. Scott died to protecting you. You're important to all of us."

She couldn't speak after that. She was wailing uncontrollably, and Caleb knelt down and clung to her. He was big and hard and comforting, but he wasn't Scott.

She wanted Scott.

She wanted her husband.

DANIEL RODE UP WITH THE DOCTOR AND THE reverend, both.

The doctor could do nothing. Two hours had passed since Scott's last breath, and they had already moved the bodies of the other men to a wagon.

The doctor shook his head sadly and gave his condolences. He offered to drive the bodies back into town. Since Daniel was the sheriff, he took over directing everybody.

The wagon was hitched and ready, but Scott's body wasn't on it. Scott wouldn't be going to town.

The Maxwell Group would take care of him themselves.

Doctor Manning checked on Jeni's foot. His gentle touch brought her out of a bottomless haze. She was no longer on the ground beside Scott's body. How had she gotten to the porch?

She'd lost a boot running in the woods and cut her foot before Caleb had scooped her up and carried her. She didn't need stitches, but the doctor bandaged her and checked her for other injuries.

The doctor offered to stay and help with the burial and ride back with the reverend.

Hank, Will, and Dr. Manning dug Scott's grave on top of the hill beside Amy's. The Maxwells, Caine and Caleb's parents, were also buried there. The view was limited from her perch on the front steps of the house. People disappeared and materialized into the inky night. Only those bodies lying in the moonlight or friends approaching the small circle of lantern-light were visible.

Jeni hardly noticed them.

She couldn't do anything but sit on the porch and stare at Scott's body.

The Maxwell men moved around her as she stared into the night. When the group moved Scott's body up the hill, she went with them.

Someone held her hand and supported her. He carried her.

She still had only one boot.

They buried Scott under a large tree on top of the

steep slope in the dark of night. The freshly disturbed dirt and boot-crushed grass smelled sweet, quelling the bloody smell emanating from her dress. Jeni sat on an old log and watched as Scott's family placed her new husband into the earth.

What a beautiful spot for him to rest.

The service was sweet, which added torment to the pain. Reverend Simon shed a tear as he blessed the grave and prayed for her husband's soul. Jeni couldn't cry. She couldn't feel anything at all anymore.

Numbness was her only safety now.

Scott deserved better.

WHEN THE LAST SHOVEL OF DIRT HAD BEEN HEFTED and the last stone set, Caine cleared his throat and stepped up beside Reverend Simon. "We have a matter of business that we need to take care of."

"I think any business can wait. We need to take care of Jeni tonight." Caleb said.

"That's just the thing. Scott said she needed to remarry tonight." Caine put his hand on his twin's shoulder. "He said she should marry you."

Caleb was taken aback. "Give her time to breathe. She became a widow a few hours ago."

She choked on a sob at the term, but didn't share an opinion.

She deserved whatever came to her.

"The fiancé that the easterner talked about is

146

coming for her. Scott said they would keep coming. He was clear, Caleb. He named you."

Caleb looked at Jeni, but she couldn't stand the question in his eyes. "I can't." She squeaked out. "I can't risk your life. I'll go back to Boston. If I'd gone months ago…" she hiccuped, "Scott deserved better than this."

"This is what Scott chose." Caine insisted.

How could she marry a second man in one day?

It was too much.

Caleb held a hand out to her. "Jeni, take my hand." His voice was gentle. His hand was warm and steady when he lifted her cold, shaky hand from her lap and pulled her to her feet. He raised her face to his with a fingertip under her chin. "Marry me?"

Jeni stared at him.

Could this be real?

No, this couldn't be real.

She couldn't say yes, but she didn't say no.

Caleb walked her in front of the reverend, and she surrendered. She didn't have the strength to fight this battle anymore.

Standing mere feet from her late husband's grave, she married for the second time that day.

Caleb's kiss was utterly different from Scott's. His lips didn't feel the same, and he brushed them against hers in so softly she thought she'd imagined it. He pulled her close and held her tight while she grieved and fought the guilt over the death of her husband. Would there be no end to the tears?

Her heart was in turmoil.

Scott deserved so much better; they both did.

Her heart broke, and once again, she sank to the ground, wrapped her arms around her knees, and prayed for her lost husband.

She prayed for her second husband. She prayed for each of the men of The Maxwell Group.

The one person she didn't pray for was herself.

She didn't deserve it.

Lost in grief, she hardly registered Caleb lifting her into his arms and carrying her toward his house.

Caleb, who'd spent months in town with her, was now her husband. Had he thought about the consequences of taking his brother's widow to wife?

She'd forced Scott to marry her, got him killed, and Caleb had taken his place.

Would she get him killed, too? It was too painful to imagine.

How many of The Maxwell Group would die for her?

Chapter Ten

W alking back to his house with Jeni in his arms, Caleb was a conflicted mess. He didn't know how to comfort her when he couldn't find any comfort himself. As her tears soaked his shoulder and chest, his own tears fell for his brother. He'd lost his best friend. The woman that Scott had loved was heartbroken, and now she was his wife. There were no words to express the snake pit of emotions writhing in his chest.

He was at war within himself.

He carried Jeni into the house and set her down in a chair. Dirt, cobwebs, and mud caked her night-gown. The delicate material was torn from running in the forest, and she still had only one shoe.

Yet she'd attended a funeral and a wedding in front of a crowd.

If she hadn't fled her marriage bed under the attack and watched Scott die before her eyes, she never would've allowed herself to be so exposed in front of everyone. She hadn't even asked for a blanket. Caleb had thrown her cloak around her when he's set her on the porch, or she would have quietly frozen without even noticing.

Caleb looked around for a solution. He'd seen a dress at the cave, but there was no time to grab it, and he'd left it behind.

The sight of his bride ate at him. Jeni's hair was had tangled with little sticks and leaves and dirt. She huddled in the chair with her arms wrapped around her middle and continued to cry. He didn't know what to do with her now that he had her home.

He put the coffee on and spotted the water bucket in the corner.

A bath. He'd make her a bath.

Maybe the hot water would soothe her.

It took time to bring in the tub and to heat water for her. Jeni sat motionless in the chair the whole time. She stared blankly at the cup of coffee he'd set in front of her and said nothing. Her tears dried up, but she hadn't recovered. That was worse, crying with no tears. It broke him to see her like that.

Caleb didn't speak as he worked to fill the tub; he let her have the time she needed.

He needed the time, too.

Caleb returned to her when the bath was ready. The sun was breaking over the horizon, and he fought his eyes to keep them open. He needed to take care of Jeni before he could think about himself.

She didn't respond when he told her it was ready.

He touched the back of her head and stroked his

hand down her hair. She didn't even move. He stopped stroking and talked to her in a soothing voice, like he would soothe a nervous mare, as he removed debris from her hair.

She was in shock.

When he finished with her hair, he took hold of her hands and stood her up. She followed him silently. She didn't move on her own, but gave no resistance.

He unbuttoned her gown and slid it down her shoulders. She had nothing else on. Under any other circumstances, it would have turned him on, but now it only made him sad.

Jeni made no move to cover herself. She didn't have enough energy left for modesty.

Caleb helped her walk the few steps to the tub and then settled her down into the water. He rested her head against the higher end of the tub and, for several minutes, sat back and let the water ease the tension from her muscles.

The hot water had an effect, because Jeni cried again. It was a haunting, sad cry that was somehow worse than her heaving sobs from earlier. The sweet sadness bit at Caleb's heart. It was a sound that reflected the feelings he struggled with inside.

It made him feel a little better.

Knowing that Jeni deeply mourned for Scott eased some of the guilt he felt for marrying her. It didn't reduce the guilt he felt for wanting to marry her all along. It didn't touch the shame he felt for his jealousy. He'd gotten what he wanted, but the cost was too steep.

With a deep breath, he reached for a bar of soap and a cloth. He spoke gently as he unwrapped and washed the dirt from her feet. He investigated several cuts and scratches on the sole of her injured foot before placing it back into the tub. The doctor had already checked it, but he needed to see, too. Caleb delicately washed the rest of her, hating the deep sadness in her eyes as he wiped filth from her skin.

When he finished, he nudged her shoulders forward to make her sit up in the tub. He washed her hair. The injury on her scalp, from when the sheriff had thrown her against the wall, poked up in a small ridge. It had healed, but a scar remained.

As he rinsed her hair, she returned to reality. Her eyes focused, and her modesty returned.

"Shh." he soothed, "I'm just trying to help."

Her voice shook, and her body trembled. Jeni wrapped her arms around herself and said, "I'm sorry," in the weakest voice he'd ever heard.

"It's not your fault. We all knew that Scott was going to honor his commitment to you. You didn't cause this."

"I planned the trap that killed him."

The shaking in her body worsened, and Caleb couldn't hold her from his position behind the tub.

He stood, removed his clothes, and stepped into the tub behind her.

She didn't have any reaction to him lowering himself into the water. When he pulled her shoulders, she turned and leaned into his embrace.

Nothing could have been more comforting to him than to hold her at that moment.

They rested in the tub until the water cooled. They needed to hold each other, and neither was ready for words. Caleb felt new guilt over receiving comfort from Jeni, and as full of guilt as she was, he was sure his comfort added to her load, too.

When she shivered, Caleb lifted her to her feet and rose to stand behind her. He picked up one towel and wrapped it around her shoulders, then took another and slung it around his waist.

He left the water in the tub and carried her to bed, then slid in beside her. They fell asleep together as the sun rose outside the window.

———

JENI WOKE UP NAKED, AGAINST A HARD, NAKED BODY. She snuggled into him and breathed in his male scent—not Scott. The night before slammed her back to reality. She was not in bed with Scott; she was in bed with Caleb.

He must have felt her tense beside him, because he sighed before he tugged her against him.

He exhaled and said, "It'll take time to get used to this."

"It feels wrong."

"I know. To me, too."

"The guilt is overwhelming." Tears formed in her eyes again. "I may never stop crying." She wiped her eye on the towel that was now open over them both.

"For me, too. I married my brother's wife last night. We both did what we had to do, but it doesn't remove the guilt."

"That's how I feel about us being here right now. I feel like I'm betraying Scott." She was comforted by Caleb, though, and so she snuggled closer to him. "I'm also worried about you. I've brought a lot of danger to you."

"We're going to handle that. You're my wife now. I will protect you. I need to know about this fellow that was mentioned last night, though. What is he to you?"

She related the entire story of Mr. Benson to Caleb, as she had the night before with Scott, but curled up in his arms with tears in her eyes. When she finished, she said, "I've never cried so much in my life as I have the last few months."

CALEB AND JENI SPENT THE DAY INSIDE THE CABIN. They discussed all the details of the situation with Mr. Benson again, and Jeni told him everything she knew about the Boston entrepreneur. It was only a matter of time before Mr. Benson himself would show up to take Jeni away. A man like that would rather see her dead than lose her to another man. Caleb expected other visitors before that happened.

It was late afternoon before they climbed out of bed and dressed. Jeni made breakfast for them while Caleb went to see if he could locate his brothers. Everyone had stayed close in case of emergency, except Daniel. He'd gone to town to keep an eye out for any trouble that might come their way.

Caleb asked the others to come in for coffee. They needed to know what they were getting into, and they needed to make a plan for how they would deal with it. He wished Daniel was there because he would be the best one to collect all the backgrounds they would need. Daniel had a knack for digging up details. His history as a US Marshall and his wide-spread contacts were helpful in situations like this.

Jeni made enough breakfast and coffee for all of them, and when the pot ran dry, she made another. They were exhausted and could use as much coffee as she could give them.

Her guilt overwhelmed her again, but her tears had dried up. She tried to look each man in the eye and answer their questions, even though she really wanted to hide.

It was most challenging for her to meet Caine's eyes. Scott was his cousin and his best friend. There was so much pain in Caine's face that Jeni avoided him. That, paired with the fact that he looked so much like her new husband, was hard for her. When Caine spoke, she answered him, but she couldn't raise her eyes above the buttons on his shirt.

Jeni and Caleb filled the others in on her history, and everyone listened carefully, understanding more of the situation. They should've been informed sooner. She'd put them in danger by keeping her secret.

When they rose to leave, Caine was the last to reach the door. He stopped in front of her and lifted her chin with his fingertip, forcing her to do the one thing she hadn't been able to — look him in the eye. "It's going to be ok."

She and Caleb spent the rest of that first day in the house, alternating between conversation and silence. Sometimes they sat side by side on the couch holding each other, and sometimes they sat across the room and kept their own company. Little by little, they eased back into the comfortable friendship that they had developed over their months in town.

It wasn't awkward.

Jeni tried several times to get Caleb to tell her more about himself, and he wouldn't. He brushed her questions off or ignored them, just as she'd done with the men at the boarding house. She wanted him to open up, but she didn't want to push him.

All he'd say was that his parents died when he was young, and that he'd worked the ranch with the others ever since.

Jeni accepted that she didn't need to know everything there was to know about her husband on their first day of marriage. It was weird enough just to think of him as her husband. She'd spent months imagining Scott in that role. Adjusting would not be easy.

When the sun set, they retired for the night. Caleb fell asleep with her in his arms. Jeni lay there for a long time, memorizing his breathing patterns. The beat of his heart was the most precious sound in the world. Even amidst her grief, she loved the warmth and strength and smell of him.

Still, a jolt of guilt followed every good feeling. Her conscience repeatedly stabbed her. Her husband had died only one day before. How could she be happy with another?

She couldn't stop feeling like Caleb deserved better, as Scott had.

All she'd ever wanted was safety, security, and love. Caleb offered those things.

Could she return those things to him?

She lay in his arms, feeling him against her, from her toes to the top of her head. His scratchy, stubbly beard poked into her scalp as she relaxed and wondered about this man. Would he ever open up to her? She wanted to know what stopped him from telling her his story.

She wondered so many things.

CABIN FEVER WAS QUICK TO DESCEND. "I NEED TO DO something." The whine in her own voice irked her.

"What do you want to do?"

"Anything. I can't stay in this house all day again. Yesterday was nice, but I need something to do."

"Until we know what's going on with Benson, we have to stay close."

Jeni paced. She was going mad. "Cleaning. I'm going to clean. Can you bring water so I can do the laundry, please? If I can't go out for a walk, I'll burn off some energy on the bedding and clothes."

Caleb helped her gather the things she needed,

and to her surprise, he helped her wash the laundry. With his help, the task was completed much too quickly, and she was stuck searching for something else to occupy her time, again.

She moved furniture and cleaned behind and under everything. She washed walls and scrubbed floors and enjoyed the ache in her muscles as she worked. Caleb continued to help as she moved around the cabin. When she washed walls, he washed above her reach. When she washed floors, he was there, moving furniture around and out of her way.

She tried to get him to talk, but he dodged her questions, as he had the day before.

They cleaned most of the cabin before they fell into bed that night.

Caleb reached for her in the middle of the night, and she came to him. Even in sleep, his warmth and embrace gave her comfort.

Caleb slept. She lay awake.

CALEB STARED PAST THE RIM OF HIS COFFEE MUG at his wife. Throughout the week, he and Jeni had fallen into a routine that was half comfortable and half frustrating. She would not stop trying to dig into his past, and he could feel her determination grow, fed by her frustration.

There were reasons to leave the past in the past, and he would not explain himself. She had to learn to live with him as he was. They were great together in the night when they curled up and quietly consoled each other. It was the daylight hours, when she wanted to talk, that were getting to him.

That morning, she'd rolled over and reached for him for the first time. He'd waited for her to be ready and hadn't approached the subject of consummating their marriage. It was a relief when she brought it up.

Jeni rubbed his chest and played with a hair. "I want to talk about something, but I don't know how to begin."

Caleb stared at her and his brows drew together. He couldn't imagine what she wanted to talk about that would make her look so uncomfortable. She turned fiery red, and he could practically read her mind. That fair skin showed blush so well. There was absolutely no hiding it.

"I know you and Scott consummated your marriage. Is that what you want to talk about?" He rubbed her back, trying to give her courage to express her feelings.

She ducked her face into his chest and moaned.

"It's ok." He started to twist a lock of her hair around his fingertip but stopped before she reacted. Something about that bothered her. Instead, he went back to rubbing up and down her back.

Jeni half-sat in his arms. "Do you want to consummate our marriage?"

Caleb chuckled. "We'll eventually have to get around to it but I can wait until you're ready. Do you want to?"

The truth was all she had to give. "I'm afraid to try."

He hadn't kissed her since their hilltop wedding, but they slept in each other's arms every night. She came to him when she needed to be held, and didn't shy away from him when he needed to hold her. Physical intimacy had come easy between them, but they hadn't pushed the limits beyond holding each other. "What frightens you?"

"I'm not sure. I think I'm afraid that it will feel the same, but maybe I'm afraid that it won't. I don't know. I'm afraid."

"Can we try a kiss first?" He waited for her to nod and then lowered his mouth to hers.

It was sweet, but not the same as Scott's kiss had been. She knew he could tell she was comparing his kiss with her experience, and she appreciated he didn't stop her. Jeni needed to feel the difference. She needed to know that it was Caleb and not Scott that she was with.

The months in town had made her and Caleb friends, but she had been so focused on Scott that she'd overlooked the connection between them. As she lay there, with Caleb leaning over her, she realized the truth. She knew him better than she had known Scott. She and Scott hadn't had any actual conversations before they married, besides her insisting on his hand in marriage and him rejecting her.

Caleb was her friend, though. They'd spent hours together over the last few months. They never had any profoundly personal conversations, but they'd developed an easy companionship that she knew she could trust.

Scott's touch was thrilling and new, but uncomfortable and unfamiliar. She was used to being close to Caleb. They'd sat side by side, strolled arm in arm, for months. They'd practically courted since she arrived in town. She just hadn't realized it for what it was.

She felt an intimacy with Caleb that hadn't had time to develop with Scott. It was different, and she needed it to be different. Caleb gave her time to think while he ran his mouth and hands over her body. When she angled up and caught his mouth, she gave her consent.

She turned herself over to him, as she had done for Scott. She would trust him; he was her husband.

Making love with Caleb differed from making love with Scott, too. Jeni could breathe easier when she realized she could separate the two. She let herself fall into the feelings that Caleb brought to her body. His scent surrounded her, so similar to Scott's but different, and she lost herself in him. Jeni moaned as he tasted and felt his way over her body.

Rather than an intense, fiery rush to each other, Caleb made love to her slowly and deliberately. He built on her passion without pushing it on in a mad rush. When the explosions came, it was emotional and took her breath away.

As the spasms racked their bodies, they clung to

each other. Both of them needed more from the other. They held on for a long time. With the morning sun streaming through the curtain, she watched his chest rise and fall, and listened to his heart rate slow.

He held her while she cried.

———

Daniel showed up with Rose and Iris after they'd been holed up inside for a week. It was New Year's Eve, and he and Jeni had been so isolated they'd forgotten. They were both ready to hear any news. At that point, bad news would have at least given them something to talk about. They had replaced their easy conversations and comfortable silence with awkward politeness and grumbling. They were both losing their minds.

They had to wait until evening, when everyone would be back at the ranch for dinner, to have a meeting. Rose and Iris helped Jeni make dinner for the group. It was hard to see the pain and loss in the eyes of the women who had been like mothers to Scott, but they were kind to her. It was also hard to see the way they looked at her and Caleb together. There was no doubt that they wanted to see Caleb happy, but they were still grieving over their loss, and they weren't able to see past their grief.

Jeni understood.

She felt the same way.

After a hearty meal of stew and biscuits, Jeni poured coffee and set a slice of pie in front of each guest. New Year's Eve dinner was a solemn affair because of Scott's absence, but time together was what the family needed.

Daniel started the conversation after dinner was cleared from the table, with no preamble. He looked straight at Jeni. "Benson is still sending scouts out after you. He's commissioned a wanted poster, so now we have bounty hunters joining the fray. I have contacted the US Marshall service and several of my old buddies back East. This Benson character is a dangerous man. His hired guns are ruthless. They're also very skilled."

"They had to be to get the jump on Scott," Will said. "Nobody's ever snuck up on him."

"Not to mention the way they shot him in the yard with his hands in the air," Caine added. "That shit's cold."

Jeni's gasp drew the attention of everyone. "I'm sorry." She threw her arms on the table and her face buried into them as sobs racked her body. It was several minutes before Caleb could settle her down.

"We're sorry," he said. "We know this is hard." Caleb took her into his arms and pulled her onto his lap. He held her until she stopped crying, and her body relaxed against his. Everyone watched them in silence.

Daniel cleared his throat and continued. "Reinforcements are on the way. I've sent for as many men as I could think of. We're going to need all the help we can get. Since Benson knows where you are, it's only a matter of time before this whole area is crawling with bounty hunters and thugs."

"I should leave," Jeni said. "It's too dangerous and I'm not worth it." She sat up straight and moved to leave Caleb's lap. He held her in place. "I know you won't want to hear it, but it's true." She cupped his cheek in her hand. "You don't need this fight on your doorstep."

"You're my wife! You're not going anywhere."

"It was selfish of me to Montana. I should have known that he wouldn't stop when I left town." She met Caleb's eyes with pleading in her own "I can't be the reason any more lives are lost. The head count against my soul is already too high. I thought he would stop when I wasn't available anymore. I promise, I did."

"You're my wife. I love you" He cupped her cheek. "You're a Maxwell, and this is where you belong."

Jeni stared at him in wonder. "You love me?"

"I've loved you for a long time. I should have said something sooner. I might have prevented what happened to Scott. It wasn't your fault, Jeni, it was mine."

She couldn't believe Caleb was saying these things with his family listening around the table. She should have realized. That was the reason for his sour attitude, and why he'd slipped out of the church right before the wedding. She thought he'd just gone to collect the horses and her belongings from the boarding house.

She patted his chest and rested her head against his. "It's not your fault."

"I suppose it's our fault. We can't go back, so we

need to focus on going forward. We need to make sure we protect anything that may have been started here." He wiggled his hand where it rested low on her abdomen. "You're more important than you think you are. You deserve safety and comfort. You deserve to be happy. Don't think about leaving me, ever. You belong here, with me." He leaned over and rubbed his lips over hers.

He must need the others to know how important she was to him. And she needed them to see that she still grieved one husband while she loved another. She relaxed back into his embrace and nodded her head.

None of the men seemed uncomfortable with the intimacy of the moment. They appeared to be comforted by it. Jeni leaned into Caleb and gave the group her full attention.

After a moment, Caine spoke. "I think you should move up to Hank's place." Caine said.

"That's a good idea," Will agreed. "Hank's got the most defensible position and with the mountain to the back, it's easiest to watch."

"Should we move tonight or wait for tomorrow?" Jeni asked. She didn't want to be stuck in the cabin, but at least they had privacy there. She wouldn't argue though. If they asked her to go, she'd go. She owed them that much. Caleb still rubbed her back in gentle circles. He always knew exactly what she needed.

"Tomorrow," Hank said. "I'll gather up some of my stuff and give you the master bedroom. There's plenty of space. We'll all be able to stay there."

"We're staying home." Rose piped up, speaking for herself and her sister. "We wouldn't be comfortable up there with so many people."

Caine nodded. "I'll stay at my place with them for now."

"We will come up if it gets bad." Iris promised when it looked like Hank and Daniel would complain. She walked behind them and kissed their heads.

Daniel smiled up at her, then turned serious again. "We should start seeing reinforcements over the next few days. As long as Benson's crew doesn't show up before then, we should be able to take anything that's heading our way." He rose and excused himself, thanking Jeni and the twins for the dinner and complimenting her pie.

The others rose and followed Daniel, leaving her alone with Caleb.

They washed the dishes together and went to bed. In the morning, they would change houses. Jeni almost hoped to find Hank's house a mess. She needed something to keep her busy so her thoughts would have something to focus on, other than hired guns and ruthless bounty hunters.

Chapter Eleven

A fter breakfast, Jeni packed her things while
Caleb shoved his into an old knapsack. It
would be a ten-minute ride from their cabin over to
Hank's, but a hum of apprehension in the air made
it impossible for Jeni to settle.

She looked around the cabin for the hundredth
time, but everything was in its place, organized and
clean. She'd checked her bag and Caleb's and gone
over the house again and again. Nothing she did
settled her nerves.

Jeni couldn't get what Caleb had said out of her
mind. What if she was with child? It was unlikely,
but not impossible, and that possibility had weighed
on her since he'd suggested it. Would it even be a
good idea to bring a baby into such an insane situation? She made another trip around the cabin,
looking for anything to distract her mind.

A baby, either Scott's or Caleb's, would be a
tremendous blessing. She pictured a little girl with

Caleb's eyes and her hair, or a little boy with Scott's smile and her eyes. Caleb would be its father. He'd be a great father.

Jeni'd always wanted children, but this was not a good time to have a baby, not with Mr. Benson searching for her. Babies deserved security and peace. She was hunted. How could she be a good mother like this? Maybe Mr. Benson would leave her alone if he found out that she'd married and started a family.

She hoped he would.

She found her hand drifting to her abdomen often throughout the morning as she prepared to leave the house.

Caleb indicated her hands. "The thought of a baby is nagging you, huh?"

"I can't get it out of my mind." Guess they were going to talk about it after all. She tried to search his expression for his feelings on it.

He relaxed in his chair, looking peaceful. "Me neither."

"I'm afraid to be pregnant with all of this danger around."

"Is that your only worry?"

"No, of course not. It's my biggest worry, though."

"Mine, too." He walked over and placed a hand over her belly. "Are you worried about the identity of the father?"

She shrugged. "I'm not worried about it, but I can't stop thinking about it. You're the father of the baby if there is one." She stepped into his embrace.

"That's pretty much my thoughts on it, too." He didn't let her go. "You know that with the way our last two evenings have been going, it's just a matter of time before we do make a baby."

"I wonder if we should stop until all of this is over. If I'm already pregnant, there's nothing we can do about that, but maybe, for now, we should keep our hands to ourselves."

"We're going to live our lives. We're married, and we're going to love each other. When we make a baby, we're going to love him or her, too. We don't know what the future holds, and we can't wait for a safe time to live our lives."

"Aren't you afraid?"

"I imagine I'm about as afraid as any man contemplating starting a family."

"What do you worry about?"

"I worry about you most." He kissed her and pulled her close. He sank into a chair and pulled her down into his arms. She didn't resist.

"I worry I could lose you — that someone will get through our line, and you'll get hurt. I worry we could lose our baby, or that you could die in childbirth." He cleared his throat and looked into her eyes.

Her heart lept to her throat, and she swallowed a lump.

Jeni could only grunt, because the words stuck in her throat.

"You are important, Jeni. Not just as the carrier of babies. You are important. Live, because I can't live without you."

He really loved her. It was overwhelming.

———

WHEN CAINE ARRIVED WITH THE HORSES, THEY'D BEEN waiting in silence for over half an hour. Anxiety, turned to agitation, had replaced their intimacy. By the time the knock had come, Jeni was ready to jump out of her skin.

She was ready to start a fight with her husband just for something to do. Caleb looked prepared to spar with her for the same reason.

Her other option was to sit and wait and think about babies.

Looking at Caleb, she could see the tension in his muscles. His position looked relaxed, but a twitch in his jaw gave away his mood. He had a talent for hiding his tension under the surface that she both envied and despised. It was annoying. Scott had exhibited the same trait, and it had annoyed her, too. Caleb sat back in the chair, his left ankle resting on the opposite knee. She wanted to know how he was feeling and what he was thinking, but she was afraid to ask.

He would tell her everything was fine. Or he would surprise her by getting all intimate again when she wasn't ready. He enjoyed sneaking up on her like that. She wasn't falling for his trap again. So she glared at him, imagining what he might be thinking, wishing she could read his mind.

They both jumped at a knock on the door and then burst into the sunlight. The short ride would be a respite from the claustrophobia of the cabin. A brief respite, she knew, but a welcome break in the monotony of her day. She hoped again as they prepared to leave that Hank would be a slob, and she would have plenty of work to keep herself busy. She didn't have high hopes, though. Hank was as neat as the rest of these brothers of his.

They had better hygiene than any other men she'd seen since coming West, too. Even the banker had left something to be desired in that department when he offered his hand in marriage. She assumed it was Rose and Iris that she could thank for the Maxwell men always smelling so good. Rose made the pine tar soap that she loved so much and promised to teach her how to make it. Jeni shook her head. Thoughts of soap making and babies were taking up mental energy that she should be focusing on safety and survival.

Caleb mounted first and held his hand out for Jeni to ride in front of him. She was still holding onto her irritation and didn't want to be close to him, even though part of her longed to be surrounded by his masculine scent and strength.

She was driving herself crazy.

He'd explained earlier that she would ride double with him, since she couldn't ride a horse. He didn't want to use a wagon because horseback was faster and safer if trouble turned up. And he was right, darnit.

Jeni didn't want to appreciate his thoughtfulness. She wanted to stew in agitation.

She gave in and walked over to Caleb's horse.

Caine lifted her into Caleb's lap, and he wrapped her in a warm wool blanket. She thanked him and nestled in, then turned up her face and kissed his neck as he nudged his horse into motion. He was irresistible, even when he annoyed her. If she was going to lose her mind over warring emotions, she might as well drive her husband crazy with her.

Caleb settled her more comfortably into his lap. As they started their short journey, he repeatedly checked her comfort and tucked the blanket around her. Caleb's doting sent butterflies fluttering in her belly. He took such good care of her. His protective-ness struck her in the heart every time.

The cold air in her lungs invigorated her when she was tucked against Caleb's warm body. She worried whether he was warm, but when he tucked her into his duster, she knew he was. He always was.

She settled against him for a pleasant ride, her frustration washed away with the cold, clean January air.

NOT EVEN HALFWAY TO HANK'S HOUSE, THREE MEN ON horseback came barreling toward them out of nowhere. Their dark silhouettes invaded the horizon and stood out against a backdrop of white. Snow flew behind the horses like water splashing in a stream. For an instant, before Caleb's body went rock hard, Jeni marveled at the beauty of the scene.

Then her breath hitched in her chest, and she

clung to Caleb as he swung the horse around. He leaned hard into the turn, offsetting her balance and moving with the animal in a choreographed dance they'd practiced throughout the years. Once he had Jeni squared in front of him again, he bolted back toward their house. She didn't even know horses could change direction like that.

Her heart and mind changed direction as quickly as their horse, and the only thing she could focus on was the thundering hooves. Hank had swung around to ride with them, but the rest of the group pulled their guns and held their ground. Their muscular bodies were tall and rigid on their mounts. She watched them until Caleb pressed her back against his chest and robbed her of any view behind them.

There was no cover; they were sitting ducks.

Jeni cringed. She'd put so many good men in danger. This was all her fault. She struggled to see what was going on, but Caleb held her securely in front of him, blocking everyone else.

The first gunshot made Jeni yelp, but Caleb blocked her again with his enormous body when she tried to look back. She fought with him to get enough freedom to see the others, but it was a wasted effort. When he put his warm hand back on her belly, she realized he wasn't trying to block her from seeing what was going on. He was shielding more than just her, and she stopped fighting.

She couldn't believe that he was still willing to risk his life to protect her after Scott's death. He'd take a shot to protect his child. She sat still for the same reason. Enough. She let go of the guilt and let him take care of her. She closed her eyes tight and clung to him, studying the rhythmic pounding of hooves on snow.

Jeni pressed herself as close as she could and said a prayer for The Maxwell Group. She said a special prayer for Caleb and her baby. She whispered, "I love you."

As soon as they reached the cabin, Caleb tossed her to the ground, knocking the blanket into the snow. He jumped down, pulled her onto the porch, and then pushed her inside. He shouted for her to get into the root cellar and stay there. Hank didn't wait for her to obey. He hauled her back into the kitchen before she could fight him. Caleb was dropping shutters and locking them in place. Every crash made her jump.

The kitchen floor opened, and Hank lifted her down into the dank hole the same way Scott had done the night he died. Her heart stopped, but her mind didn't. The nightmare of a week ago played in her head, only this time she was alone in the hole, and there was no tunnel to safety.

Jeni couldn't let herself crumble and cry. She focused on taking slow, deep breaths, trying to get her emotions and thoughts under control. She felt around for a safe place to sit and tucked herself into the corner behind the ladder, wishing she had Caleb to keep her warm.

Something moved over the door, and dust drifted down over her head. They'd closed her in and hidden the opening. Jeni could do nothing. Her man was up there, risking his own life to save hers. She should have told him she loved him. She should've made sure he'd heard her on the horse.

Could she stand to lose a second husband? It had only been a week, but the thought of losing Caleb tore her to pieces.

She hadn't had time to kiss him—really kiss him. To tell him she loved him. She had so much she needed to say.

Jeni wrapped her arms around her knees and prayed.

She listened to the scraping of their boots on the floor, then the eerie silence in the cabin, and she prayed.

"Two," Caleb said.

"Right."

"Left."

Both men knew what to do. They'd practiced together for most of their lives, and they worked as a team. Jeni hadn't, though, and Caleb hoped she was ok in the dark root cellar. It was cold down there, and she was alone. He wished he'd thrown a blanket down with her.

Shaking off the distraction, he focused back on the men in front of his house.

The bigger man pulled a knife from a sheath as the smaller man checked the chambers on his revolver. The bigger man walked left, and Caleb followed him with his eyes.

When the riders snuck around toward the back door, Caleb and Hank followed their progress from inside, catching their shapes through the curtains and gauging their positions by moving with them. Their footsteps were silent as they glided around the interior of the house. He couldn't say the same for their visitors. The fools stomped and made enough noise that tracking their locations was too easy.

It must be a trap.

If it wasn't a trap, these were the dumbest gunslingers he'd ever seen. Nobody would go around stomping like that if they were trying to sneak up. Hank must've had the same thought, because he moved to look out of the front window and held up two more fingers. Caleb nodded to the back door as he crept toward it.

The odds had changed to four on two. He hoped his brothers would arrive soon. The first three gunmen they'd seen on the road, plus the four here, might be a larger party than he and Hank could handle. He'd expected a lot of men to try for the reward on Jeni's head, but if they kept showing up in full-fledged posses, this would be a hard-won fight.

He wanted to rip that Benson's heart from his chest. That reward poster would have every asshole bounty hunter in the territory after her. They needed to get her out of this house. Hank's place was easier to defend. It was designed it for this. Caleb's cabin was not. He resisted running his gaze over the trap-door. He needed to focus.

Caleb forced his mind to stay on the men outside.

Jeni was afraid and cold. He wanted to protect her and the baby he suspected was growing inside her. He needed to get rid of these assholes so he could hold her.

The man he'd followed was as big as he was, and he had a knife in his hand instead of a pistol. He wanted a fight.

Caleb would happily give him one.

The backdoor slammed open, the big man charged Caleb. A quick jump to the side dodged him. The shadow of his feet under the door had announced the attack. Caleb shot, but missed.

Hank cleverly kept his eye on the other door. He knew as well as Caleb this big guy was only a distraction.

Hank leveled his gun and took his first shot. Caleb heard a body drop outside as the smaller man charged through the back door.

One down.

The big guy jumped in front of the smaller one and charged again. Caleb knocked him back with a fist to the jaw. His knuckles throbbed, but his shoulder burned. The knife had found flesh. Warm blood made his shirt stick to the wound and tugged at the gaping edges.

Before the big guy could regain his balance, Caleb shot the smaller man. He dropped to the floor, his gun flung across the room.

Two down.

The big man roared and charged a third time.

Caleb landed a hard punch to the man's ribs and darted out of the way. He felt that impact all the way up his arm. Shaking out his hand, then opening and closing it, he watched as the big man turned for another go. He panted. The man had size and strength, but no endurance. The lumbering giant was panting like an overheated hound. He had size and strength, but no endurance. The big man startled when the front door burst open, and the last of the gunmen entered the fray.

The door's crash against the wall was all the distraction Caleb needed. The big guy looked up, and Caleb took him out with one shot.

Three down.

Caleb turned as Hank landed a punch on the new opponent's jaw and sent him sprawling. His gun flew six feet in front of him, and he scrambled to get it. Caleb kicked it out of the way and hauled the man to his feet. The asshole swung for Caleb's face, but he ducked and sent him reeling with a punch to the gut. He landed on the floor beside his gun. In the space of a heartbeat, Hank shot him.

Four down.

Hank's speed and marksmanship never ceased to amaze him. Caleb had lost a fair amount of money, pitting his own skills against Hank's in the old days. That was something he didn't do anymore. Hank had only missed once and never would again,

The immediate threat had been neutralized, but they weren't ready to get Jeni yet. They needed to make sure there were no more surprises—that the other three attackers hadn't made it past their brothers.

The sweet sound of a hoot owl heralded the arrival of horses. Caleb and Hank sagged with relief. The Maxwell Group was all there and in one piece.

Will entered first, followed by Daniel and Caine. Caleb punched his brother on the shoulder, happy to see him.

"You got three?" Daniel asked.

"Four." Hank nodded to the back door where the smaller man had dropped.

"Let's get the bodies out of here," Caleb said. "I don't want Jeni to see them."

They carried the bodies out of the house and lined them up in the snow.

Daniel grabbed the wool blanket that Caleb and Jeni had left behind and tossed it over them. "Let's get you and Jeni to Hank's. I'll come back with the wagon for these ruffians later. I want you both settled before it gets any later in the day."

Caleb waved the others out the door and walked back to the kitchen. He pushed the table out of the way and lifted the door. Jeni crouched in the corner, and when she looked up at him, his heart stopped. The fear and worry on her face hurt to his soul. Her red-rimmed, tear-filled eyes broke his heart.

He needed to hold her.

***

JENI STOOD AND CLIMBED THE LADDER UNTIL CALEB could reach her and pull her out of the hole. She sobbed and threw herself into his arms. He was safe. She'd prayed and begged and bargained with God to save him. Seeing him and having him in her arms again filled her heart.

"I love you, Caleb. Oh my goodness, I love you so much." She brought his mouth down to hers and held him as tightly as she could, then she buried her face into his neck. "I love you."

She stepped back and took a good, assessing look at him. He was bleeding!

In a flash, she changed from a frightened woman in need of support to a wife needing to take care of her injured husband. With a strength that made Caleb's brows lift and his eyes go wide, she forced him back into a chair, pulling and pushing at his shirt to get to his wound.

He tried to brush off her attentions. "We don't have time for this now. We need to get up to Hank's place before we run into another posse."

"You're bleeding." If he thought she'd let him bleed to death on the ride, he had another think coming. Every gunshot that had rung out above her, every thump and grunt and wheeze, had fed her fear and sent her imagination reeling. She'd pictured him lying in the dirt, bleeding to death, like Scott. There was nothing she could have done for him, but Caleb's wound was different. She wouldn't let him refuse her aid now that she'd dodged the horror of a second dead husband.

Caine leaned in through the doorway. With his hands pressed against each side, he blocked all the light. "We need to get going."

"He's bleeding."

"We'll take care of it at Hank's. We need to get out of here."

"He's bleeding."

Caleb wrapped his gigantic hands around her little ones and stopped their prodding. "I'm ok."

"I could have lost you." She broke down.

Caleb lifted her into his arms and walked toward the door, cradling her as they went. When he reached the side of his horse, he handed her to Caine and mounted. He lifted her up into his arms again, then pressed a kiss to the top of her head and whispered, "I love you, too."

Caine tossed a blanket up to Caleb. She tucked in, but not so tight she couldn't keep an eye on his wound. He stroked her face and kneed his horse into motion.

She gripped him as they rode hard for Hank's place.

Caleb nudged her and pointed ahead as they approached the house. It was a log cabin like Caleb's and Scott's. They'd built it into the side of the mountain, and they said it was bigger than it looked.

As the other two houses had been, Hank's home was well cared for. Everything looked strong, and she could see why they wanted her in this house. Not only was it backed up to the mountain, but it was also high on a hill, and from that perch, they could see around it in every direction.

Caleb took her inside to the settee near the fire. He went outside to talk to the others for a minute before returning. She removed his shirt to assess and clean his wound. It could use a few stitches, but it was not as bad as she'd feared. It only took a few minutes to have him stitched up and bandaged.

Reality warred with Jeni's sense of relief. Caleb's good luck didn't erase the fact that she'd come dangerously close to losing another husband.

Chapter Twelve

H ank's house was as large as the men had
said. Larger. The backside of the house went
deeper than she thought possible for a house built it
into the mountain. Hank's house had a second floor
with several bedrooms upstairs. Those rooms had no
windows, but they weren't as dark as they should've
been. Clever use of mirrors and lanterns reflected
the light into the dark spaces.

Caleb gave Jeni a tour of the house, showing her
to their room. "It started with a cave." It would be
fun to explore the place by herself, when she'd have
time to peek into all the rooms and take it all in.
Caleb walked her from room to room and rattled on
about the construction. "We used dynamite to blast
into the mountain and expand enough for everyone
to fit. We wanted the house would provide a lot of
protection and this way we only need to guard it
from three sides."

He went on and on about air circulation and reservoirs of hot water, but after the emotional morning, Jeni couldn't listen. She didn't care. The only thing she wanted to know was if everyone would be safe.

If the house offered that, nothing else mattered.

Hank gave Jeni and Caleb the biggest bedroom on the second floor, and the other men all moved into the house and took their own rooms.

Over the next week, they settled into a routine. The house gained new occupants by the day. Men arrived in ones or twos to join in the fight to protect her. It horrified Jeni to think of the number of lives being put on the line for her.

She wasn't that great of a sacrifice.

It was a little better when she realized that some of them were the usual ranch hands. They'd been called back to work early and would stay through the autumn. The bunkhouse wasn't ready for them though, so they were camping in the house while work was done to repair the section of roof that had caved in when a tree fell.

By the end of the week, men slept all over the place. Every morning, they'd all roll up their bedrolls and tuck them away. But walking down to make coffee and start breakfast became tricky, with bodies sprawled around the house.

She spent her days with Caleb. When he wasn't keeping watch or organizing the men, he helped Jeni with the cooking and cleaning. The number of men in the house made Jeni uncomfortable, so she stayed as close as possible to her husband. Caleb understood, and he rarely left her side.

Jeni got a kick out of how the men relaxed and enjoyed each other's company while they didn't have an enemy to fight. They rotated in and out of the house as they took turns guarding the property and working the ranch.

Jeni couldn't tolerate losing any more people she cared about, so she tried not to get to know them. She limited her conversation as much as possible to Caleb or the other men of The Maxwell Group.

A vein of humor flowed through the group that tickled Jeni. She couldn't help a chuckle as one man, Brian Dennehy, who had a tendency to lean back in his chair, lost his balance and hit the floor. He later learned that Mark Webb had weakened the legs. In retaliation, Brian had put a fish inside of Mark's bedroll and set it close to the stove all day. It reminded her of Elenor's little pranks, but on a bigger scale. The fish prank hurt the entire company, because the house reeked for days, and Brian suffered just as Mark did .

If they didn't have the threat of violence looming over them, they had a downright good time. It was too cold outside, even though the snow had held off, so they spent their free hours either in the barn or enjoying camaraderie inside the house.

Around the dinner table one night, they were all sitting and laughing together when Brian spoke to Jeni. It was unusual for any of them to address her. Even though they were there to help her, they didn't put her at the center of attention often. She appreciated that.

"I spent a few days in town before heading out here," Brian said. "Thought I'd try to catch all the rumors."

A few men nodded. So Jeni nodded.

"I've been dying to know something," he said.

"What's that?" Jeni asked.

"They say at the Christmas party, you were stunning in a dress to kill."

She ducked her head, feeling the familiar heat rushing up into her face.

"They said you danced and sparkled, and nobody had ever been so beautiful."

Her trembling hands latched on the fabric of her skirt and twisted it under the table. Where was he going with this?

"I heard you were a witch, because there was no way for a human woman to be so beautiful. They say you cast a spell over the entire town," Brian laughed.

Mark chuckled. "I did the same. I heard that even with your beauty and obvious attempt to get Scott's attention, he refused when you proposed in front of the town."

That was a sobering reminder of the worst day of her life. Her head dropped to her chest, tears stinging her eyes. She didn't respond to his comments. He was there to help her. He deserved to know whatever he needed to know about her. She would answer any questions he proposed. She owed him that.

She nodded, straightened her spine, and raised her eyes to his, waiting for him to continue.

"But," Brian smoothed his red beard in a useless attempt to hide the redness moving up his face, "then you whispered something into his ear, and he changed his tune."

Jeni's face flushed as red as Brian's, and she turned her head and hid her face in Caleb's arm. There was no malice in these men; they weren't trying to hurt her. They were joking, teasing, and enjoying her mortification. He wasn't trying to remind her of how her choices had gotten her first husband killed.

"What did you whisper to him?" Brian laughed and sipped his coffee.

"I'd forgotten about that," Caine said. "I want to know too." He chuckled, enjoying her embarrassment.

"Oh my God!" Jeni gasped. If she could have crawled behind Caleb, she would have. Truth be told, she'd been happy that nobody had ever thought to ask her about that.

She couldn't even look at the men. She knew they were smiling and enjoying her blush. She continued to hide her face in Caleb's shoulder, and his body shook with laughter.

"I'm pretty curious about that myself." Caleb laughed out loud and threw his arm around her shoulder when she squealed.

Rose watched from where she sat, with a curious smile on her face. Jeni did not want to tell, but especially not with Rose and Iris listening. What would they think? Why had they come for breakfast on the day when this conversation happened? She hoped they wouldn't feel any differently about her if she told them.

Jeni sat up and smiled, full of embarrassment but also of humor. These men wanted a laugh, and she was going to give it to them. It was the least she could do. She looked around the table at all the men surrounding her and smiled as brightly as her face must've been glowing.

She opened and closed her mouth several times before she worked up the courage to speak. "I needed him to marry me because I knew I was being tracked, and it was just a matter of time before the bounty hunters caught me. I was sure that Scott was the only man that I could marry." She rubbed Caleb's arm and continued. "I hoped that jealousy would cause him to give up his game of refusing, but it didn't, even though I could see that he didn't like me with other men.

"When making him jealous didn't work, I put him on the spot—to force him to accept or deny me in front of everyone. I couldn't believe it when he rejected me even then. That whisper was the last card up my sleeve."

She couldn't go on and hid her face in her hands.

"Why was he the only man you could marry?" Brian asked.

"Because Scott sent for me without ever seeing what I looked like. I've never wanted to be married for being beautiful. I wanted to be accepted as a person. Beauty is the least interesting thing about me."

"I know that about you." Caleb ran his fingertip down the side of her face in an affectionate touch that had her blushing anew.

Caine grinned. "You can't leave us hanging like that."

"Everyone heard him whisper that you'd pay when you got home. Nobody heard what you told him, though." Brian piped back in.

"You might as well just come out with it now," Caleb said with a smirk. The jackal was enjoying it.

Jeni threw a glare of mock reproof his way. "You're the one who's going to be paying for this later. I thought you'd protect me from being ganged up on by men." The laughter in her voice was new. She'd been serious for so long that it felt good to be a little silly.

Once again, she sat up straight and looked around the room. She took a deep breath and finished her story.

"I was desperate. If he named another man, I was prepared to marry him. When I pulled him down, I... Ugh!" She took several deep breaths as she tried to find the courage to tell these men the thing she'd whispered to Scott. She went on before she lost her nerve. "I told him that the dress I was wearing buttoned up the back. I would need help to get out of it. Whichever man he chose was going to have the honor of undressing me."

With a moan, she threw her arms around Caleb

and buried her face in his neck. Everybody, including herself and Caleb, laughed. His body shook as he rubbed her back and kissed her hair. Hands banged on the table and boots stomped on the floor.

Hank laughed from his spot near the fire. "I figured it had to be something like that."

"Oh yeah, that'll do it," Caine said, heading to the stove to top off his coffee cup and deposit his plate into the sink.

"You pulled out the big guns," someone said from the back of the room. "He couldn't have said no to that."

"Ace up your sleeve." Will joked.

She didn't know Will well. Caleb was untrusting of his youngest brother. He wouldn't tell her why, but he hadn't left her alone with him all week. The others she'd spent a few minutes with, here and there, while Caleb was out discussing ranch business, but never Will.

The group had a friendly laugh at her expense, and the teasing would probably never end. It was ok though. She had Caleb, and he loved her.

Caleb kissed her head and rested his hand on her belly, as he always did. As always, the move caught the other men's attention.

"Are you expecting?" Brian asked.

"You're full of questions tonight." Daniel said.

Brian shrugged and smoothed his beard, then sipped his coffee.

"Are you?" He asked when Jeni hadn't answered for a few minutes.

Jeni met eyes with Caleb before she answered. "I think so."

A chorus of congratulations met her, but all she could hear was Caleb's excited heartbeat against her ear. He kissed her senseless and cradled her to his chest.

***

THE NUMBER OF PEOPLE LIVING IN THE HOUSE OFFERED no privacy. After another week and a half, Jeni wanted to be alone with her husband. She thought back to their discussion about not trying to get pregnant until they were through this crisis. Caleb said they would live their lives, but in this house full of people, they couldn't live their lives as husband and wife.

They slept together, wrapped in each other's arms, but they couldn't make love for fear someone would hear. The one time they had resulted in an awkward and embarrassing breakfast the following day.

Not embarrassing for Caleb, of course; he couldn't have been more gloating.

Men!

A week and a half was a long time, and Jeni got edgier by the day. She enjoyed the company and the laughter and camaraderie of the group. Still, she was desperate for her husband's attention.

Morning sickness confirmed her pregnancy. Jeni was happy and stressed and every other emotion all at once, all the time.

Caleb showed mixed emotions, too. When he held her, he didn't relax right away. But his hand always found her belly, and that calmed them both.

The possibility of a child soothed and stressed everyone. Every man had a soft look in his eyes when Caleb's hand rested on Jeni's middle, but one that was tempered with gallantry.

One day, the house was quiet when Caleb came up to bed. The bunkhouse was nearly finished and most of the men had moved outside. He said the others were all on a late guard. What a fib. The men had all moved out for the night so she could be with her husband.

Mortification overwhelmed her as it always did, but she wouldn't waste an opportunity. She needed him.

That night, they reached for each other. They took their time and soaked up every kiss and caress, knowing they might not have a chance again for a while. Caleb's passion fed Jeni's, and her love fed his. They were both wild and hungry, and sweet and savoring.

The following day, they arose, and together they did what they had been doing for weeks. Made breakfast and pot after pot of coffee while men poured in and out of the house.

Knowing that a battle was coming but not knowing when or how was the hardest part. Part of Jeni hoped it would just go ahead and come, so they could get it over with. She worried about how long the men could stick around waiting. It had already been weeks, and it could be much longer. Caleb said the men were there to work for the summer, but a few would leave after the spring roundup for cattle drives. They would return after, though. The normal business of ranching would go on.

While washing dishes one day, she caught a piece of conversation and realized that they hadn't been waiting; they just weren't telling her about the battles that they were fighting.

Jeni stormed into the conversation, angry as a wet goat. She was used to being frustrated, irritated, embarrassed, but she was not used to this kind of outright fiery anger. Woman's moods could swing during pregnancy, but this was more than she was prepared for. She stomped her feet and pounded on the table. They would not leave her in the dark.

When she cornered Caleb and Caine in the sitting room, they weren't prepared for her fury, either. Daniel entered as she was losing steam, and she turned on him and fired right back up again. She grabbed his hand and dragged him over to where Caine and Caleb sat in shock. She held his feet to the fire and demanded that he tell her everything he knew. He was the one with the most to share, since he was the sheriff. The badge on his shirt got her attention, and she pressed her finger into it, insisting that he tell her what had been going on while she was inside playing house, like a little girl.

Quite a few men had tried to attack the property and been subdued or killed. There were so many men up here that it would be impossible for anyone to make it through their line. She hadn't even heard gunshots.

They explained that a few men had come close to the house but couldn't get past the guard. Those were bounty hunters, carrying her wanted posters, and they'd encountered no more of Benson's men.

Jeni's fury simmered. They'd been keeping this from her. In bed, she fumed at Caleb. She didn't let him hold her and apologize. Everything he said was stupid, and she wasn't ready to forgive him.

He said he hadn't wanted to upset her in case it was bad for the baby.

Please!

He was using the baby against her now.

She hated that.

When they'd been up at Hank's house for three more weeks, a man rode in to join the resistance. Everything about him made Jeni uncomfortable, and she told Caleb. She couldn't point to what it was about him, but there was something. She stayed as far away from him as possible. He was an old friend of Daniel's, but Jeni hadn't caught his name. He stayed to himself mostly. He had a slight limp and a very southern accent.

When she was alone with Caine, she told him how the new man made her uncomfortable. Caine promised to ask about him. It was strange that Caine didn't know him. Caine seemed to be always in charge. Even when Daniel was giving orders, it seemed like Caine was driving the wagon.

At dinner, several days after arriving, he watched her so closely it made her skin crawl. The hairs on the back of her neck stood on edge, and she wanted to curl up into her husband and hide.

The man addressed her before she could. "You really are as beautiful as they say you are, aren't you?"

She turned to Caleb.

He glared at the other man. "Do you have a question for my wife?"

Caleb threw his arm around her shoulders and held her to his side, his protective instincts rising to meet a new challenger. She tried to soothe his tense muscles with a hand on his chest. He didn't relax, though. He glared over her head at the newcomer and waited for him to explain himself.

"I've been hearing about her beauty all over the country. They're talking about your wife and how she's the most beautiful woman that has ever been. I didn't believe it." He swallowed hard, but didn't break eye contact. "I also heard that she was a whore."

She jumped and leaned even further into Caleb, hiding her face in his neck and clinging to his shoulders. She breathed him in and fought to slow her racing pulse. It was bad for the baby; Caleb would take care of it.

Caleb's arms tightened around her, and his hand cradled the back of her head to his shoulder. Caleb surrounded her as much as he could, but Jeni wished to be closer still.

She was never quite close enough. Jeni clung to Caleb, afraid he'd jump out of his chair at any moment. Caleb glared back and forth between Daniel and the new guy.

"I've been here for a few days now," the man went on, "and it's easy enough to see that the second part isn't true. The needle of her compass points directly at you, but she is the most beautiful woman I've ever seen."

"The day you arrived, my wife said she was uncomfortable with you. She's mentioned it several times since. What's your deal?"

"She's said the same to me," Caine added.

"Your instincts are dead-on, aren't they?" He was looking straight at Jeni, causing her to twist in Caleb's arms, pushing him to see the stranger. "I heard that about you, too."

Puzzled, she lifted her head, then followed with her shoulders, sitting straight up, but still as close to Caleb as she could be. She waited for him to continue.

"When I picked up the telegram from Daniel," he nodded to his friend across the table, "I wasn't far from Boston. I thought I'd head over there before coming out here. That's why I was so late for the party. I wanted to check out the situation from both ends, so I could make up my mind on which side was right."

"That's always been his way," Daniel cut in.

The man offered Danial a small-but-grateful

salute with his cup. "Benson has several stories that he's selling, depending on who he's talking to. He's an excellent salesman, good at reading people.

"To some, you are his beloved fiancé. In that version, these men kidnapped you, and you're desperate to get back to him. He misses you and will do anything to have you home." He sipped his coffee. "The second story is that you left him at the altar and broke his heart. He only wants to make sure you're safe. He can't live without knowing that you're being taken care of.

"The story he prefers—the one he is sharing with mercenaries—is that you seduced and tortured him with your beauty until he gave you his heart. Then you robbed him and left him behind. He wants his $10,000 back, and he wants revenge."

Jeni didn't break eye contact with this stranger. "What's your name?"

"Dean."

"Is that your first or last name?"

Daniel laughed, "If you get that out of him, I'll give you a million dollars." He tipped his mug to Rose, who filled all the cups around the big wooden table.

The man glanced at Daniel with mirth in his eyes. "Just Dean."

"How do you know all this about Mr. Benson?" Jeni asked.

"I let him hire me as a gunman to come get you and bring you home."

"I figured I might as well hear the man out before I went to war against him." Dean shrugged.

Her anger was back. She didn't need to hide from this man. She'd see this conversation through. She swatted at Caleb when he looked like he would take over and stared at Dean.

"So, what now, Mr. Dean?" She demanded.

"Just Dean. I told you, I came to observe and to decide for myself. You aren't a criminal, and you're not a whore. I don't think you're a witch.

"I visited your friends Sarah Forbes and Denise Miller. They're a pair!"

"You talked to Sarah and Denise?"

He nodded. "I showed them the telegram from Daniel and explained that I was coming to protect you. They told me your side of the story and showed me your letters. When I arrived in Hope, I spent a few days getting the lay of the land and listening to the gossip, as I assume most of the others did." A few nods around the table confirmed it. "I met an interesting little mouse named Opal Whitfield, who was happy to fill me in."

Bless Opal.

"You sussing me out shows you have excellent instincts, as Miss Miller said you did. I knew Scott Maxwell, and if I were in your position, I would've done the same as you. He would've respected you and protected you, as Caleb will. Like I said, your instincts are spot on."

"I'm not sure what to say." Jeni wrung her skirt in her hands.

"That's fine. Have you felt distrustful of any of the other men who've ridden up? I know I'm not the only man that Benson sent this way."

Jeni's eyes darted left and right. She scrunched her eyebrows up tight and pursed her lips, trying to look back into the last few weeks. "I can't think of anyone."

"If you feel even a little uncomfortable, get to your husband or one of the original men of The Maxwell Group. Don't trust anyone else here, me included, because there is just no way to be sure." He cleared his throat and added, "There were two men back in town getting ready to head back to Boston. They'd been up here, and after spending a few days with you, they couldn't take you from your husband. There were probably others who've made the same choice.

"Knowing that, I waited to test your instincts and to see your loyalty to your husband before I said anything. Daniel and I are making a list of men who've come and gone already. They won't be back." He cleared his throat and took another drink of his coffee. "I get a little soft for pregnant women. I imagine most of us do. Your part in all of this is to trust your instincts and stay by your husband. Let us protect you."

Jeni looked into Caleb's eyes and leaned forward and rested her forehead on his. The fight went out of her, and she settled into his embrace.

THE FEEL OF JENI RELAXED AGAINST HIM EASED CALEB'S ire about the fact that two enemy men had got close to her, and nobody told him. She sighed and fell asleep. Caleb kissed the top of her sweet head and cherished the feel of her in his arms. She was his world. She and the baby were everything.

Dean looked on, his eyes sad as Caleb rubbed small circles over her growing belly.

Caleb considered the other man. His ethics impressed him, but Caleb wouldn't trust anyone around his wife anymore. He'd thought she was safe to be left among the men who'd come to help. Now he learned that he'd been in the dark too. Not as much as Jeni, but it pissed him off just as much as had her.

If she wasn't sleeping in his arms, he might stomp his boots and shake his fists as she had. Her anger was a surprise, but it was also sort of cute. He'd never be stupid enough to tell her.

Caleb wouldn't leave her alone again. He thought he could feel the first signs of her belly warming under his palm. It was fascinating and so damn beautiful.

He spent a lot of time watching his wife; she was captivating. Jeni was sweet and considerate, but there was a fire that burned beneath the surface, which intrigued him. She was beautiful, but she was more than that. She never stopped trying to be helpful, proving that she could be more than a pretty face.

When she didn't think anyone was watching, she bloomed. The special smile she saved for when her hands roamed over her belly took his breath away. When her guard was down, and she allowed herself to feel the joy bubbling up inside, she took his breath away.

Whenever she caught the attention of the men, her guard shot back up. Caleb's heart hurt to see her allow them to steal her joy. He hated that she felt the need to make herself small and invisible. She was the sunshine; she should not have to hide behind clouds.

Alone at night, when the house was quiet, though, she didn't hide. That was the best part of his day. Every night, Caleb slept with one hand over her belly. Her stomach was still flat, but when she was naked beside him, he thought he could see some roundness there. His protective instincts ran on high. He'd love nothing more than to hide her away in safety and hold her forever.

There were still attacks on the ranch at least a few times each week. Caleb asked the men to stop discussing it in front of her again. Whenever the conversation had turned to danger, her joy faded to worry.

He didn't want her to worry. He wanted her happy. So he decided that ignorance was to be her bliss. At least for a little while.

It would piss her off if she found out. Last time she nearly ripped him and Caine to shreds. The image of her jabbing her finger into Daniel's chest was almost comical. The top of her head didn't even reach his shoulders, but she stood toe to toe and poked her finger into his badge and demanded answers. It was the same as she'd done to Scott only a few months ago.

She was something.

Ignorance was the best thing for her, though, and for the baby. They wouldn't lie to her if she asked a direct question. That was going too far. He just wanted them to avoid the subject of her safety as much as possible.

Chapter Thirteen

J eni obsessively calculated the dates and tried imagining when she had conceived. It could have been any time since Christmas and her two weddings. The baby could be Scott's. Or it could be Caleb's. She was desperate to know.

How had 8 weeks passed?

She slept all the time now. She'd never been a person to nap during the day, but it had turned into a daily event. It was not uncommon for her to crawl into Caleb's lap after supper and fall asleep with conversation rumbling around her. In the night when they could lie together without the burden of clothes, Caleb always pressed a kiss to her lower abdomen and told her that he loved her before he pulled her into his arms to sleep. They marveled together at the small bump, which she sometimes thought they were probably imagining.

Not everything was all happiness, though. Jeni became extremely sensitive to smells, and that increased her nausea to knock her off her feet some days. The smells she found herself most sensitive to were strange. It wasn't the body odor of the men, the smell of cooking meat, or even the strong coffee that was always at the ready. It was the smell of cooking eggs that took the wind out of her sails. Who would have thought?

Caleb had to take over breakfast preparations, because if she was in the kitchen when the eggs hit the pan, she'd have to run to the chamber pot in her room. Vomiting always left her weak and exhausted. It became her habit to sleep in later in the morning and come down after the breakfast had cleared to help with cleanup. The men had all joined forces to make her chores as light as possible. With the number of them around, it wasn't a big job for any of them, but she was grateful.

Iris brought a tea that she mixed herself. It helped with the morning sickness when nothing else had. Jeni still had to avoid the kitchen, but it was better.

Her breasts swelled and grew tender. They became so sore that she couldn't stand the feel of her dress pressing against them. One afternoon, she took herself to her room to remove her dress and lay down. When Caleb had come in a few minutes later, his eyes popped out of his face in the funniest expression. She was too sensitive to cover up. Even Hank's soft sheets were too much for her poor nipples. Caleb had a great time teasing her about that for days on end, making subtle little jokes that nobody else could decipher.

They laughed together more and more with time passing. The fear remained, but she was happy.

Whenever she thought about the baby, she thought about both Scott and Caleb. Looking back at her relationship with Scott, she was tormented by the unfairness of it all. She would probably always wrestle with guilt and grief.

She and Scott hadn't known each other, really. They hadn't ever had a chance to talk and had only actually laid eyes on each other a couple of times. She'd been so focused on his refusal to commit that she ignored the fact that she didn't know more about him than he'd written in his letter. He'd told her what would happen, and she hadn't listened. His death was her fault.

Sitting at meals with Caine was still difficult sometimes. He felt Scott's death so deeply he couldn't hide it, and the guilt ate away at her. Talking to him and making eye contact had taken weeks to manage. Caine's burden of grief was harder for her than anyone else's. She could feel that he blamed her and avoided her. He was kind and protective, like the rest, but he resisted her friendship.

Caleb had been her friend before he was her husband. They'd had time to get to know each other. The love and passion they had now were built on a foundation of trust and companionship. She wished she'd realized the depth of Caleb's feelings before the Christmas party. If she'd switched her interest from Scott to Caleb while they were in town, Scott would be alive.

She wondered if Scott would have been ok with the change. Even while she tortured herself with these thoughts, she knew that she wouldn't have changed her course. A groom that didn't know what she looked like was one of her reasons for becoming a mail-order bride in the first place. She probably wouldn't have accepted Caleb if he had asked.

No matter how she'd ended up with the man she married, she tried to remember to be happy in the moment. She loved her husband, and she knew that he loved her, and together they loved the baby that grew inside of her.

There was one piece missing to Jeni and Caleb's relationship that nibbled at her confidence. He'd told her the basics of his past, but he wouldn't share any details with her.

He and Caine were twins. They'd grown up on the ranch and when their parents had died, Rose and Iris took care of them, and the boys worked on the ranch. They were thirteen in the summer when Scott came to join them. He was the same age.

The next summer, Hank and Will showed up together, and the sisters took them in as well. Hank was fifteen and Will was sixteen. Daniel had been last to join the group. He showed up a few months after Hank and Will; he was thirteen. Beyond that, all Caleb would say was that he'd farmed. He grew most of the crops that fed the livestock.

She'd heard the name Amy a few times, but whenever she tried to get details, conversations stopped and she was left hanging. Opal had mentioned to her that Amy was Caine's wife, and she'd died, but that was all she knew. Nobody seemed to know what had happened to her.

Jeni asked about Amy one quiet evening after dinner. The hired men had retired to the bunk house and just The Maxwell Group remained. The reactions around the sitting room were unmistakably uncomfortable. Men shifted in their chairs, swirled their drinks and generally avoided eye contact with her or each other.

It wasn't only Caleb who was sensitive about the topic of Amy. All the Maxwell Group men clammed up when she'd asked. Caine's reaction was the strongest of them all, which made sense. The rest of the men shook their heads and turned away from the topic, but Caine became angry and stormed out of the house. Jeni was sure that the mystery of Amy was harder to accept than any reality would be.

She determined that she would try to get it out of Iris and Rose. Rose, really. Iris wouldn't tell her, but Rose might. She'd ask next time she saw them.

She wanted to know about Amy. The mystery wouldn't leave her alone. It nagged at her. The more she tried to learn, the less they shared. Her digging was hurting them and they were risking their lives to take care of her. She stopped asking about Amy and after a few days, the mood around the house picked back up.

Even Rose wouldn't talk about Amy.

She'd wait until she and Caleb were in bed to ask again. It was always easier to talk to her husband in the dark.

When they lay together with his hand over her belly, they relaxed and opened up.

"Why won't you tell me about Amy?"

Instead of answering, he turned away from her, leaving their baby without the warmth of his hand.

"Did you love her?" she whispered into his back as she wrapped herself around him from behind.

"We all loved her."

"Who was she?"

"It's hard to talk about her. It's hard to think about her. With everything that's going on, it's not the time to get into this."

"I don't understand, Caleb." She kissed the middle of his back. "Were you in love with your brother's wife?"

At that, he turned and pulled her against his chest. "You're the only woman I've loved."

"Then why can't you talk about her?"

He shook his head, his scruffy beard scratching against her forehead. "I just can't."

The speed of his heart and tension in his muscles made her to let it go. He'd already opened up to her more than he had before. There was a story, and it was a sad one. She'd give him the time he needed, he deserved that. She kissed his chest and let herself drift off to sleep.

———

WHY WOULDN'T JENI ACCEPT THAT THEY COULDN'T share everything?

There were some topics too painful to

discuss—especially with his wife and child in danger. Caleb didn't want to think about loss and hurt of his past, he wanted to focus on getting his family through one nightmare at a time.

It was getting harder to put her off now that she'd decided to question him in bed. It had been easy enough to shrug her off before, when she only hinted at it, but now she asked directly, and he had to tell her to leave it alone. He had to either lie to her, or openly refuse to talk about it.

He hated treating Jeni that way, but he couldn't talk about Amy.

It wasn't just that he didn't want to talk about Amy. The others struggled with their own feelings about what happened to her, too. Amy had been special to them. Thinking about their failure to keep her safe didn't help them focus on the situation at hand. The Maxwell Group had never openly discussed what had happened to Amy, even between themselves. When her name was brought up, it was always as a reminder of what could happen.

They never spoke in specifics.

It he couldn't talk about it with men he'd known his whole life, how could he talk about it to Jeni? In her condition, and in her situation, she had to accept that there were things they couldn't address. Eventually, she would need to know, but that conversation couldn't happen now.

He hoped that she would understand and let the subject rest.

JENI HAD WRITTEN SEVERAL LETTERS TO HER FRIENDS IN Boston several times throughout her incarceration at Hank's house. She left out her name, even though Mr. Benson already knew where she was.

She hadn't received any responses, and it drove her crazy. With the winter upon them, she knew going back and forth to town was difficult, and mail was even slower than usual. She tried to be patient, but she missed her friends.

There was a chance that her letters were not getting to her friends because Mr. Benson might still be confiscating them. Regardless, whenever a man left, either for a short trip, or if he had to get back to his own life, she sent him off with a letter to post.

In her letters, she shared the news of her pregnancy. Maybe if Mr. Benson was reading her letters, that would change his mind, and he'd leave her alone. She could hope.

She shared news of the attacks against her, and she shared her struggle to get to know her husband. She also shared her love, excitement, and hope for the future. She didn't mention Amy specifically, but she did hint that there was something going on that these men didn't want her to know about. Her letters grew softer as the weeks turned into months, and the house developed a routine. Sometimes her letters felt more like journal entries, but she mailed them off just the same. She felt safe and happy, and after a while, her letters were all about the baby.

Life developed into an easy rhythm again.

Winter faded, and as the temperatures rose, peace settled around her. Caleb was there with her every day. He helped her and held her and told her in little actions how much he loved her. They grew closer to each other with every week that passed. Caleb never walked by her without touching her in some way, and she couldn't keep her hands off him either.

As spring came to the ranch, Jeni's happiness grew. The fearful feeling of being hunted down was replaced by joy at becoming a mother. It was the most beautiful thing she'd ever experienced. Her growing belly was now visible through her dresses. Everyone enjoyed seeing her grow by the week.

The men who had been accommodating from the beginning doubled down their chivalry, and Jeni was hardly allowed to do anything. They cooked, they cleaned, they worked together to take care of the chores that she should be doing. She was so distracted by herself that she hardly noticed. If she weren't pregnant, she would've insisted that they allow her to do her share. She wasn't used to being taken care of like this, but she was too absent minded to notice.

She walked around with her head in a fog. The most blissful fog. Rose and Iris spent several afternoons each week with her, talking about the baby and sharing dreams for the future. The thought of two loving grandmothers for her child touched her. She'd never had a family, but her sweet cherub would have a large, protective, and loving family.

One day, she was presented with a package of fabrics and sewing notions. She'd been thinking about her child's needs, but was afraid to ask. Caleb had asked Iris to make a list and then sent someone to town to get her everything she would need to create a wardrobe for their child.

Sewing was one of her favorite pastimes, and she'd missed it. She loved everything about making clothes, and making tiny ones for her own babe was precious. She created the little patterns on paper and carefully cut out the shapes. She sewed every delicate stitch with love and a prayer for her sweet infant. As she worked, she dreamed, and she wove her hopes through each garment.

Opal visited the ranch several times as the weather warmed and the snow cleared. She pestered Daniel for a ride if he was heading out for a day. Jeni never said anything, but she suspected her energetic friend had set her cap for her stoic brother-in-law. She just shared her knitting and sewing and listened carefully for hints. Jeni cherished Opal. They had the best visits, full of laughter and female companionship.

The men stopped giving their daily reports after supper, leading Jeni to believe the threat might finally be over. Then they dragged Will into the house with a gunshot wound, and reality jumped up to bite her like a coiled snake. The threat was as real as ever. They'd simply kept it from her. All the happiness that had been building around her crashed back to reality and she realized how much she'd been living in dreamland.

The wound ended up being a small graze, but it was the reminder that she needed. She kneeled on the floor beside his chair and cleaned the wound on his side with brusque movements, not bothering to spare his feelings in her rage. When he hissed and his body clenched, she looked into his face, and remorse settled over her anger. She gentled and finished cleaning and stitching Will's injury without causing more pain than was necessary. He'd been shot protecting her. He didn't deserve rough handling.

The knowledge that they'd coddled her for months, and allowed her to dream away her time in ignorance, kept her anger at a steady boil. How dare they leave her in the dark?

Jeni turned on the men who'd become her family. "You've been hiding the truth from me."

Will answered for the group. "We thought you deserved the peace of mind. Even if just for a little while."When she focused on his face, he winced and cradled his hand over his side. Was he was faking to get a softer reaction from her?

Little did he know, he risked being given another injury.

No matter how sorry she was for him, her anger burned. He was putting himself at risk to keep her safe, but that didn't give him permission to manipulate and lie to her. She mentally bounced back and forth between excusing every last man in the room and pummeling them.

"How much have you protected me from the truth?" Jeni asked as she lay in bed with Caleb.

"We never meant to make you angry. We wanted to give you a chance to enjoy your pregnancy."

"I've been selfish. You're all out there risking your lives, and I'm in a safe little bubble, sewing and dreaming of rainbows. You've taken care of me, and I haven't been allowed to help."

"Watching you glow and enjoy your pregnancy reminds us of what's important." He rubbed her back and twisted a lock of her hair around his finger. "With the snow and cold, there have been fewer attempts, and they have been easier to stop. It isn't like it was in the beginning, with attackers showing up almost every day. We haven't had anyone within miles of the house for weeks. Today they had a little trouble, but Will's fine, and they stopped the attack."

"How many men have come?"

"You mean since we moved up here?"

"Yes."

"I don't know. I don't want to speculate either. I want you to focus on the baby and not on the danger. Your job is to grow and give birth to a new life. Ours is to make it possible for you to do that. I don't want to see fear and anxiety in your eyes all the time."

"I can't live with anyone dying for me."

If Caleb's face was any indication, her words had had a powerful impact. "We moved to Hank's place for a reason. We can defend it." He moved down her body to rest his forehead on the growing mound of her belly. "This is the most important thing."

"You expect the springtime to bring more attempts, though, don't you?"

"It's hard to say. We keep guard, and we work our ranch. Just because the others aren't here doesn't mean they're doing battle all the time. We're preparing for the spring. I promise that if you're in danger, we'll tell you."

Chapter Fourteen

Jeni awoke on a horse with a pounding head and screaming muscles. She rode in front of a stranger with her wrists bound and resting in her lap. His tight grip on her waist bit into her ribs. Terror made her shiver despite the sun directly overhead. No armed men gathered on the ridge, and no chorus of hooves pounded the ground behind her.

Dear God. She'd been kidnapped, and no one knew she was gone.

Her abductor must've knocked her out. She had no memory of how she'd gotten here. One minute she'd been cleaning dishes, and the next she was on a horse, in pain, and afraid.

"Who are you?" Jeni tried to twist around to look at the stranger, but his iron grip kept her facing forward.

He said nothing.

"Where are you taking me? If Mr. Benson sent you, all of his stories are lies. Please. Please take me home. I didn't run away from Mr. Benson. I was never engaged to him. I promise I haven't been kidnapped, and I didn't steal anything from him. Whatever reason he's given, it's a lie." No matter how she begged, nothing in his demeanor changed in the slightest.

He rode in silence, as if she weren't sitting in his lap with her baby kicking away at his too-tight arm. He wouldn't be able to feel it through his jacket, but she could. She had to shake herself to focus on the stranger and not the baby.

The sky was clear, no rain or late snow on the way. The wet smell of spring was too pleasant for the situation. Melted snow and mud would leave an easy trail for Caleb to follow. She strained to catch any sound in the distance. Nothing.

An hour must have passed before the man stopped his horse and unceremoniously threw Jeni to the ground. She braced her arms around her belly and took the impact to her shoulder and knees. Her head struck a rock, and she saw stars. She tried to get up, but only got as far as her knees and elbows before the man crouched beside her.

He grabbed an ankle and pulled her leg out from under her, sending her sprawling so she had to roll sideways to protect her belly. The impact on her shoulder and hip jolted her. He ignored her scream and tied her ankles together. With her hands bound, she had no way of protecting herself or her baby.

The man walked away and left her lying in the dirt. It took a fair amount of effort, but she turned herself over and sat up. Everything hurt. She forced herself not to cry. This was not the time to cry.

He went about untacking his horse and lead it away. She memorized everything, praying for a chance to escape. She'd need to remember where he hobbled the horse. She cringed when he stalked back her way, trying to make herself as small as possible and shield her belly with her arm.

He scooped her up and carried her into a clearing that was more like a ledge on the side of a mountain, and dropped her to the ground by the rock wall. He left her alone. She didn't know if she would rather he leave her tied up there alone or come back. He was back, though, after about ten minutes.

She studied the man as returned with supplies and moved around the small clearing. One would expect a man who treated her like this to be big and strong and dirty like the other gunslingers that had come for her. He wasn't. He wasn't as tall or strong as any of The Maxwell Group, and he wasn't dirty like the other gunmen she had seen either. Even his clothes looked too neat to be a gunslinger.

It was as if he'd purchased a bounty hunter costume, and pressed it neatly, to wear for her kidnapping.

The more she studied him, the more certain she was that he was not what he was trying to portray. His posture and mannerisms were precise, not casual as one found with western men. The Maxwell Group men all had excellent hygiene, but this man was perfumed. She hadn't considered it from that perspective while she was sitting on his lap. She'd smelled it, but she was too busy trying not to be sick. His hair was neat under his hat, and even his hat was brand new and spotlessly clean.

Who was this man?

She could picture him as an accountant or lawyer more easily than a gun for hire. He was a terrifying mystery. How had he gotten past the men guarding the house? Was Caleb ok? She had to remind herself to remain calm and keep a cool head.

She couldn't afford to panic.

He didn't care about her safety; that was obvious. The way he'd handled her, even with her obvious pregnancy, showed a coldness of heart that she wondered if even Mr. Benson could have matched.

It was also odd that he didn't speak to her at all. When he looked at her, it was only to glare. She hadn't heard his voice. They'd ridden for at least an hour after she'd awakened to get to the camp. And the entire time, he hadn't said a word. He hadn't even told her to be quiet. He'd crushed his hand over her mouth once to silence her when she screamed, but he hadn't uttered a single word.

She wondered if he could speak.

Jeni turned her attention from the man to the campsite. He must've come here and prepared it earlier. There were bedrolls and weapons strewn around the small, flat area. He didn't start a fire, and she saw no food or equipment for cooking. He must not plan to camp here long.

They were in the mountains on a ledge. Not a

narrow dangerous ledge, though, a flat spot on the side of the mountain. Large boulders created a fascinating, natural railing protecting them from the cliff's edge. Rock surrounded the clearing on all four sides. Jeni's back rested against a cold rock face that went straight up over her head for at least twelve feet. To her right, a narrow gap between boulders worked as the only entrance and exit from the landing. Along the opposite edge lay six large boulders guarding the drop off. The boulders wrapped around the campsite, protecting them from every side.

Deep, narrow gaps between the large boulders provided cover from bullets while giving a good place to shoot between. It all combined to make protecting the clearing easy, even for a single man.

He was smart.

He'd chosen this position carefully. Attacking from behind would mean attacking from above, and that was impossible. Defending from every other direction would be simple. With his weapons spread around, he could hold this position by himself for a long time. If anyone showed up to help him, she didn't think even the most skilled rescuer would be able to get to her..

Beyond the boulder railing, another mountain rose sharply on the other side of a deep narrow canyon. She scanned the area repeatedly, hoping to see any sign of rescue or escape. She searched her mind for any sort of plan to save herself, but nothing came to her.

She was helpless, and she hated that.

The late afternoon chill seeped into her body, and she folded her arms more firmly into her chest and shuddered. She was tired. She'd become used to napping in the afternoon, and at five months pregnant, her belly caused her discomfort in the best of circumstances. The pain of being bound in such a way and sitting on the hard ground intensified every ache and pain. She was afraid to complain, though, so she forced herself to remain quiet and as still as possible. The less attention she drew to herself, the better.

She sat there for what she assumed was about two hours before she spoke. It was growing dark, and she was starving and needed to relieve herself. As much as she didn't want to get his attention, she had to.

"Excuse me."

He looked at her, his eyes so cold they made her shiver.

"I need to relieve myself."

"You can wait." His voice was as sharp as his stare, clipped and cold. Not a warm growl, like she was used to with the Maxwell men. But his accent gave away his home.

Boston.

This *was* one of Mr. Benson's men.

Maybe direct speaking would get through to him. "Being pregnant means I can't wait. If I could, I promise I would. If I sit here any longer, I'm going to have an accident, and we're both going to suffer from it."

"I won't suffer from it."

"You're downhill from my seat." She shivered and then shrugged. "I have little time. I've been sitting here trying to will myself not to go, just so I wouldn't have to speak to you. Pregnancy makes these things emergent." She wanted to keep reminding him she was pregnant.

He probably wouldn't soften, but she hoped.

He huffed in an odd, gentlemanly way that was again in contrast with his gunman costume. It reaffirmed her impression that he was not an outlaw. He was dangerous, but this was a city man. He pulled her to her feet. Her balance depended entirely on him, and his hand on her arm was her only support.

Soft hands. He had no calluses to abrade the fabric of her sleeve.

"Can you please untie me?"

"No."

"I won't run away. As much as I hate it, right now my safety depends on you. You're my protector at the moment."

His eyebrows drew together as he considered her statement.

"I'm heavy with child. I can't run. Even if I could, I wouldn't know where to go. Getting lost in the wilderness isn't exactly appealing to me. I know there are wild animals out here, and with no way to defend myself, I entirely depend on you."

He still didn't speak more than needed, but he removed the ropes from her wrists and ankles carefully. Rather than cut them off, he unknotted them and set them aside.

He would probably tie her back up.

She left the clearing, and he pointed towards a thicket. Instead of letting go, he walked with her.

She was horrified. "You don't mean to go with me, do you?"

There was no way she could relieve herself with this stranger watching. It was bad enough when Caleb walked her to the outhouse and stood there waiting for her to finish.

She'd drop from mortification.

He stayed with her, though, and she did what needed to be done. Her blush was hot enough to light the entire forest on fire by the time she finished.

He escorted her back to the camp and pointed back to her spot beside the wall. Thank God he didn't tie her back up, but she couldn't look at him after that very personal experience.

She didn't expect him to respond, but she continued with her interrogation. "What's your name?"

CALEB WATCHED AS THE SON-OF-A-BITCH PULLED JENI to her feet. His breath caught with fear that she'd fall. She had no balance with her feet and hands tied like that. She couldn't catch herself if she fell.

The stranger held her arm and steadied her against the rock wall. To Caleb's surprise, the kidnapper untied her wrists and ankles. Jeni stretched her joints with a wince, and even from his perch Caleb could see the damaged skin and her painful wince when she took her first testing steps.

God damn it!

Jeni stumbled toward the edge of the camp. She probably needed to empty her bladder. It was the only reason her abductor would take such a risk. She'd been in this man's custody for almost five hours, and she usually went much more often than that. She must be so uncomfortable. He couldn't take his eyes off of her as they moved away from him. She waddled a little. Something that he'd considered cute at home looked unsteady and vulnerable out here.

Tension drew him up tight when he realized the bastard intended to watch her. He wished he could fly across the gaping canyon and rip the man's head off. The only thing that restrained him was that Jeni needed him to stay calm, rational.

He'd get his chance to knock the bastard's dick in the dirt.

The Maxwell Group and a handful of others from the ranch were currently gathering down below. They'd scoped out the situation from every vantage, then returned to the horses to plan their approach. They knew the area well—this clearing in particular. It was an excellent position to defend. The rocks where her captor sat completely sheltered him. There was no angle where they could get an unob-structed aim.

The weakest spot in the clearing was against the rock wall where Jeni sat. Bullets could hit her from any direction. She had no protection at all.

With his heart full of hate, Caleb returned to the group.

"Jeni's ok," he let them know first.

Several others had also seen her. They nodded.

"Something's weird about this guy," Caleb said. "He's not like any bounty hunter I've ever seen." He pulled his saddle from his horse as he talked, tossed it over a stump to keep it off the ground, then looped his reins over a low branch. "I saw two guys to the left of the clearing. Sharpshooters maybe."

Daniel loosened his horse's girth, but didn't remove the saddle. "One more up top."

"One below." Hank added. He tossed his saddle bags over his shoulder and moved to the center of the group.

Caine clapped a reassuring hand on his brother's shoulder. "Two more on the other ridge. Not sure what they're doing up there, there's no shot from that far away. Lookouts probably."

"Something's not right about this asshole," Caleb pressed.

"Too pretty," Daniel said. "I'd guess him as a gambler or lawyer, maybe. I've never seen him before. He's not local, that's for sure." Again, there was a round of nods.

"I think our opportunity'll come when Jeni has to relieve herself again. He just took her. Son of a bitch didn't give her any privacy, but he did remove the ropes. And he didn't put them back on."

"Damn." Caine threw his hat on the ground and kicked a rock.

Caleb had to force himself to keep his head in the game. Daniel put his hand on Caine's shoulder and gave him a grounding shake.

"We need to stay focused here," Hank said. "This won't be like it was with Amy." Looking at Caleb, he added, "We'll get her back."

Caleb nodded, but the fear didn't ease. Every minute without Jeni was fresh torture. His hand ached to be pressed against her belly.

He needed her.

Opening and closing his fist several times, he dragged his thoughts back to the situation at hand. Focus had never been so hard to maintain. "I'll go with Dean and sit in that thicket. If he brings her out, we'll be ready." Caleb pulled his gun from the saddle holster and formulated his plan as he armed himself for the hike back up the mountain. "Caine, take two guys and head up on that ridge. Get rid of the lookouts. Hank, I want you in the tree line I just came from. You can get a line on him if he stands up. If not, at least you'll be able to watch Jeni." Turning to Daniel, he motioned up the hill with his rifle. "I want you up above. Will can pick off the one below, then stay with the horses. Hopefully, there'll only be the six but keep your eyes open."

"I think we need to keep a few men below for distraction." Caine tossed over his shoulder as he waved to Brian and Mark to start up the ridge. "Go on. I'll catch up." They had the furthest to hike to get into position—he wasn't wasting any time.

"That makes sense." Daniel said, nodding for two men to start up the ridge ahead of him.

"Anyone gets close enough to grab her," Caleb said as they gathered their weapons. "take her and run. Don't come back to help. Get her to the ranch and send someone for the doctor.

"She won't want to go, so just remind her of the baby and tell her I need to know she's safe. Every time she wants to turn around, remind her of the baby. It's the only way she's going to go, and even then, she will fight you." He wanted to be the man to get her out of there. He wasn't so arrogant that he was going to stop someone else from doing it. A lot more than ego was on the line.

They spent fifteen minutes making sure the plan was solid and everyone knew where they needed to be. Fifteen minutes was an eternity, a necessary eternity.

With a last shared look, the brothers dispersed.

WHO KNOWS HOW MUCH TIME PASSED? IT WAS probably another hour or two, anyway. It was too dark to judge anymore. She was cold and hungry and tired. Sitting against rock chilled her to the bone. She was so sore that her body was numb. She didn't even have a shawl.

"Would you please make a fire?"

"No."

"I'm freezing…" She shivered and wrapped her arms around herself. "I'm hungry too."

He shrugged.

Heartless.

"A blanket then?"

After a minute, he tossed a bedroll to her. She

wondered why he wouldn't have given it to her earlier. She was obviously cold, and he had been watching her shiver all afternoon. She should've thought to ask for it hours ago.

"Are you going to kill me?"

"Maybe."

"Maybe? You haven't decided?"

"You have value."

"You're going to sell me? To Mr. Benson?"

Shrug.

"If you kill me and my baby, there is no amount of money in the world that'll protect you from my husband."

Another shrug.

Could he really not care?

"What's your plan? Up here in the mountains, alone, freezing to death, with no fire or food, or even a roof. How do you intend to seek ransom?"

"Who says we're alone?"

"I only see the two of us here."

"Good."

That shut her up for a minute. Were there men hiding out here? She'd spent her day hoping The Maxwell Group would show up to rescue her. Now she feared that they'd walk into an ambush. She wished she had a way to let Caleb know there were more men. Jeni's heart and mind raced with fear.

She held her belly and wished to be in bed with her husband, warm and safe. She wanted to watch his face as he tried to feel their baby moving against his hand. They'd been so happy just twenty-four hours earlier.

It was terrible how quickly things could change.

———

CALEB APPROACHED FROM BEHIND AND TOOK OUT THE first guard as Dean came up behind the second. Caleb hooted to let the others know they'd taken out the first two. He and Dean worked together to move the bodies of the men, then settled themselves into place to wait.

A bird call came from above. The man from up top was taken care of. Five minutes later, the call sounded from below. That was the four on this side of the clearing. The two on the ridge would take longer, but they were too far away to shoot Jeni. They were too far away for birdcalls, too, so they wouldn't know if Caine got those two.

His brother was lethally accurate. Caleb didn't worry.

Pieces of Jeni's conversation with the dandy-outlaw floated through the forest. The rocks around the clearing were a natural amphitheater. Their years of birdcall communication came in handy Caleb knew that everyone was in place, and they'd taken out all the gunman's backup. Hank could see Jeni, so she must be against the rock wall again. Daniel and several men above might see the stranger, but he wasn't sure. It wasn't an exact science, but he could judge fairly well everyone's positions.

When Jeni asked for a blanket, Caleb held his breath. If the stranger walked over to her, Hank would shoot. Hank was a sharpshooter; the best he'd ever met. He had only missed once, and that miss would torture him for the rest of his life.

A soft thump and not a blast of Hank's gun crushed his hope. The stranger must've tossed her a blanket.

Damn.

The son-of-a-bitch didn't know they'd taken out his backup, though. If they could line up a shot, this could end with relatively little fighting.

Jeni couldn't know any of this, and he had no way to tell her he was there. She was afraid, but when she had threatened the guy, Caleb smiled.

She was feisty.

He loved that about her.

It also frightened him.

THE MAXWELL GROUP WAS OUT THERE! NOT ONLY that, they'd already taken out some back up. She hoped they'd gotten all the backup.

Jeni suppressed a smile, but rejoiced inside.

While waiting for Scott to marry her, she and Caleb had killed time with months of small talk. He'd told her about their birdcall language. Jeni had been so impressed by his hoot owl call that she'd made him perform it for her every day for weeks.

The sound of that call sent her heart soaring. Caleb was out there!

Cold and fear fled, but now her mind raced.

He was somewhere behind her. She needed to get to him. Jeni sat there for at least half an hour trying to find a way before her scattered pregnant thoughts returned to the simplest solution. She wanted to shake herself. Jeni had sat there planning all manner of conniving plots in her mind, when she could use what had already worked.

She didn't have to go, though. She hadn't had water since the last time she went. Would she be able to make herself go again if there was nobody over there to rescue her?

And what if she was wrong, and Caleb wasn't on the other side of this opening? She exhaled with a low groan. She had to at least try.

"I have to go again."

"You're fine."

This again? "I'm pregnant."

"So."

"I'm not a doctor. All I know is that since I've been pregnant, I can hardly go a few hours without taking care of this particular business. My poor husband is about worn out by walking me in and out of the house all day and night."

The callous scoundrel huffed. "Just go," he bit out at her

"I can't see."

"Then you can't run away."

She was ok with that. It would be easier for Caleb to get her without this man by her side.

She couldn't get up. Darn it! She was so stiff and weighed down by her belly she couldn't get herself up off the ground.

She hated to ask him, but… "I need help."

He grumbled when he wasn't happy.

He huffed again and rose from his crouch.

An explosion ripped through the forest. Jeni jumped so hard her head knocked against the rock wall. Stars invaded her vision and, for a moment, she sat, completely stunned. Her hands flew to her head. She was bleeding in the exact spot that had healed after Sheriff Danes' attack.

Before she could refocus, the kidnapper hauled her up into his arms. His arm was strong around her neck, and she held on to his forearm with both of her hands to get air. She could smell the coppery scent of blood, his blood. It couldn't be hers. The cut on her head was too small, but she smelled a lot of blood.

She felt his blood soaking into the back of her dress and cringed.

She tried to pull his arm away, but stopped, worried that he might shift and hold her around her waist instead. She quit fighting for another reason, too. He held a gun in his free hand. Jeni didn't know if it would go off from moving too much.

Maybe she could appeal to his sense of self preservation. "We need to put pressure on your wound."

"*We're* not doing anything."

"You're bleeding too much. Let me bandage that."

"Just shut up and stop fighting."

"Please don't kill me."

"Shut up."

"Please don't kill my baby."

A hard knock to the back of her head registered before blackness surrounded her.

Chapter Fifteen

"**M**axwell! I've got your woman."

The bastard hauled Jeni back against him and moved, so her body blocked any further shots from Hank. He couldn't get back across the clearing to the rocks that offered protection. His only option was to back up into the corner and use her as a shield.

Caleb cursed. Snatching Jeni was no longer an option. He'd have to lay out the facts and hope the cornered mongrel would either pass out or surrender.

Caleb poked his head around the corner and pulled back. Catching a glimpse of Jeni, then losing it again. "We got your backup," he called. "You're alone and you're surrounded."

Caleb stepped forward into the clearing but stayed back. Blood poured from the wound on the man's side, and the side of Jeni's limp body pressed into the gory flow.

Jeni wasn't moving, and the side of her dress was covered in blood. It wasn't her blood, though. Only one shot had gone off, and Hank had hit his target. The blood on her belly ripped at his heart just the same.

The man shook his head and looked into the darkness. "All five?"

He was smart, buying time to think, hedging.

"All six."

"They promised me they were better," he admitted.

"Guess not."

"Why isn't she moving?" Caleb asked after a few seconds.

"She's alive. Knocked out. Fighting too much. You want her back, make a deal." He was wilting, stammering and gasping for air through the pain.

"You harm one hair on her head, and I'll kill you slowly."

He pressed his hand into his side. "I'm dying, anyway."

"What do you want?"

"Your word that you'll help me."

"I'm listening."

"Roger Benson took my daughter. If I get this woman back to him, he'll let my Maggie go." His breathing grew shallower.

"What's that have to do with me?"

"You have to promise to rescue Maggie."

"What's your name?"

"Carl Jacobs. Banker." He gave Jeni a shake. "I

need your word, or I won't die alone. This girl has always been more trouble than she's worth."

"What does that mean?"

"I need your promise."

"Why you?" Caleb was racing against time, but he'd been trying to figure out how this man fit into the picture. He wasn't big or strong. He looked like a banker. "Why'd he pick you?"

"Wasn't always a banker." He leaned against the wall, barely supporting Jeni over his arm. "Have a talent for getting in and out without being seen. Don't know how Benson discovered it. Held it over me for years." He gurgled and stumbled again. "Made my fortune stealing jewels and art. Changed my ways, though."

"What made you change?"

"Maggie." He couldn't put Jeni down—she was his shield—but his strength was fading fast. If he dropped her, it could hurt her.

"I'll find your girl. But only if Jeni's ok. If my wife or my baby are hurt, I won't do a damn thing for you."

It wasn't true. In going after Benson, Caleb would help the other woman and get revenge on the man who'd terrorized his entire family. He couldn't know she was out there and not help her.

The gun hit the dirt, clattering off a stone as it fell. Caleb took a cautious step further into the clearing, his own gun trained on the kidnapper. Jeni, unconscious, dangled by her neck from his arm. Caleb raged. He reached for the mother of his child with one hand while he punched the man who held her in the face with the other.

The man went down, and Caleb saw the blood weeping from the wound.

Son-of-a-bitch deserved it.

"You promised," he uttered with dwindling breath.

"I'll find your girl." Caleb scooped his wife into his arms and walked away.

Caine entered the clearing with several men as Caleb left with Jeni. Caine cradled her head and then squeezed Caleb's shoulder. His brother would finish questioning Mr. Jacobs. Daniel would take the bodies to town and collect the weapons left behind.

The other men surrounded Caleb and Jeni as they made their way back down the mountain. They couldn't be sure that there were no other bounty hunters hiding out in the forest. They'd picked off all the conspirators they could see, but that didn't mean there wasn't more.

Halfway to the horses, Jeni stirred, screamed and lashed out as though she fought for her life in his arms.

HE WASN'T GETTING AWAY WITH HER AGAIN!

Jeni fought and battered at his head with her fists as she kicked with her feet. She raked her nails down his neck and twisted in his arms, trying to bite him.

The piney scent of her beloved reached her at the

same time as his soft, growly voice, and her bones melted. Tears overwhelmed her. She threw her jelly arms around him and buried her face in his neck.

Caleb sank to the ground and held her.

She was ok.

They were going to be ok.

Caleb carried her all the way to the horses. He was tired and she could walk, but he didn't put her down, and she didn't ask him to. His muscles twitched and shuddered under her weight, but he clung to her as she clutched him. Between them, their baby fluttered.

The men wanted to hunker down and camp for the night, but Jeni wanted to get back to the ranch. She couldn't get warm, and she needed to eat. They didn't argue. The men packed up and rode for home.

Will took her from Caleb's arms long enough to allow Caleb to mount his horse. Before he passed her back, he squeezed her and whispered, "I'm so damn sorry," into her hair. His voice shook, but she didn't have time to question him as to why, because he passed her back into Caleb's arms and turned to mount his own horse.

As they rode toward home, she studied Caleb's face. She traced several long scratches, sorry to have attacked him when she'd woken up. He needed comfort as much as she did. She removed his big, work-hardened hand from the reins and placed it on her belly.

"Can you feel the baby?"

"No."

"I can. He's kicking at your hand." She smiled and kissed his neck. "It's the sweetest little flutter."

He took her mouth and poured all of his passion into her, then he pressed a kiss to her head as his child kicked against the wrath of his hand..

"I missed you," he said.

How was this protecting her?

Rose and Iris had been at Hank's house when the party arrived the night before. The women had taken action right away. They had fixed her a bath, fed a warm meal, and tucked into bed before an hour had passed. They both agreed that she needed to take some control over what was happening to her.

Not for the first time, Jeni appreciated these two amazing women. She wished they could be around more often, but they preferred being at Caine's house, and didn't leave often. But when they heard she was missing, they'd packed up and headed over to the house to prepare for her return.

Their counsel was what she needed. The women treat her like a useless decoration around the house. They agreed that Jeni should have some skills to protect herself in case anything should ever happen to her again.

In less than twelve hours, Jeni's anxiety settled into irritation. Frustration replaced her fear, and she saw everything these wonderful men were doing wrong. She saw how their love and protection had weakened her to the point of complete dependency.

They'd coddled and kept her in the dark. Not only was she learning nothing, she had been sitting around growing weaker rather than stronger.

That ended now.

She wasn't stitching another diaper or gown. They were going to teach her how to fight for her baby. She would learn how to fight for him and her husband, too.

Darn it, she was going to fight for herself.

Worse than her anger at these men, self-hatred engulfed her. She'd been the most pathetic victim. Jeni hadn't had the power or sense to fight. She'd cried and prayed, tried to wish away the reality of her situation. She raged at herself, as she raged at these men who she loved like brothers.

Jeni waited through breakfast, seething. Her blood boiled as she watched them sip coffee and cut pancakes. Concerned glances and sad eyes around the table added to her irritation until she was ready to jump out of her chair.

Pregnancy might help fuel the anger, but she wanted to punch every one of them in the face, including her handsome husband. Her spine pulled tight, her knee bounced under the table, and she forced herself to wait for her moment.

She was five feet of fury by the time the dishes had been cleared.

"Enough is enough." She spat, drawing everyone's attention. "You've put me in a terrible position, and this ends now."

The guilt was thick enough to choke on.

Every man focused on his coffee cup.

"I sat there, leaning against a rock half the day yesterday, looking at weapons that I couldn't use. How can you hide me inside this house, month after month, and not have thought to teach me how to use a gun?" She didn't mention that she had never thought to ask.

That was not the point right now.

Caleb placed his hand on her belly. "You're pregnant."

"No kidding." She swatted his hand away. She'd had enough of being consoled and coddled. She didn't need a reminder of what was at stake; she needed some respect. They were sweet and accommodating, and it had been nice for a while, but that time was over.

Now she needed their instruction, not their pampering.

"No kidding." She wasn't used to being this aggressive. The pregnancy hormones supported her anger and pushed her to continue. She liked these power-giving hormones.

"It's ok," he soothed. "You don't have to worry. We'll double down on guard. Nobody's going to get in again."

More placating. Jeni slammed her fist on the table, wincing from the pain that shot up her sore arm and reminded her of exactly what she was fighting for.

She jumped up and began pacing and rubbed at a bruise on her shoulder. "Sarah would've killed that man before he even had her on the horse." Everyone knew about Denise's grace and Sarah's fire.

"How'd he get you on the horse, anyway?" Caine asked.

"I think he hit me over the head. When I came to, we were nearly in the mountains. I didn't know how to help myself, and all I could think was to stay as still as possible, so he didn't hurt the baby. He wouldn't tell me how he got in. He wasn't exactly answering questions."

Will could barely meet her gaze. "It was my fault he took you. I fell asleep. I'd had a little too much fun in town the night before. Winning streak."

That explained the apology in the mountains. He looked terrible, like he hadn't slept in weeks. She wouldn't have been surprised if he crawled under the table to hide from his shame.

"Son of a bitch!" Caleb and Caine both roared at the same time. Caleb sprang to his feet. His chair crashed to the floor so fast that Jeni hardly had time to spring away from him before he jumped on Will. "Amy and now Jeni?"

Hank grabbed Caleb at the same time as Daniel threw himself on top of Caine. Jeni hadn't even seen Caine get up, and here he was, on top of Will.

Will didn't fight back. Caine landed a punch or two before Daniel wrestled him off of their friend. Caleb fought and roared, trying to get away from Hank so he could get back to Will.

Jeni was stunned.

What just happened?

For half a minute, the room was in complete chaos. Everyone shouted and struggled at once.

And over Amy again.

"ENOUGH!" she bellowed. "Sit down!"

The first command got their attention. They weren't used to her boldness. Caine and Caleb both continued to glare at Will as they shook off Daniel and Hank. But they backed down and returned to their seats. The others did as well. The room was silent for a minute before Jeni continued.

"Tell me about Amy?"

"Now's not the time for that," Caine said.

"Oh, yes, it *is* the time for it. I can see that you're all trying to protect me. But when you look at me, it's not always me you see. Especially when I'm in danger. I need to know what you're struggling with. I can tell that she was important. What happened to her?"

Caine exhaled a labored breath. "Amy was my wife. She was killed three years ago."

Jeni's heart pounded. She wanted to cry for Caine. She stopped herself from turning to Caleb for comfort. Her crying days were over. Jeni placed her hand on Caleb's shoulder and turned back to the others at the table. Every man hung his head in defeat. It wasn't only Will; they all looked guilty.

Swallowing the lump in her throat, she pressed on. "I'm sorry, Caine. I know that much, but what happened to her?"

"Not now."

"Soon, then. I'm only letting this go now because

it's off point. We need to come back to this soon, and you all know it."

She needed to stay on target. She wanted to push their resolve.

"I'm sorry, Caine. You must see that I need to learn to protect myself. They haven't stopped coming, and if someone gets through again…"

"They won't."

"If someone gets through again, I want to be able to help myself." She looked at Hank. "I want you to teach me how to shoot." To Will she said, "I want you to stay home. I need you close to the house."

Caleb's fists clenched where his hands rested on the table. "He's not guarding you ever again."

"Yes he is."

Caine turned his hands out in appeal. "You can't go shooting guns and wrestling men when you're five months pregnant."

"I'm not asking for your permission." She looked at each of them. "I sat in that clearing, looking at weapons and wondering if I could pick one up and shoot it. I didn't know how to check if it was ready to shoot or if it had bullets or anything. I sat there, wishing I was Sarah. She could've handled that situation and saved herself. All I could do was sit there and wait to be rescued or die. My big plan was to ask to relieve myself and hope that the bird sounds were you."

"You knew we were there?" Caleb asked.

"How many times did I make you do that impression for me? Did you think I wouldn't recognize it?"

There was an appreciative nod around the table.

Was that respect? Was that all it took?

Men were a confusing bunch.

"I won't be helpless anymore. I'm pregnant, but that means I have more to fight for. It's time to learn."

THINGS WERE QUIET AROUND THE RANCH FOR THE NEXT few weeks.

Jeni's belly grew, and her confidence grew with it. Pregnancy empowered her. When she thought back to those sweet months of sewing baby clothes and dreaming of motherhood and family, she smiled. She treasured those months. She couldn't think of them as wasted. She had learned nothing helpful, but she and Caleb had grown closer to each other.

The bond they had was precious, and she cherished it. Her motivation had changed, and she felt good. She grew in endurance and skill every day. She grew up in a way she didn't know she needed to grow up. Sarah and Denise would be proud. She couldn't wait to write and tell them of everything she was doing.

She spent her mornings with Hank, learning how to care for and use various types of guns. "It's important to know how to clean and load every kind of gun." He had laid out a selection of weapons on a table in the barn. "You don't know what types of guns you may encounter, so in an emergency, it is important to know how to use them all."

Jeni ran her hand over the butt of a gun. "You have quite a collection."

"These are the guns from the mountain, and those are from the cabin attack," he pointed as he spoke. "As we go along, I'll even show you the weapons carried by the other men around the ranch."

Jeni'd known there were many types of guns, but she hadn't expected such an extensive education. He wanted her to shoot big guns and small guns and guns with hair triggers and guns with double triggers.

"This is a lot more education than I bargained for."

"I don't do things halfway. Follow me and we'll get started."

Rather than teaching her to shoot a gun, he taught her how to clean and load all the guns. He said that some guns were being made with safety mechanisms, but he didn't have any to show her. As they worked, he talked about guns, and after a few days of lessons, Jeni had to insist on some actual shooting practice.

Hank chose a rifle for her to start with. After a lecture long enough to have her tapping her toes, he led her out to the firing range. He'd warned her, but the kickback bruised her shoulder, and she narrowly missed a black eye more than once. If it weren't for Hank's insane reflexes, she would have hurt herself several times. She did not want to know what Caleb would do if she returned home with her eye blacked.

Hank reminded her daily that shooting took time to learn. She hadn't expected to be an expert marksman from the first day, but it frustrated her when she wasn't.

Hank had become her friend, and she enjoyed her morning routine with him. She enjoyed his sense of humor, even when he was being serious. He was easy going, and it helped her to relax and work with him. Of all the brothers, he was the biggest, but the gentlest. He spoke to her in a soothing voice that made her comfortable and gave her courage. His quiet humor and peaceful personality made her mornings fun.

As her self-defense skills grew, Caleb stopped hovering and trusted her to the care of his brothers. She couldn't ask or expect him to stop worrying, but his effort didn't go unnoticed. He worked on the ranch again. There was much to do in the spring, and she was glad to see him have the freedom to do some of his own work. Jeni could feel how much the physical labor helped him work off the stress. She hadn't considered how hard it was for him to be bound to the house for all of those months.

As his muscles bulked back up, Jeni realized being holed up in the house had weakened him, too. It'd happened so gradually that she didn't even notice when he softened. It wasn't until his muscles hardened and his skin tightened over his abdomen and chest that the reality hit her. He'd barely had the stamina to endure her rescue, and this was why. She had been so self-absorbed that his sacrifice had gone unnoticed.

Caleb was proud of her—he told her all the time—and Jeni vowed to make a habit of telling him as well. Their marriage couldn't be one-sided anymore. She needed to give to him as he gave to her.

It was hard for him to stand back and let her be strong, but he did.

Caleb celebrated her growth.

His pride fed her determination.

At night, they held each other. "Do you think we'll be able to go back to your house soon?"

"Our house."

"Right." She played with a lock of his hair.

He nuzzled his face into her belly. "A little privacy would be nice."

Jeni laughed.

"I have something for you." He shifted half off the bed to reach for a box under the bed.

"You do?" Jeni shifted to sit up, tucking pillows behind her back. "What is it?"

Caleb presented her with a little pistol and Jeni cried. "You're working so hard. Hank helped me pick one that you could wear like your friend Sarah does. You two are going to start practicing with this tomorrow."

It was the first time she'd cried in a month. The gift was a beautiful symbol of his support.

She spent the next few evenings adding pockets to her skirts to hold her new firearm. It was an easy enough alteration, but she cherished each little stitch. She wrote to Sarah and asked for instructions to create her own holster. Sarah had worn a gun and carried a knife before any of the boys at school, and she'd designed a custom holster to wear under her skirts.

The solid weight of the gun in her pocket boosted her confidence immeasurably. As she completed her regular daily tasks, the solid weight against her thigh was a reminder that she was capable of defending herself.

Jeni was careful not to overdo it. She wouldn't risk the baby. She napped every day, and if she became tired throughout her exercises, she stopped. The men watched her like a hawk, but they didn't tell her what to do. They no longer treated her like a delicate bird egg that would shatter.

She'd never been respected before.

It was heady.

When Jeni entered the barn, Caine was shifting hay bales. "How was your nap?"

She sighed. "It's still weird that I need to take a nap, but I feel great afterward. You probably get me at my best."

Caine's smile was half-hearted at best, but at least he tried. "Are you ready?"

"Yes."

"Ok, I want to focus on staying away, rather than fighting off an attacker." He walked around the bales he'd placed in a block in the middle of the barn.

"How's it going?" Will asked. He sauntered over with a cup of coffee in his hand. "I was waiting for you in the house. You must have snuck right by me."

Jeni's, "It's fine." came at the simultaneously with Caine's, "Seems to happen to you a lot."

Caine didn't wait for the fight though. He turned back to Jeni and focused her back on the lesson. The exercise was to just stay out of his reach for as long as possible, but her skirts tripped her constantly. She couldn't run away and she couldn't fight with yards of fabric tangling around her legs.

The belly was enough of a challenge. She didn't need her clothes to hold her back, so she altered her skirts again, this time into split skirts, which would be useful when she convinced her husband to teach her to ride a horse. It still wasn't as good as pants would have been, but she couldn't bring herself to go that far.

Caine didn't want to teach her how to wrestle. "It's more important to focus on dodging and evading. Your size and strength are no match for a man, even a small man like Jacobs."

Jeni sat on a bale of hay and tried to catch her breath. Another thing that slowed down her progress, the baby took her breath away with even the smallest amount of exertion.

Will leaned against a horse stall and scratched the ears of the animal, watching the lesson with him. "If she gets caught, she needs to be able to fight."

"Her intelligence is a better weapon against capture than any self-defense we could teach her."

"She's right here." Jeni struggled to her feet. "I agree with Will. I will do everything in my power not to be caught, but if I am, what do I do?" She stretched her back and watched Caine.

She had to push, but he eventually agreed to do some wrestling with her. He was so gentle, though, she became frustrated with him and Will stepped in.

Will was her shadow. He'd assumed that role ever since the night of his confession. If she went shooting with Hank or working with Caine, Will was there. He escorted her from place to place and dedicated himself to her. The tension remained between him, Caleb, and Caine, but nobody would talk about it. The only information she'd learned was that Amy had been kidnapped and killed and it was somehow Will's fault. Nobody would go into detail beyond that. She couldn't even get it out of Caleb in the middle of the night, when they were most likely to bare their souls to each other.

As time passed, Will became dear to Jeni. He was careful of her, but he didn't coddle. His patience was penance for his part in Amy's loss. He spent hours teaching Jeni how to use her size against an enemy. Caine taught her how to use her brain. And Will taught her how to use her body mechanics. He taught her how to twist and angle and move so that she could use an attacker's momentum against him. When he grabbed her, he was careful not to hurt the baby, or to put too much strain on her body, but he used enough force to give her the experience that she needed.

While she grew close to Hank and Will over the weeks, her relationship with Caine remained awkward. He was kind and helpful and he shared an enormous amount of knowledge with her, but he never became her buddy. He never hesitated to remind her that she should let the men protect her. No matter how she tried, she couldn't change his mind.

Scott's memory was always between them. Jeni grappled with her guilt over Scott's death. The pain of loss never left Caine's eyes.

He never said anything to her, but Jeni was sure that Caine blamed her for losing his cousin and best friend. He was right. It was her fault. She wished she could go back in time. For Caine as much as for herself, Caleb, and the baby.

But mostly for Scott.

Morning meetings became a regular event at the house. After breakfast, the men would all sit with their coffee and discuss their day. Jeni was happy to be included. They still tried not to give her too much work to do, but she was happy to be helpful. She liked to know where everyone would be throughout the day.

With the summer approaching, many of the men were preparing to leave for the spring roundup and cattle drive. Things were quieting down and settling into a rhythm.

Danger still lurked, but life went on. Jeni was still guarded, but after weeks of self-defense and weapons lessons, she had confidence in herself.

She felt respected and understood.

It was all she had ever wanted.

Chapter Sixteen

J eni convinced Caleb to move back to their own
house, but it took a veritable act of congress.
She was tired of the lack of privacy, and she
wanted to feel like they were living their own lives.
The other men weren't able to concentrate on their
own work because they were busy watching over
her, and that wouldn't do. She eventually got her
way by insisting she needed to get settled into her
own home before the baby came.

Caleb opened a door and Jeni's eyes landed on a
crib and changing table on the opposite wall. He'd
built a small addition to the little house and turned
it into a nursery.

When had he had time to do that?

The little gowns she'd sewn were pressed and
folded into a chest and the diapers were stacked
inside the changing table. There were little knitted
blankets and a lovely new braided rug on the floor.
A rocking chair sat in the corner, with a small table

beside it. She could see herself sitting there for hours with a baby in her arms and a book in her hands.

Going around the little room, she had to touch everything. Rose and Iris had put this together. There were baby things everywhere, and she hadn't made them.

Grandmothers.

That's how she saw them. She hoped when things settled down, she'd be able to spend more time with them. They were the sweetest ladies. Iris was quiet and unobtrusive, but she was so interested in Jeni's pregnancy and would speak to her to ask about the baby. She could see in Iris's eyes she was delighted to have a baby on the ranch. Rose didn't leave her feelings in question; she expressed every thought and emotion, sharing all of herself and with love.

Jeni threw herself into Caleb's arms and let the happy tears flow. She couldn't imagine being happier than she was when she was with him. Whenever he held her, the world faded away, and it was just the two of them. She pushed him through the door and towards their own bedroom

They could finally be together, in complete privacy.

"Don't you dare shush me." She wriggled her eyebrows and started tugging at the buttons on his shirt as they stumbled through the door.

"I wouldn't dream of it." He laughed and tugged pins out of her hair.

She tipped her face up to his, and he claimed her lips, sucking her bottom lip into his mouth. He crushed his mouth back down on hers, and she moaned. He nipped and tasted her mouth, delving deep and savoring as she savored back. His tongue slipped inside while his hand took her sensitive breast.

He had the most amazing hands.

He plundered her mouth as she worked the last few buttons on his shirt. She pushed the fabric open and splayed her hands over his chest. He was so hard. The little hairs tickled her palms and she couldn't resist giving a little tug.

He groaned and swatted at her hand.

They undressed each other, standing in the middle of their bedroom. When she was naked, Caleb stepped back and stared.

She saw wonder in his eyes.

She saw love.

For a moment, he pressed his hand to her belly and held her gaze. Sparks flew between them. Both hearts raced as the pot bubbled over.

His mouth was back and his hands burned her alive.

All thought ceased.

He moved her backward until the backs of her legs hit the side of the bed. He pushed her playfully, but caught her hands as she tipped and lowered her gently to the mattress. He kneeled in front of her and kissed her another way he knew she liked.

Jeni moaned and arched her back and ran her hands through his hair. She squirmed as the first climax came over her. Caleb gentled and slowly brought her back to earth. Then he nipped her thigh and crawled up to kiss her mouth again.

When he rose over her, he stopped for a puzzled moment. Her expression mirrored his. They hadn't realized how much the belly had grown to be in the way. They both laughed at their conundrum. It was a sweet second, laughing in bed over a moment of private humor with her husband. Then he kissed her deeply with feeling before he lifted and smiled at her again.

Caleb winked at her and rolled onto his back. He lifted her over him and helped her slide down to take him in. Jeni experienced a surge of boldness straddling him. She could control the entire experience, and she loved the freedom of his hands to run over her body.

She set a rhythm and closed her eyes. Every day she discovered things about her body, even after these months. She fed off of the sounds she could pull from her gorgeous husband. When he moaned, it was her that gave him pleasure.

It was potent.

It was pure joy to have his hands on her. Sensations from all over her body crashed together, overwhelmed her, and drove her to a passion that she didn't know she could experience.

She had never been in control like this before.

She loved it.

Not fighting to be silent, or trying to keep the bed from rocking, not worrying about the looks around the breakfast table in the morning all added a satisfaction to already unencumbered passion.

There was nothing between her and the bliss that she knew she could have from Caleb's body.

She dove into the experience and let the waves of emotion and pleasure carry her further away. As the pressure built, she leaned over and took his mouth. Locked together, she rode until they both exploded.

With a scream that was his name, she came crashing around him. Her body wracked with shudders as he shuddered within her.

His kiss went from fierce to soft and loving. He cradled her against him as they both caught their breath. She didn't know she could love someone so much. This man was the most amazing person she had ever met.

With her still straddling him, the baby kicked. They both chuckled at it.

"I guess he doesn't like being squished." she said.

"Guess not."

She slid down next to him and snuggled in. Her belly resting against his side as her head rested on his shoulder.

"I love you."

"I love you."

In her pregnant condition, she wouldn't have thought it possible, but they reached for each other two more times in the night. Caleb showed her new ways that they could please each other, and she was willing to try anything with him. They weren't making up for lost time, they needed to be connected to each other in their own home. It was normalcy that they both needed.

CALEB WORKED, AND JENI TOOK CARE OF THE HOUSE. She could finally prove herself as the useful wife that she'd always wanted to be. She could've been more useful if she weren't struggling around her swelling middle all the time, but she was happy to do what she could.

Jeni cooked meals, kept the house and washed their laundry. She even planned and started a little garden and took care of the chickens.

It was so normal.

Her husband left early every morning and worked late into the day. She cooked breakfast while he milked the cow. Then he was off until lunch time. He came home after work looking tired and happy. They had their evening meal and went to bed together.

Caleb never wandered far from the house. If any work needed to be done out of sight of the house, he assigned it to someone else. Will was always around, but Caleb still wouldn't trust him to be her guard and he wouldn't say why. Will did a lot of work in the back fields so Caleb could be close to Jeni.

He was a good friend.

With the new routine, Jeni felt secure. It was the first time in her life that she had felt like she was living a normal life. She wasn't out of danger, but it wasn't a constantly pressing shadow either. She enjoyed her new life.

Will popped in mid-morning every day, claiming to need coffee. She pretended not to know he was checking up on her. They spent a half an hour chatting, and if she needed anything heavy or difficult done, he would take care of it before he left. He'd be back in the middle of the afternoon, again, begging for lunch. She enjoyed his company, but she knew that part of the reason he was devoted to her was his guilt over her kidnapping.

"It's not your fault," she blurted out one day.

"What?"

"My kidnapping."

"It is."

"There were plenty of men on the ranch. That kidnapper had experience getting in and out of guarded places. It's what he did. He got past everybody, not just you."

"If I hadn't been sleeping, he wouldn't have gotten by me."

"You can't blame yourself forever."

He pressed his lips together in annoyance. "What do you know about Amy?"

Curiosity replaced Jeni's frustration and softened her tone. "Just that she was Caine's wife. She was kidnapped and murdered. Nobody'll talk about her. Caleb won't even talk to me about it."

"I failed her, too. I wasn't there when she was taken. I was supposed to be, but I'd been in town all night. Poker game. Drank too much and didn't come home. Sound familiar? Caine left to round up a few stallions for the breeding program, expecting me to be there to escort Amy to town. That's why she was alone when the riders showed up."

"Oh, Will. You made a mistake." She reached out and took his hand. "Let yourself have some peace."

He didn't look up from his coffee, but he clung to her hand. "It's hard to talk about." His voice shook. "Amy was special. Caine loved her like Caleb loves you. Strong and passionate and sweet. That's how Scott loved you, too. Amy was gentle. She was beautiful. I never heard her raise her voice. She never needed to. She was easy to love.

"You're special to all of us, too. Not just because Caleb loves you, you know?" He met her eyes. "Instead of crying about the unfairness of everything, you took charge. You made choices, and you followed through every time. You handled that kidnapping the best you could, and when you got home, you are the one who took control of your training. You're strong, Jeni, and we're all amazed by you."

Jeni choked up, not sure what to say. She had no idea they saw her this way. She surely didn't.

They thought her courageous and strong?

"I don't know what to say."

"On top of all of that," he continued, "you're a damn fine cook. You take care of everyone around you, and you're beautiful."

Jeni sniffled, and a few tears escaped.

He moved his hand up as Scott, Caleb and even Caine had done, and brushed it away with his thumb.

"Thank you, Will. I needed to hear that."

He nodded in a very Maxwell Group way, then he drained his coffee and left.

Caleb was home early, and! good grief! she'd never heard him clomp around like that. She grabbed a towel and dried her hands. Her first thought was that he might be hurt. He never stomped, even when he was tired or angry.

She turned and started forward as the door opened and a stranger filled the threshold. She froze. Their eyes met, and for an instant, her mind went blank.

When he moved through, she snapped into focus. All of her training rushed back to her at once. Caine's firm command that she not let him get close enough to grab her rung out in her mind. The key point was avoiding hand to hand battle. She remembered him telling her to use her voice.

Scream!

She could get no sound out as she leapt to the side. Dodging his grasp, she found her voice and let out a peal. Jeni moved to the other side of the table as he crashed into the counter. When he turned, she screamed again and evaded him when he tried to get around the table to get to her. For several moments, they chased each other around the table, her staying just out of his reach.

He shoved the table into her, and it threw her off her feet. She hit the ground hard on her hip. He shot around the table before the pain of landing had fully bloomed.

Jeni remembered Will's wrestling practice and stayed on the floor until he was close enough. She kicked with as much force as she could manage, aiming for his knee.

The sickening crack made her skin crawl as he came crashing down beside her. He reached for her, but someone pounced on top of him.

Will. Thank God. Will was there.

And Jeni was still screaming. What was so hard to start seemed impossible to stop.

The stranger couldn't get up, but he fought hard. Will wrestled him away from Jeni, and the two crashed together on the floor. The stranger was no match for Will, with a broken leg. Will pounded the man in the face and body until he was unconscious and then removed his weapons. Then he ran to the front door and fired two shots into the sky.

He turned to Jeni and drew her into his arms. Sitting on the floor with her in his lap, he held her tight and rocked her as she sobbed into his chest. He whispered into her ear that she had done a good job, and he was proud of her. He kept telling her he was proud of her.

She clung to him.

CALEB RAN INTO HIS HOUSE AND FROZE. A MAN LAY bloody on the floor in the dining room. Chairs were overturned, and the table was halfway into the sitting room. Broken dishes scattered the kitchen.

Will sat on the floor with a sobbing Jeni. Will passed her into Caleb's arms and then stood.

Caleb was overloaded with fear, anger, and

something else that he couldn't name. He held his weeping wife and stared at his friend.

Guilt was thick in Will's eyes.

"Thank you," Caleb said.

Will tipped his head toward the bedroom and Caleb took her in. Hoofbeats thundered closer. The others were coming. They'd take care of the intruder and put the house back to rights.

He needed to take care of his wife.

Jeni shook. She held him tight. Caleb didn't put her down right away. He needed to hold her, and he sensed she needed it, too. He sat on the edge of the bed and cradled her until he felt both of them relax and their heartbeats slow. He was so focused on comforting his wife that he lost all sense of time.

Through the door, Will directed the others. He sent Hank to town to bring back the doctor for Jeni. Caleb appreciated his brother, who finally seemed to have grown up.

He laid Jeni down on their bed and ran his hands down her legs and arms and over her body in search of injury. She watched him as he leaned over her.

"I'm ok."

"Just lie still and we'll see what the doctor has to say about it." He ran his hand through her hair and kissed her head.

He didn't expect her to talk about it yet. She would have plenty of time to tell what had happened later. He leaned down and kissed her, desperate for the connection. Caleb needed more. He couldn't settle his feelings. He was overwhelmed, choking. He needed to hold her. He needed something.

He rested his hand over her belly and waited. She stiffened, waiting too.

They sighed a collective breath when the baby kicked at the familiar weight. Caleb leaned forward and rested his forehead against hers. Neither of them moved. He thumbed away the tears that rolled down her face.

THE DOCTOR'S VISIT WAS BRIEF. HE CHECKED JENI ALL over and found only bruises. He assured all the Maxwell men that she was fine. Jeni was too exhausted and relieved to laugh at the scene in front of her. The town doctor facing down all five Maxwell men.

It took him longer to convince the men that she would be ok than it had taken him to examine her. She watched them, and she listened and she realized that they truly did all care.

They loved her.

She was important.

Will caught her eye, and they stared at each other. He was probably her best friend in the world, and she suspected that he felt the same. He'd come to her rescue, but once again, guilt etched into his beautiful features. He blamed himself for this attack, too.

Darn.

She motioned him over with a crook of her finger

when the doctor finally got away. He sat on the edge of the bed when she patted the mattress and picked up her hand, rubbing over the knuckles and studying the dust on her floor. When she took his hand with both of hers, he clung to her.

"You're blaming yourself again."

"I should've been closer."

"You saved me."

He winked and grinned at her, easing up a little. "You looked like you were doing a pretty good job of saving yourself when I came in."

That didn't fool her. He still needed her reassurance.

And his brothers needed to know what a hero he was. What heroes they all were.

"I evaded him as much as I could," Jeni said loud enough for them to hear.

The other men silenced and turned to listen. Caleb moved closer and laid his hand on her head.

She didn't release Will's hand when he tried to get up and let Caleb take his place beside her. "I kept hearing Caine's voice in my head." She looked at him over Will's shoulder as she spoke. "When he charged the first time, I waited until he was too close to stop before dashing out of the way. I got myself on the other side of the table and kept away from him as much as I could. We chased each other around the table and I screamed my head off, like you told me to."

She held Will's hand the whole time she spoke, twisting her fingers through his.

Caleb stood next to her head and watched her, but said nothing.

"When he shoved the table into me, I lost my balance and fell backward." Looking at Will, she continued. "I waited until he was nearly on top of me, and then I braced myself against the floor and kicked out his knee like you taught me. I was about to scramble away when you arrived, but I couldn't. Then I saw you, and I knew I was safe." She turned her face up to her husband. "I couldn't get away from him. I couldn't move fast enough. Will saved me."

"I know."

"I should've been closer. He shouldn't't've gotten into the house."

She turned back and locked gazes with Will. "You can't be everywhere. You can't control everything. You've been here. Every day. Helping me and protecting me. You're my best friend, and I need you to find some peace. You took a bullet for me. I'm worried about you." She poked at his side, where she knew he wore a scar from the bullet crease received not too long ago.

The spot was still tender, and he jerked from her nudge.

"Will." Caleb waited until Will met his eye. "Thank you."

Will didn't speak. He was on the spot, sitting in the middle of the room, holding her hand. He couldn't escape.

Jeni pulled his face to hers, kissed him, and then released his hand. "It's not your fault."

Will snapped his eyes to Caine's, and Jeni was shocked when the big man crumbled. She pulled him back into her arms and held him as he cried into her shoulder.

Caleb reached around her and pressed his hand to Will's heaving back. Caine laid a hand on him, gave a firm shake, and then left the room. They all left, one by one, as Will finally allowed himself to grieve.

It wasn't from her attack he was grieving.

Caleb was the last to go. He leaned down and kissed Jeni on the forehead before he gave Will one last pat and then joined the others outside. Jeni ran her hand up and down his back, and let him unloose the feelings he'd been holding close for years.

Once he'd unwound, he kissed her cheek. "I'm sorry."

"You needed that. Will, you deserve more than you're allowing yourself. What do you want from your life?"

"I don't know."

"Start there, then. Figure that out, and then get it."

He nodded, gave her a small smile, and then stood to leave.

Before he walked away, she squeezed his hand one more time. "I love you, Will."

"I love you back."

T hey were back to making decisions for her.

Jeni was furious when they informed her that The Maxwell Group had held a meeting without inviting her to take part. Not only had they met and discussed a plan, they'd cemented the plan and were ready to act on it.

That irked.

She understood their need to protect her and the baby. Jeni couldn't blame them for that. She'd been attacked in her home, and it was eating at them. And the old guilt over Amy's death fueled their anxiety. Still, they shouldn't make decisions that regarded her safety and security without consulting her. The group knew better.

They'd reverted to their 'hide the pregnant lady' routine. The 'respect for the strong lady' bit they'd been working on had vanished.

They couldn't wait for attackers any longer. She understood that. The bounty hunters would keep coming for her until they got rid of Mr. Benson for good.

She felt the same.

Something needed to be done. When they sat her down at the table and ran through their plan for her, none of them even noticed her anger. She expected more from Caleb or Will, at least. How would they feel if she made plans that affected their lives and didn't tell them? She couldn't stand it.

Caine spoke first. "Caleb, Will, and I are going to Boston to flush out Benson."

Caleb chimed in next. "We're going to track him down and take care of this once and for all. We can't sit here waiting for another attack."

"Dean's already in Boston," Caine explained. "His last telegram said that nobody'd seen Benson in weeks. He should have some information waiting for us whcn we get there."

"You can't go to Boston," Jeni said to Caleb before looking at Will as well. "I need you here." She depended on both men. Caleb was her love, her husband, and her life. Will was her best friend. She didn't want them on the other side of the country while she was here worrying about them.

"Hank's staying," Caleb told her. "He's got work that he can't leave, and Daniel will be close by if you need him. You'll move back up to Hank's place, and Rose and Iris are coming up with you." He smiled. "You'll all have a pleasant time. You can finish working on the baby's things."

It was surprising how matter-of-fact this was to

these idiots. Caleb was talking to her like she was a child.

That did it.

"Did you ask Rose and Iris if they wanted to move up there, or did you just tell them what they had to do, as if they were a couple of children? They don't enjoy being away from their house for too long. Surely, they wouldn't want to be up at Hank's for weeks on end."

"They'll go," Caine said.

"I'm six months pregnant. I'm not going anywhere." She looked at Caleb and threw her hand in the air. "Neither are you.

"Did you forget that we're going to have a baby? You can't go running all over the country and leave me here to worry about you." She slapped her hand on the table and then shifted away from him when he reached for her. She turned away from Will, too.

Caleb tilted his head and looked into her eyes. "You won't be unprotected. I'll be back before the baby comes. It shouldn't take more than a month."

"A month?" She jumped to her feet. "Are you out of your mind?"

"Jeni…"

"Don't you Jeni me! I'm not sitting on my hands for a month while you're traipsing all over the country." She paced back and forth between the kitchen and the sitting room. There was no way he was leaving her for a month, neither of them.

"I don't think it'll take that long. I'm just saying a month is the longest. If it takes longer, I'll come home and let the others handle it. I'll be back as soon as I can. I won't miss the birth of the baby."

He reached for her, and she ducked him again. She wouldn't make him feel better about treating her like a child. He sighed and dropped his hand.

Jeni rounded on him and planted her hands on her hips. "You're not dumping me at Hank's house and running off without me. I'm going with you." She nodded; that was a better idea. She could stay with Denise while they searched for Mr. Benson and Mr. Jacob's daughter, Maggie.

"You can't come with us. You're six months pregnant. It's too much of a risk. See reason, Jeni."

"I'm unreasonable? You're having secret meetings that affect my life and safety without including me. You want me to be reasonable about it? If I stay behind, you stay too. Hire men to go after Mr. Benson like he hired men to go after me. I know you have enough contacts to get other people to do this for us."

"I have to do this myself."

"I need you home."

"I will be back as soon as I can."

"And if something happens to you? Am I to lose another husband? Which of The Maxwell Group is to be my next?" She knew she was going too far, but she couldn't pull back. She wanted to rage at them all. Caleb had the guts to speak, but the rest of the men stared at their coffee. She knew they would happily jump up and run out of the house if they could.

Bunch of cowards.

Caleb cast the same look at her that one would give a feeble elder, long-suffering laced with pity. "It's not like that, Jeni."

"You don't know that," she said. There was no way she would let this go. "You're not going anywhere, Caleb Martin Maxwell."

———

SHE WAS WRONG.

Two days later, Caleb packed her a bag, and they stowed her at Hank's place with Iris and Rose. They gave the women no choice. Rose and Iris didn't like it, but accepted the men's need to protect them.

Jeni couldn't. She couldn't get past her anger.

The nights after that little family meeting had been cold and lonely. Every time Caleb reached for her, she turned away from him. She was so upset with him she couldn't stand to let him touch her. He felt helpless in his own way, but she could not bring herself to comfort him.

She felt disrespected and abandoned.

Jeni furiously unpacked her bag in Hank's master bedroom. She'd insisted that he keep his room, and she would take one of the spare rooms, but on this, she was overruled, too. He was another man treating her like she was some delicate figurine, to be put under glass and protected. She tossed clothes left and right and let the steam build.

They might as well call her pretty.

Caleb pulled her into his arms and kissed her gently before he left. He pressed his big stupid hand over her belly and said he loved her. She didn't respond when he laid his forehead on hers and breathed deeply. He needed the connection that she couldn't give him. She didn't want him to go, and she'd made her feelings clear. It hurt that he didn't take her concerns into consideration.

She felt abandoned.

He turned and walked away, but stopped at the door. "Daniel brought a letter for you. I hope it cheers you up. I'll miss you."

She hadn't kissed him back or held him tight, and she hadn't returned his love. She was too angry with him to hold him.

Sending him away without her love was a knife in her ribs, but Jeni couldn't bring herself to make this easier for him. She hardened her heart even though dark thoughts plagued her. What if it was the last time she'd see him? The ache of losing Scott engulfed her; how would she survive losing Caleb?

When the carpetbag was empty, her finger struck against the trick bottom. She remembered the money from Sarah and Denise that she'd hidden inside. Sarah and Denise, they were what she needed. She crossed the room and snatched the letter off the dresser. She sat on the edge of the bed and read with a heart that grew heavier with each paragraph.

Someone was after Sarah, and Denise had been abandoned when she'd informed her fiancé of her pregnancy. They were both in danger, and they needed protection. Jeni flew down the stairs and out the front door, but she was too late to stop Caleb and send him to take care of her friends. She watched the dust settling and realized she wouldn't have any trouble following them to town.

Her mind raced. She knew she shouldn't, but she made a quick decision. Jeni was going to Boston. She bolted back up the stairs. She had little time.

Jeni listed all the reasons that it was a good idea for her to go, knowing full well they were weak at best. She could help end all of this sooner if she was there. She might even be able to deliver her baby in Boston with Miss Samantha as her midwife. That alone would be a million times safer than delivering at home with only Caleb to help. Of course, Rose and Iris could just as easily help, but she wanted to cling to her justification. Miss Samantha was the best midwife in Boston. She, alone, was worth the trip.

Jeni tossed her clothes haphazardly back into her bag and slipped her little pistol into her pocket. The money, she stuffed into her reticule. She pulled her big cloak over her shoulders and settled her ugly old bonnet over her hair.

The thought of gunslingers along the way gave her pause.

She grabbed a book from the stand and slipped out of the room. Hank was in the kitchen with the sisters. They were discussing dinner and laughing over some old memories. It was a homey scene, and if she weren't in such a hurry to go, she would have enjoyed being a part of it.

She eased past them and left the comfortable scene behind her. She couldn't sit here and enjoy the casual chatter while her husband was miles away, risking his life for her. No matter how angry she was, she loved him with all of her heart, and she needed to be close to him.

She saddled her horse. Another useful thing she'd learned after her kidnapping. While she was no expert rider, she could saddle and ride Sassy well enough to get by. She'd spent hours with Daniel or Will in the barn making friends with Sassy. They were meticulous in their training, and she knew how to do everything. Hank chose Sassy for her, and Jeni adored her. Sassy did not live up to her name at all. She was gentle and easy to direct, but she was big and fast. He'd chosen her specifically to outrun captors.

Jeni needed fast today!

She worked quickly but quietly to tack the horse.

As she led Sassy to the mounting block they had constructed for her, Hank called out to her from the porch. *Here goes nothing.* She leaned into the horse and flew.

She was out of the barn and heading down the road when she looked back and saw Hank bolt for the stable. He wouldn't be far behind. She needed to get to the train station and board the train before he reached her. Once they were on the train, they could find the others.

She couldn't let them go without her. Jeni needed to tell them about the letter. They had to protect her friends. They had to bring her friends home with them.

She feared what Hank might do, so she held on and rode hard—harder than she probably should have in her condition.

At the train station, she finally exhaled. It was a hot afternoon, and she wished she could remove her cloak, but she wanted to be as invisible as possible. The large sunbonnet shielded her face and protected her from the heat of the sun at the same time.

She purchased a ticket and hid in the corner until the train arrived, puking smoke and screaming with steam as the brakes stopped it at the platform. With her sizable brown bonnet and cloak concealing her, she cowered to make herself look smaller and turned away from her men, who stood less than ten feet from her on the platform.

Sarah had told her she could disguise herself as an old lady by doing this, and Jeni hoped that was the impression she gave. She kept her head down with the brim of the bonnet over her face and waited.

When the train was ready to board, she rushed on and pressed herself into a seat at the back of a car. She kept her face lowered and hunched over her belly. She pulled her favorite copy of Jane Eyre from her bag and held it while she spied men and women board the train. When she saw Caleb, Will, and Caine board and walk through to the next car, she relaxed. She'd be able to find them, since she knew which direction they'd gone. When Hank and Daniel entered the car, her anxiety kicked up again.

If they found her before the train pulled out of the station, they would take her off and bring her home. She made herself smaller and hid. She could not go home and wait on news from them. Jeni couldn't live without knowing how or where her men were.

She rubbed her belly; even the baby couldn't keep her home. She worried about the risk she was taking. The stakes were high, but she couldn't bring herself to turn around. She needed to help her friends, and she needed to be with her husband. She couldn't stop thinking about the husband she'd already lost.

And she couldn't lose another.

Caleb was her world.

After an eternity of apprehension, the train lurched forward, and Jeni could think. They couldn't take her home now. Caleb would see that she was an asset and should be with him. He'd understand once she explained about her friends.

The car smelled of smoke and dust and dirty people. Travel gave little opportunity for hygiene, and the car was full of offensive smells. She'd never been more grateful that morning sickness had only lasted a few months; she wouldn't survive a trip like this with morning sickness.

She let herself relax against the back of the seat a little. Still keeping her head bowed to hide her face behind her bonnet, she let the anxiety ebb. She wouldn't seek out the men too soon. There were several stops, and she didn't want them turning her back around.

The weight of the gun in her pocket gave her a sense of security.

She turned her attention to her book and let her mind wander for a while. Sweat poured down her body, but she kept her cloak over her. She looked out the window to her right and watched the scenery pass. Then she settled in and enjoyed her book for a while.

Chapter after chapter flew as she counted the hours. Two stops had come and gone, and she still kept her seat. Nature called, though, and she had to get up and use the closet.

Knowing that she risked discovery if she moved around, she waited until she had no choice. She tucked her book into her carpetbag, stood, and hunched over. The toilets weren't far, and she made the trip there and back without incident.

Returning to her seat was an immense relief. She settled herself back into the corner and reached to pull out her book again. It took some work to bend over enough to reach into her bag. On the floor between her feet was a lot harder to achieve when six months pregnant. The baby objected to her bending, kicking, and rolling around inside of his cramped space.

She took a moment to love the fluttering little person struggling to push her body back into a comfortable position. Caleb would be so proud. This tiny person was already trying to boss her around. Like father, like son, she thought as she sat up with her book.

A man slid into the seat close to her, too close. He wedged the cold barrel of a gun against her swollen abdomen.

Her baby!

She didn't move a muscle, but she mentally kicked herself repeatedly.

What had she done?

Caleb was right. She should've stayed home where she and her baby were safe. This was more risk than she should've taken in her condition, and she'd waited too long to join her husband. Every piece of her poorly constructed plan crumbled around her; she sat there with a gun pointed at the most precious piece of her world.

Jeni chastised herself as she dragged her thoughts back to the present. "What do you want?"

"You know what I want."

"Who are you?"

"Just sit there and be quiet. Read your book and look natural. If you make any kind of scene, I'll shoot."

She looked at him. He was clean cut, like her previous kidnapper, but he wasn't as well dressed as Mr. Jacobs had been. She guessed him about average height and slim, not as big as any of the Maxwell Group men. His brown hair was short, clipped close to his head and neatly combed to the side, and his beard was cleanly groomed.

He had a long, narrow face with close-set eyes and a straight nose. He scowled and drew his neat eyebrows down in the center threateningly. His clothes suggested he was from the city. He could be one of Mr. Benson's henchmen, but she suspected that he was more like a hired gun. He lacked the familiar Boston accent, but he was working for Mr. Benson.

Jeni cursed herself again.

So much for going along to protect Caleb and her friends. She'd served herself up on a silver platter.

Jeni didn't make a scene; she didn't even breathe, but her mind raced at breakneck speed. The only thing she could think to do was stop hiding and hope that one of her men would see her. She lifted her face and looked around, then untied and removed her bonnet and cloak.

"God damn it."

Hank ran his hands through his hair. "I'm sorry, Caleb. She rode that buckskin out of the yard like a bat out of hell. There was no way I could catch her."

"Just once, I wish she would do what she's told."

"She was already on the train when I got to the station. She's here somewhere."

"She damned well better be here," Caine said. "She's getting off at the next stop, and you're taking her back."

Caleb's face was red, and the muscles in his jaws and hands worked. He wanted to punch something. "What the hell was she thinking?"

"Let's just split up and find her," Will said.

Caleb ground his teeth and nodded.

Jeni wouldn't listen.

She knew the danger.

She'd put their baby in danger because she didn't want to be left out?

They'd spent the last two days fighting this

battle, and he thought they had settled it. The only thing he hadn't expected was for her to take off and follow him. Looking back, though, he should have expected even that.

Selfish, this was selfish.

She should think about the baby, not her damn ego. He didn't want to leave her behind any more than she wanted to, but this is how it needed to be. And now she'd messed it up for all of them. He wanted to shake her, but he'd never be able to do it.

His anger would have no outlet. And his soul would have no peace.

His heart was broken, too. She hadn't even said goodbye.

He'd find her, and he'd send her back. He was going to protect his child, damn it, with or without her cooperation. Caleb fumed as he stalked through train cars. He looked into every seat before he moved forward to the next car. The others did the same.

They had stalked back and forth looking for her. They disembarked at every stop and returned to their search when the train pulled away. Caleb was beginning to think she hadn't boarded the train at all.

Will jabbed an elbow into his ribs as they walked by the last seat in a car near the back. A stranger sat uncomfortably close with his arm slung over her shoulder, and the hand in his pocket was holding a gun on her belly. It took every ounce of self-control they both possessed to walk casually by, especially when Caleb saw tears on her down-turned face.

Guilt was written all over her.

It should be. And yet it slayed him.

He was pissed at her and worried about her, and in love with her. She was driving him crazy. He was so full of emotion he couldn't think straight. They waited a minute by the toilet and headed back toward the center of the train to meet up with the others.

Caleb wanted to signal to her, but he didn't want to alert her companion. He kept his calm and didn't alter his casual pace down the train car. He doubted she'd seen them with her head bowed and her eyes full of tears.

He wanted to hold her, and his hand itched to slap that gun away and cover her belly. He cursed her in his head for getting into this mess.

What the hell was she thinking?

"What's your name?" Jeni demanded.

"Why?"

"If you're my companion all the way back to Boston, I think I should know."

"Charles James."

"You work for Mr. Benson?" She already knew the answer. His name sent chills down her spine. Jeni'd never seen Mr. James before, but his reputation was infamous, and terrifying.

"Just read your book and shut up."

Caleb and Will walked through the car, but they didn't see her. She agonized over how Caleb must be feeling. By now, Hank had found him and told him she was on the train. She couldn't stop beating herself up. She tried to think of a way to signal to him that she was there, but the gun to her middle kept her mute.

Mr. James turned out to be a chatty traveling companion after a while. He wouldn't answer any of her questions, but he liked to go on and on about his nasty exploits and plans for what he would do with her. Every story was worse than the last, and his graphic accounts made her skin crawl. Each minute dragged by, and her palms became clammy as the image of what he planned to do to her formed in her mind.

The weight in her pocket was a constant reminder that she was a capable woman. She just needed a chance to pull the weapon. She couldn't do that until he let his guard down, and he never did.

Mr. James sneered and laughed at Jeni's discomfort. When she wiped a tear or dried her clammy hands on her skirt, he seemed to find extra enjoyment in his effect on her.

Jeni prayed for escape before he could do any of the horrible things he teased her about.

CALEB AND WILL GATHERED ALL THE MEN TOGETHER IN the closest car to Jeni. Will explained the situation while Caleb fumed. Caine put his hand on Caleb's shoulder, but nothing would calm his boiling blood.

The bastard had a gun pressed against Jeni's belly, and it was her own fault for being there.

It was his anger at Jeni that he struggled with most. He could kick the gun slinger's ass, but he had no outlet for his outrage against his wife. He didn't know how to deal with that anger, and it writhed like a den of vipers inside of him.

He turned his rage toward the situation and channeled it into a firm plan of action with his brothers.

When evening came, they climbed into bunks, spaced out around the sleeping car, and waited. Once Jeni was tucked into a bunk, they'd take out her captor.

Then her ass was going home.

Chapter Eighteen

J eni sat bolt upright on the seat with Charles James's arm across her shoulders. To anyone walking by, they looked like a normal, expecting couple. He hid the weapon in his jacket, but she felt it, and he poked her with it as a reminder or to punctuate a threat.

Jeni's head spun. She tried to remember every-thing she'd learned from Caine.

First on his list was always to stay calm.

With a deep breath, she forced her heart rate to slow, but with Mr. James beside her, it took enor-mous effort. Jeni wrapped her hands around her belly and closed her eyes, focusing on steadying her thoughts.

"Good job. You just stay calm, and everything will be just fine."

"Why are you doing this to me?"

"Taking you home. I don't think your fiancé is going to be too happy to find you in this condition, though." He poked the barrel of the gun into the side of her round belly, making her flinch again. His grin and raised eyebrows said he enjoyed her reaction to him. Jeni flinched again, on purpose. She kept showing little signs of fear until he was ready to talk.

Mr. James was a well-known accomplice, or as some called him, 'henchman' of Mr. Benson's. He was a freelancer, going wherever the money was. She wouldn't have recognized him, but she knew his name. He was reputed to be cold and deadly, and he took pleasure in playing with his victims.

What kind of man could press a gun into the belly of a pregnant woman?

Jeni schooled herself not to react too excessively to anything he might say, giving him just enough to tickle him into sharing his plan. So far, he was living up to his reputation.

"Mr. Benson was never my fiancé; but you know that."

"Not what I heard." He leaned close to her, bumping shoulders companionably. Jeni resisted the urge to wretch and sat still. The thought that onlookers might think them a cute little family turned her stomach and added to the weight on her chest.

How could she have been so stupid?

"I'm a married woman, and I love my husband," she said in a voice for his ears only. "We're expecting our first child, as you can see. I don't belong with Mr. Benson. I belong at home with my husband."

"When a woman's promised to a man, she has to

follow through. Can't just change her mind and run away." Mr. James reached his hand under the cloak on her lap and caressed her thigh.

Jeni squeezed her eyes shut and focused again on controlling her reactions to him. She wanted to run away. When her voice was as steady as she could manage, she continued.

"I never promised Mr. Benson anything, ever. I'm a married woman now. And pregnant. I'm not available. No matter what, he can't marry me."

"Not my problem. I'm in it for the reward… and maybe a little fun on the way. You sure are as pretty as reported."

Jeni fought the urge to gag.

"I'll take you back, and then Benson can decide what he wants to do with you." He shrugged and ran his hand up and down her thigh again. "Maybe he'll feel sorry for you and send you back," a cruel glitter sparked in his eye. "Or maybe he'll make you available and marry you after all."

She couldn't hide the disgust on her face, no matter how hard she tried. Keeping her temper was a struggle that she worried she would lose. "You don't care that you're taking me from a happy home and delivering me, in this condition, to a monster?"

Mr. James chuckled.

"You're a beauty. That's what everyone says. I didn't believe you could be as beautiful as they say, but even with that enormous belly, you're still gorgeous. A man wouldn't want to lose you. Benson wants you back. He's not happy that you left him the way you did. You'll have to discuss this with

him. You know he can get rid of this easily enough."
He nudged her belly with his gun again.

She wrapped her arms around her stomach and
resumed beating herself up for her own stupidity.

He'd called her beautiful.

A thing that she had once heard every day was
now something she only heard when she was alone
with her husband. She hadn't even noticed that
nobody called her that anymore. When the Maxwell
men praised her, it was for her accomplishments, not
for her appearance. Iris and Rose didn't compliment
her on her appearance, either. They praised her for
cooking, her endurance, her sewing, or any of her
other skills. She hadn't seen the shift but it had long
since happened. It bolstered her and reminded her
how much she wanted the respect of the people
who'd become her family.

She wouldn't take it for granted ever again.

Thoughts of family sent her questions in a new
direction. "The last man Mr. Benson sent for me was
trying to save his daughter. Did he kidnap someone
that you love?"

"No."

"If he did, The Maxwell Group can help you
rescue them."

"You think you can make promises for The
Maxwell Group?"

"I am a Maxwell. If I promise, they'll see it
done." She felt the truth of her words in a surge of
confidence and hope.

She was a Maxwell.

"No blackmail. I'm in it for the reward."

Jeni's heart hurt, because she knew the truth of his words. He would use her and hurt her and then turn her over. Not even threatening Mr. Benson's wrath would save her from the terror that this monster planned for her.

"Money is significant enough that you'd trade a happy, pregnant woman to a monster for a reward?"

"Looks like." He shrugged again. Jeni wished she could slap the satisfied smirk off his face. He genuinely enjoyed the position he put her in.

The position she'd been arrogant enough to put herself in.

Jeni didn't know what to say to that. She'd hoped that if she kept reminding him how happy, married, and pregnant she was that he would let her go back to her husband. She'd hoped he would have sympathy for her by pointing out that Mr. Benson was a monster.

He didn't care.

She abandoned trying to sway him and watched and prayed for a sign of rescue or any opportunity to escape.

She bided her time.

Side by side, they bumped shoulders in the rocking train, hour after hour. He took her to the dining car for dinner, and she searched for escape, but no opportunity came. He didn't leave her side for a second, even waiting outside the closet door when she had to use the latrine.

When he rose to usher her to a sleeping car, she thought she'd have her chance. She planned to wait until he fell asleep and climb out of her bunk and slip away. Instead of settling into another bunk, he climbed into the bed beside her and put his arm over her.

Jeni almost stopped breathing, and her heart skipped a beat. "You need your own bunk, Mr. James. You cannot sleep like this with a married woman."

"I'm not going anywhere. Our fun starts now."

Jeni was fast losing her grip on maintaining her composure. "Mr. Benson won't like you touching me. Not to mention that my husband is going to rip you to shreds for it. If I don't get the chance first." Trembles took over her body as she revolted from his touch.

"Benson wants you back. Your husband's not here. Just settle in and keep quiet."

"Remove your filthy hands from my body." She pushed his hand off her breast and raised her voice. "I'm going to enjoy seeing my husband tear you apart."

He hissed in her ear, sending goosebumps running down her neck. "Your husband has already forgotten about you." He nuzzled his face into the back of her neck. 'It's just you and me here."

She jerked her head back and nailed him in the nose.

"Bitch!" He pulled her hair, making her cry out.

"Ow… Let go of me. If you don't let go, I'll scream."

He pressed the gun to her back. "You scream, and you will die. His hand slid around her body and he cupped, squeezing her already sensitive breast to the point of pain. "We have three more days on the train and three more nights together." He rubbed his hand down her back to her bottom and squeezed. "I've never been with a woman this big and at least we don't have to worry about you getting more pregnant."

"My husband is definitely coming." Jeni cursed the tears she heard in her voice as she tried to pry his vice-like grip from her bruising breast. Jeni couldn't hold back and cried out against his painful grip. He shushed her. "Shut up. Just go to sleep then. He stopped groping her, but he didn't move away.

He still sniffed and rubbed his nose, and she wondered if she'd broken it.

She hoped she broke it.

Serves him right if she did.

CALEB LAY IN THE BUNK AND LISTENED TO THE ANGRY, whispered conversation between his wife and the stranger he was going to kill. She called him Mr. James. He couldn't see them, but he could hear them well enough. He did a short birdcall, hoping to get her attention and let her know he was there. No matter how angry he was with her, he wanted to offer her any comfort or reassurance he could.

His hands shook, and he heard an extra warble in his birdcall. It was a struggle to keep still. Slowing his heart rate was even more difficult. The man had his hands on his wife and he was hurting her. It made him seethe. He narrowed his eyes in the dark and focused on the fear and courage in her voice.

She sounded strong, her voice steady at first, but even though her words remained bold, he heard tears. He wanted to yell at her and kiss her in equal measures as his pride and frustration grew.

What the hell was he going to do with her?

As long as she was fine and the baby was fine, he would figure it out later. He'd never fought with Jeni, but he was going to have to learn how to do it soon. He didn't know how he was going to forgive her for this.

"YOU DON'T KNOW MY HUSBAND. HE'LL NEVER STOP looking for me."

"Maybe so. You're pretty enough; it would be hard to give up this ass." He rubbed her again and reached around and grabbed the front of her dress. "Or this."

"I'll gut you myself if I get the chance." She wished she could kill this man. She thought of Sarah, who'd used that threat before and nothing had ever suited her feeling so well. Jeni wanted to gut the beast who would take such liberties.

She was lying on top of the pocket that held her gun, making her feel even more impotent against the threatening monster. The gun pressed up under her thigh, reminding her she had power, but that she didn't have enough. She felt weak and strong simultaneously, frustrating the situation even further. It bruised her hip where she lay on it. She had to wriggle to get it out from under her, and relieve the painful pressure.

"I like that." Mr. James wriggled his pelvis against her bottom in response.

"I'm not trying to turn you on. My skirts are twisted, and my belly is sore." Jeni jerked away from him, but he pulled her close again.

"Don't let me stop you. You just wriggle that sweet little ass as much as you want." Mr. James continued to caress her as if they were lovers.

"Don't flatter yourself. Ugh." To get into any position that would allow her to get to her gun, she'd have to turn over, and she would not lay face to face with this horrible man. "Turn over. I need to roll over to get comfortable."

"You can roll over here into my arms if you want."

"You're disgusting. Roll over. Neither of us is going to get any sleep tonight if you don't."

"I enjoy this wriggling against me. I'm in no hurry to move."

"Turn over!" The order was louder, and he looked over his shoulder to see if anyone had heard.

"Keep it down!"

"Then turn!" Jeni sent an elbow back into his ribs to punctuate her command.

He grunted and rolled over with his back to her.

She awkwardly flipped, grunting and groaning and making as much noise as possible. She then pulled her skirts into a more comfortable position. Wrapped around her legs, as they were before, she wouldn't be able to spring out of the bunk and run. She was glad she'd worn the split riding skirt. It was the only right thing she'd done. She wrapped her fist around the handle of her gun just before she heard the light birdcall that told her Caleb was near. The call repeated from a bunk close by, but in a different pitch.

Was that Will? Hank, maybe?

She sighed.

They were there.

"You hear that?" He bumped into her with his shoulder like they were friends.

"What?" Jeni pulled back away from him, further into the bunk until her shoulder hit the wall.

"There's a bird in the car."

"It happens. At stops."

"You just settle down back there now and sleep."

Pulling her gun out of her pocket, she pressed the barrel into his back instead and said. "Drop your gun to the floor."

Her heart soared, and she hoped she wouldn't actually have to shoot him, but if she had no other options, she would.

"What do you think you're doing, bitch?"

"What do you think I'm doing? I'm rescuing myself, and I will shoot you if you try anything stupid. Drop the gun on the floor and slide out of the bunk."

This was another of those moments in life where everything happens at once.

Caleb and Will jumped from bunks above as

soon as Mr. James's gun hit the floor. Jeni filled her lungs with air and blew it out.

She was safe! She and her baby were finally safe.

Mr. James spun around, but instead of having his arms jerked behind him to be bound, he pointed his gun at her and pulled the trigger.

HE'D DROPPED A FLASK, NOT HIS GUN.

Before either of them could stop him, he'd spun on Jeni and shot her!

Blood seeped through her dress and stopped Caleb in his tracks. He had nowhere to channel his rage. As the stranger turned with his gun again, Caleb was on him. Another shot rang out, but it went wild, splintering the carved wood trim of the train car. Will wrestled the gun from the stranger and landed a heavy blow to his jaw before he turned to Jeni.

Will managed Mr. James as Daniel charged toward them from the back of the car.

With Caine heading their way, Caleb dropped into the bunk with Jeni and scooped her into his arms. They could handle the stranger. He needed to help his wife. She was unconscious, bleeding and pale, so pale. He clung to her and begged her to wake up.

Caleb ran his hands over her and kissed her head. He couldn't think straight, with blood draining from her belly and over his hand. He pressed his palm into the wound, hoping to hold back the flow. The baby kicked his bloody hand, as he always did, but there was so much blood.

The cocking of a pistol brought him back to attention, and he turned around when the cold steel pressed into the back of his head. Will, Caine, and Daniel stood against the wall with their hands up. How had someone gotten past them?

Goddamnit.

"Let her go and stand up. Slide out of there and join your friends."

"She's my wife, she's hurt, and she's pregnant. That son-of-a-bitch shot her." He looked at the man on the floor, beaten to a bloody pulp. His ragged breathing and whimpering were proof that he lived, but wouldn't live long.

"Step away from the woman and join your friends."

"I can't. She's my wife. She needs me. I can't let her go."

The pistol came down hard on the back of his head, and Caleb fell out of the bunk, crashing to the floor. The unknown man was a beast. He was bigger than any of the Maxwell men, and he looked mean. He pointed the gun at Jeni and told everyone, "drop your weapons and get over there." He indicated with his hand for them to sit on the floor along the wall.

Caleb's head pounded.

He couldn't do anything with the gun trained on Jeni like that. He couldn't take his eyes off her. She was still bleeding, still unconscious. Her skin was flushed, rather than pale, as had been moments earlier. He wondered if she was sick. Could she have a fever? He wanted to hold her, to check her wounds. He needed to have his hands on her.

Instead, he moved away from his weapons and sat down next to Caine and Will against the wall. Hank and several other passengers gathered around, but he didn't alert the stranger that he was part of the group. Hank watched the crowd, searching to see if anyone else might be part of this gang. He'd wait until he was sure before revealing himself.

He didn't want to lose his guns, too.

"Git back to your business," the gunman told the watchers.

They dispersed without argument. Hank also turned, but he climbed into the bunk closest to the hulking gunslinger.

The big man kicked at the man bleeding on the floor with the toe of his boot. "My brother," he said.

"He had his hands on my wife. He shot her."

"Deserved it, I guess. Shouldn't put hands on another man's wife. Gonna kill you, though. Can't let it pass. Family."

He was raising his gun when a shot rang out. The giant went down for a minute and came up roaring.

Hank burst from the bunk, pulled his gun, and smashed it down on the back of the big man's head. It wasn't Hank who'd shot him.

Caleb spun around. Jeni had shot him with her little pocket pistol.

The Maxwell Group sprang to their feet at once. Caleb jumped into the bunk with Jeni while the others tied up the big stranger and collected his weapons.

As soon as they had control of the scene, The Maxwell men formed a tight half-circle in front of Jeni's bunk. They still didn't know if more men were waiting to attack.

Jeni gasped and winced. She dug both of her hands into Caleb's shirt and clung to him. He held her and whispered words of love into her ear as he kissed her face and celebrated that she was alive.

He held his handkerchief to the wound on her belly and pressed hard. Holding it there as she buried her head into his shoulder and wept.

Daniel and Will carried the bigger man out of the car while the other man continued to rasp and wheeze on the floor where he'd fallen.

Will returned and stood over the other man. Even if the man could get up, Will wouldn't let him. If there were others in cahoots with this duo, they did not show themselves.

When Jeni had insisted that Will be her guard, she'd been right. Will had needed her confidence in him as much as she'd needed all of their confidence in her.

Will's show of bravery had healed a bit more of their past.

"I'M A DOCTOR. LET ME IN." A LITTLE MAN CARRYING a black doctor's satchel pushed through the group. "I'm Dr. Jones, Elijah Jones. Let me in. I heard the shot and grabbed my bag." He eyed Mr. James on the floor and shrugged. "Hmph. Won't need to bother with him. There's no saving him now. Good for her."

Dr. Jones approached Jeni, pushing past all the much bigger men in his way.

Caleb moved aside, but didn't leave her. Jeni was awake. She had said nothing, though. She was softly sobbing, and terror shone in her eyes. Caleb watched her struggle to remain calm. Her worst fear was the same as his.

Caleb took the gun from her hand and handed it to Hank behind him. He kissed her as he ran his finger down the side of her face. "You did well." His hand stroked over her hair and settled on the back of her head. Caleb massaged circles on her scalp with his fingers. The ridge of the newly healed scar rippled under his fingertips.

She was constantly in danger.

She deserved safety and happiness.

He was going to give it to her.

Jeni was the center of his world; he would do anything to protect her and their baby. His fingers itched to hold her belly, but the doctor pushed him aside even as he reached for her. He needed her to be ok; he needed their baby to be ok.

Dr. Jones didn't hesitate to shove Caleb over and out of the bunk. He climbed in beside her and took Caleb's place. Caleb was fine, kneeling on the floor beside her head.

Dr. Jones was a busy sort of man. Everything about him was dynamic. He had wild hair that stood out in all directions around his head. Fuzzy, untrimmed eyebrows and darting eyes. He was rumpled and disheveled all over. Even his whiskers were unevenly shaven. Like maybe he'd been distracted from the chore and forgotten to finish. He babbled and set about his business in a methodical sort of way, though.

The doctor had her dress unbuttoned and opened in an instant. He didn't hesitate, even with Caleb sitting beside him, looking like he'd explode if the doctor made one wrong move. The Maxwell men stood guard and blocked the bunk as much as they could to preserve her modesty. She appreciated their effort, but she couldn't even think about herself at that moment. She held tightly to Caleb's hand and waited for the doctor to tell her how their baby was doing.

Dr. Jones reached out and pushed Caine and Will aside. The little man shoved them, just stuck his small hand on their hips, and drove them out of his way. If she hadn't been in pain, afraid and bleeding, she would've found it funny.

The two big men looked down at him, but their questioning glares didn't intimidate him. "I need the light." A second later, a lantern was handed to Caleb so the doctor could see. Jeni remained quiet, her eyes narrow and her breath shallow from pain. She focused on Caleb's face and tried to keep herself calm.

Her only worry was about her baby.

"It's a flesh wound… Just a crease." The doctor announced as he removed medical items from his bag. "I'll stitch it. How far along are you?" he asked.

"Six months," Caleb answered.

Looking pointedly at Jeni, he asked, "Is this your first child?" When Caleb looked like he would answer again, the doctor shook his head and waited for Jeni to speak.

Pain was etched in her voice. "Yes, this is our first." Jeni ground her teeth and nodded.

"This your husband?"

"Yes." She reached out for Caleb and cupped his face. He turned and placed a kiss on her palm. She closed her eyes and let the tears roll down her face. "Is the baby ok?"

"You were fortunate, my dear. The bullet grazed your belly but didn't go deep. I don't think you lost too much blood, and I've felt no sign of contractions since I sat down. Are you feeling any sort of cramping?"

She shook her head.

"I think you're going to be just fine, then."

More tears.

Caleb's eyes swam, too. She brushed a tear from his face and winced as the doctor placed the first stitch. Caleb bent to her and pressed his lips to her forehead. Watching her in pain, watching her bleed, was killing him.

With every stitch came more tears. Caleb did his best to offer as much support and love as he could. She kept telling herself that the baby was fine, she was fine, and Caleb was fine. They were all going to be ok.

They'd been lucky.

Again.

What would she have done if they'd lost the baby?

Her heart couldn't take the question.

When he finished, Dr. Jones spoke to Caleb. "You get her somewhere to rest a few days. If there's a hotel at the next stop, I don't even know where we are now; get her off and stay there. She needs at least three days before you take her home. Bedrest as much as possible. Keep the stitches clean and dry. If she has even the smallest sign of cramping or bleeding, you find the doctor. I think your biggest worry at this point is going to be an infection." He turned to her and added, "I'm impressed with how well you handled that situation. You're going to be an excellent mother. I wish you the best of luck. I'll be close by if you need me before we reach the next stop."

He slid out of the bunk and shook hands with Caleb. "Take care of her. Move her over to a clean bunk and then keep her still. I'll see to this man here, and then I'll be close enough to hear you if you call." Before he walked away, he shook his head and added, "She's really something."

Will helped Caleb move Jeni to the next bunk, and an attendant arrived to collect the bloody laundry. Once everyone was settled, and they'd made a plan, Caleb climbed into the bunk with Jeni and pulled her into his arms. He absorbed her sobs into his body as he rubbed her back and finally rested his hand on her belly.

He only had to wait a second for the familiar little kick against his palm.

The kick was the balm they both needed.

Chapter Nineteen

W hen the train pulled into the next station, they moved Jeni to the hotel. Caleb and Will stayed with her while Caine, Daniel, and Hank went back to the ranch.

They were all frustrated with her for ruining their plans. They were also all worried about her and the baby. She'd broken their confidence. They'd have to regroup, and then they could go again the following winter, when things quieted down. They'd have to protect her at the ranch for the rest of the summer, whether she liked it or not.

Caleb carried Jeni into the hotel room Will reserved for them and tucked her as gently as he could into the bed. With his emotions in turmoil, he sat with her and watched his wife sleep with his baby kicking away at his palm. She slept the better part of the first day. With the white covers pulled up to her chin, her red hair and pale complexion were all that was visible. Her face had no color, and no amount of reassurance from the local doctor would be as good as seeing her open her eyes.

As he watched her sleep and felt the life inside of her, it refueled his anger. He couldn't think of anything but the fact that she'd put herself in danger. She'd risked their child so selfishly. The more he watched her sleep, the angrier he became. He tried to reason with himself, to talk himself out of his anger, but every time it came back to the same thing.

She'd risked the baby.

Her selfishness was something he was not prepared to forgive.

When she awoke and reached for him, he left the room. He couldn't speak to her or look into her eyes. He still had no outlet for his anger. The choking sob he heard before the door slammed cut him to his core, but he didn't stop.

He found his way to the woodpile outside the hotel and helped himself to a little manual labor. He burned off some fury at the chopping block, but as soon as he set the ax down, his rage returned.

Selfish.

WHEN JENI OPENED HER EYES, CALEB WAS BESIDE HER. He'd pulled a chair up next to the bed, and his hand was resting in its favorite spot. The baby played with his warmth. She smiled and reached down to cover his hand with hers. Before she could, he'd pulled back and stood.

"Caleb?"

He turned and left the room.

Her heart broke.

It was several minutes before she could control her breathing and stop the sobs that racked her body and pulled her stitches painfully. The busy floral wallpaper and evening sunshine gave her plenty of things to stare at. She needed a distraction, and counting flowers became her hobby. She clutched at the white bedspread and stared at the wall.

"You scared us," Will said, startling her. He sat amongst the shadows, in an armchair in the corner, watching her. She hadn't seen him.

"I'm sorry."

"What the hell were you thinking?" Anger burned off of him, as it had from Caleb.

"I guess I wasn't." She stared at the door her husband had slammed. "I needed to be with him and I had a letter from my friends."

He didn't let her finish. "You derailed the entire mission."

"I wasn't trying to derail anything. I wanted to help. I hated being left behind, sure, but it wasn't just that. I couldn't watch my husband and best friend leave together to go into danger while they expected me to stay behind and knit booties."

"The baby needed you to be at home knitting booties, and we both know this isn't about me. It's about him." He leaned forward and rested his elbows on his knees, and continued. "You're going to have a hard time getting through to him. I've never seen him so angry."

"I know."

She groaned as she rolled onto her back. Her hands rubbing over the stretched skin of her stomach and pressing against the stitches as they pulled even tighter. Red flashed behind her eyelids with a shot of pain, but after a moment, it passed, and she moved more slowly onto her side.

"When Mr. James slid into the seat next to me, I knew I'd made a mistake and should've stayed home. I couldn't see it before that. I only saw the danger that my friends are in. But by then, it was too late. He caught me."

"You need to learn to follow directions, Jeni."

"Don't patronize me. That's half the reason I'm in this position. Maybe if you men hadn't made these plans without including me, I wouldn't have had my anger up in the first place."

"Protecting you and patronizing you are not the same things."

"They are the way you guys do it."

She braced herself and rolled away from him, then closed her eyes. Before she fell asleep, she heard him say, "We can't lose you or the baby, and you know it."

"You have to talk to her."

Caleb glanced at Will then resumed pacing the hall outside Jeni's room. "I will. I need to figure out what to do with all of this anger first."

"It would be so much easier if she were a man, and you could punch her."

"Tell me about it."

"You don't think I feel the same? She's so frustrating. But Jeni loves you, Caleb. She wasn't thinking, and she made a mistake. Give her a chance."

"Shit. I love her too. I love that baby growing inside of her. She risked my whole heart when she lit out of Hank's on that damn horse."

"Go back and talk to her. She said something about her friends being in danger. I'll go see what I can find to eat."

"She got a letter before I left. I'll go in soon. I'm not sure I can talk to her yet."

"Try. She still needs you."

He growled deep in his chest and turned back to the hotel room door. When he'd worn himself out at the woodpile, he'd come back but couldn't bring himself to go inside. He sat on the floor in the hallway. He still had to protect his family, even mad as hell.

She sat up in the bed when he entered. She had her book open but turned down in her lap. He couldn't help the glare he shot at her. He could not get past his fury. The tears on her face and her red-rimmed eyes added another element of struggle to his already stressed emotions. He wanted to shout at her and hold her tight at the same time.

Her lips trembled. "I'm so sorry."

"I don't want to hear it."

She blinked. "Are you going to hate me forever?"

"God damn it, Jeni. You know I don't hate you. I'm mad as hell, but I love you and our baby." He stalked over to the chair and threw himself down, his elbows tented on his outstretched knees and his head in his hands. "I'm not sure if I can even talk to you yet."

"Does it help that I know it's mostly my fault?"

"Not really. It fixes nothing. It takes nothing back. It doesn't change the fact that I saw a bleeding gunshot wound in your belly where my baby is growing. Do you have any idea what that did to me?"

"I have an idea." She rubbed a hand over the bandage. "I imagine you felt about the same as I felt when the bullet ripped through me.Or maybe you felt the way I did when I saw Scott bleeding and dying in the dirt. Or maybe you felt like I felt when Will was shot in the side. I think I can imagine how you felt."

She closed her eyes, swallowed twice, and fought back more tears. "I didn't know it was a graze. I only felt pain and blood and fear. I thought he had killed both of us." She held her belly with her hands and shuddered.

"You shouldn't have been there."

"I know."

"What were you thinking?"

"I keep trying to go back in my head. I was angry that you made plans for me without consulting me. I'm still angry about that. I should be part of the planning. Especially if your plan is to leave me behind and rush into danger. All I wanted was to be with you, but then I read Den's letter and I had to catch you. I had this idea that I could help every-body and protect my friends if I could just be with you. I hate the thought that something could happen to you. I… We need you."

"I need both of you. Safe," he said.

"What do we do now?" she asked.

"I don't know yet. The doctor said to keep you here for a few days, and that's what we're going to do. Any sign of trouble with the baby, and we'll get the town doctor. Will went over and let him know the situation, in case we need him."

"And after a few days?"

"We'll go home. We'll figure the rest out from there. This won't be the end, though; we can't leave Benson out there to hunt you. You've only delayed the inevitable and hurt yourself." He couldn't look at her. He turned and paced on the other side of the room. With Will gone, he needed to stay, but being close to her was driving him crazy.

"Feels like I hurt us more than I hurt myself." She broke, and he fought to keep from rushing to her and holding her. He wanted to go for another round at the woodpile.

"Will went to get food," he muttered as he left the room. If he had to sit there another minute with her crying, he would have pulled her into his arms. He ached to hold her, but he still itched to shake the shit out of her. The contradicting emotions were pulling him in every direction.

THE THREE DAYS PASSED WITH UNCOMFORTABLE tension. There was no evidence of distress to the baby, and Jeni was fine. They boarded the train that would return them to the ranch the following day.

"I'm not going back," Will said.

"What?" Caleb and Jeni blurted in unison.

"I'm heading on to Boston. I wired Dean two days ago, and he sent me a telegram back today. I'll connect with him, and then we're going to find this Benson character, rescue the Jacobs girl, and finish this."

"No," Jeni said. Tugging on his hand to bring him closer to her.

"It needs to be done. A promise is a promise, and we can't live like this forever. I'll be able to check on Denise and Sarah for you. You've been talking about them for days."

"It's a good idea," Caleb said. "Dean's already in with Benson. Maybe the two of you can get close enough."

Jeni clearly didn't agree. "Will, please. Please come home with us. Send a telegram and ask Dean to check on my friends."

Caleb watched as his brother and his wife shared a moment. It was strange that the sight of Will cradling her head in his hand didn't bring feelings of jealousy. Her hand cupping his face didn't either. They were close, and they had a special bond he appreciated and respected. There was no romance there, just pure friendship, and it felt good to him that his wife could have another man that she trusted.

Will had needed a relationship like this, too.

Caleb was still angry at Jeni to show such signs of affection. He couldn't bring himself to touch her unless she was sleeping, and then only to check on the baby. He didn't know what it was going to take for him to forgive her.

He knew he would, though. Eventually.

He loved her.

Will straightened up. "I'm going to take on the hunt for Mr. Jacobs's missing daughter Maggie. We promised him, and it's already been weeks since he died. We can't leave her in danger any longer." He ran his hand down Jeni's hair, and she turned her eyes pleadingly up to Caleb.

He shook his head. He wouldn't help her change Will's mind. Will was right, and she needed to trust him.

"I'm going to miss you so much," she said to Will.

"I'll miss you, too. Especially at breakfast time."

She laughed. It was one of their private jokes, Caleb knew. They had many jokes like that, but she didn't share them all with him.

"You'll keep in touch, right?"

"I'll telegram at least once a week." He kissed the top of her head. "I promise."

"Take care of her," he said to Caleb.

They gave a one-arm hug and patted each other on the back. "You know I will."

THE TRAIN RIDE BACK WAS EXCRUCIATING. SHE AND Caleb were together, and yet not together. They were miles apart emotionally, though they were sitting side by side.

Jeni's entire body hurt. But the emotional pain was worse than the physical. The crease from the gunshot and stitches on her already stretched skin took her breath away every time she moved. Caleb tried to help her be as comfortable as possible. Still, there was no warmth or affection in his gentle touches. He was helping the mother of his child, not the woman he adored.

It sliced her heart wide open.

The day was long, but the night was an eternity. They huddled into the bunk together with no intimacy between them. Their bodies spooned, but the sparks were gone.

In the middle of the night, she whispered into the dark, "I miss you."

Behind her, he whispered it back to her. "I miss you, too."

"How do we fix this?"

"I have been trying to figure it out all day."

"Me, too."

He placed his hand on her belly. "This is still the most important thing."

She placed her hand over his. "It is."

They agreed on that, but the coldness between them didn't go away. By the time they reached Hank's place, they were more on edge than when they'd boarded the train for home. They wanted the same things, but they didn't know how to manage it.

They hadn't even been able to really talk to each other.

―――――――

JENI'S APOLOGY TOUR BEGAN AT BREAKFAST THE NEXT morning. She started with Rose and Iris, while they all prepared the morning meal together. Rose had been more business and less friendly than usual, and Iris had taken the trouble to ignore her. They wanted to go home, in fact. But Caine had asked them to stay one more day to make sure that Jeni was ok.

"I'm so sorry to have caused you so much worry." Jeni placed her hand on Rose's shoulder and turned her. Iris looked at her, but Rose tried to avoid her. She saw Rose's eyes were swimming when she finally relented.

"We know."

"I wasn't thinking. Everyone warned me, and I didn't listen." She hugged Rose, who softened and hugged her back. Jeni felt Rose's tears on her cheek, and guilt overwhelmed her.

Iris reached out and touched Jeni's arm. "It's frustrating when the men decide for us and don't talk to us about it. Imagine how it feels for Rose and me when we raised the men making the choices for us!"

"I hadn't thought of that. How frustrating. Why do you listen to them?"

Iris approached and put both of her hands on Jeni's belly and said, "Because we listen to more than what they are saying with words." She rubbed a slow circle on either side of the abdomen and smiled when the baby kicked at her hand.

Jeni wilted at Iris's insight. She'd been so bent on rebellion, she hadn't thought to look deeper. "It was too late when I realized they were right, and I was risking too much."

"You can fix things now. Just be patient." Iris kissed her cheek and then left.

Rose kissed her cheek and squeezed her shoulders."It will be ok, sweetheart. I'm not mad, just anxious. You take it easy, and we'll all work it out." She followed her sister out of the room.

Jeni tracked Hank down, and then Caine, to apologize to each of them as well. They were both happy to have her home, but both said she had shaved years off of their lives. They hugged her and told her they were glad that the baby was doing ok and assured her that they loved her.

They were family.

Some of the chill had gone out of Caine's reaction to her, and she hoped they were going to be friends. He was her husband's twin brother; they sometimes felt each other's pain. She could not go through life with a gap between herself and her brother-in-law.

She had to wait two more days to talk to Daniel. Their conversation went much like she'd expected. He said all the same things as Hank and Caine. He loved her and worried about her and the baby. He was sweet and didn't lecture her about safety and better behavior. He knew she'd already received that lecture several times. She kissed him and knew they were fine.

Caleb was the holdout. She couldn't get him to come around.

It took a week for Jeni to get Caleb to move back to their house. He didn't want to be alone with her, she could tell. No matter what his excuses were, that was the real reason. She wanted to be home, and she wouldn't take no for an answer.

The first few days were exceptionally awkward. They moved around each other as if in a daze. Painfully polite and impersonal.

"Will you help me get the big tub in and fill it so I can take a bath?"

"Sure."

"Caleb?"

She waited until he looked up at her. "I want you back."

"I know. I do, too. I just don't know how to get back."

"Will you try something with me?"

He raised his eyebrows.

She walked up to him and put both hands on his firm biceps. "Kiss me."

He didn't move.

"Please, Caleb. I need you. I can't fix this alone." She leaned forward and pressed her belly against him until the baby kicked.

"You're not doing anything alone. We're all here for you."

"I've never felt more alone." She didn't let go of him. "I need you to love me."

"I love you. You know I do."

"I need you to *make love* to me."

He groaned and put his hands on her shoulders. When he pressed his forehead against hers, she felt like they were going to reconnect. He sighed and took a step back. "I'll go get the tub."

She didn't cry when he turned and left the room. She moved water to the stove to heat and collected her towels and soaps and things she wanted for her bath.

It took a long time to get the tub in and filled. It was a lot of work, and she appreciated he did it for her, even if he was still not ready to let her off the hook.

He sat in a chair near the fire when the tub was ready for her bath and watched her as she undressed and climbed in. She took a moment to check her side before lowering into the water. The stitches should be removed. Jeni wondered how long they were supposed to stay in. She hadn't thought to ask the doctor.

Caleb would know.

Jeni relaxed against the back of the tub and let the warm water wrap around her tired body. She let her mind wander to those happy months of sewing baby clothes and sleeping in her husband's lap.

A soft thump got her attention. Caleb stood next to the tub, naked. His clothes dropped in a heap on the floor.

"Slide up."

She moved forward, and he lowered himself behind her and pulled her into his arms. Neither of them spoke. They cradled each other in the warm water and enjoyed being close again.

When the water cooled, Caleb added more buckets of hot. He wasn't ready to end the closeness with his wife that he had so missed.

"You scared the shit out of me, Jeni. I can't get the image out of my head, the blood seeping out of your dress, the color draining from your face. It haunts me."

She turned her face and kissed his chest. "I know."

He let his hands roam over her body in lazy strokes.

Fire shot from his fingertips to his groin. The passion that he'd been suppressing ignited and spread through him in a warm glow. With a fingertip under her chin, he lifted her mouth to his.

The kiss they shared was soft, deep, and slow. The instant their mouths touched, everything changed.

He pushed her hair behind her shoulder and pressed his lips to the curve of her neck. "I want to get back to how it was."

"Thank God." With just a few words, they were on their way to healing their broken relationship.

Jeni turned in his arms to get better access to his mouth, and he took advantage of the position.

Jeni shifted, and he slid inside of her. There was no hurry as they both needed the slow simmering build and the connection. Caleb drank from her lips and let the love wash over him. He let the anger go. He needed his wife more than he needed his anger.

Her hands moved over his body in slow tracks of lava, melting the hardness away. With every touch, he softened. They didn't speak. They didn't need to. They let their hands stroke comfort into each other as their mouths mated.

Caleb helped her to stand up, and wearing only towels, they went to bed together.

WAKING UP WRAPPED AROUND HER NAKED HUSBAND IN the morning was the most amazing miracle of Jeni's life. Everything felt natural, safe, comfortable.

She was happy.

She reached for Caleb, and they came together again before breakfast.

"I missed you so much." She said with her hand rubbing the prickly stubble of his morning beard. "So much."

"I missed you, too." He kissed her in that long, slow way that she loved.

Jeni made breakfast, and Caleb made coffee.

Things were going to be ok.

Chapter Twenty

"You've got a letter." Daniel tossed it on the table as he walked into the kitchen, took a mug from the cabinet, and reached for the coffeepot. "I had a telegram from Will, too."

Jeni reached for the letter, laughing when her belly bumped the table. She had to walk around the table to get her hands on it. She recognized the handwriting. Denise. Oh, how she missed Denise. She cradled the letter to her chest and smelled it, hoping to get a whiff of her dear friend or a smell of home.

"How's Will?"

"He's back in Boston now. He and Dean were over in New York for a few days, but that turned out to be a dead end."

She missed Will. He'd kept his word so far and sent at least one telegram home each week. Caleb always left for work after breakfast, and every day, about an hour later, she got a pang of loneliness, missing her morning chat with her favorite friend. She sighed, hoping he'd find Miss Jacobs soon and come home to her. Every time she thought of him missing the birth of her baby, it made her sad.

She shook herself and turned to give her attention to Daniel.

Daniel took two plates from the cupboard and loaded one at a time before bringing them to the table. "They're following some other leads now. Looks like Benson has gone underground, but nobody is sure why. Some rumors floating around are that he's dead. Either way, people are letting go of some of their fear and beginning to talk."

Caleb entered and grabbed a mug and the coffee pot, set both on the table, and then heaped his own plate full of breakfast before taking his usual seat at the table. "Any news on Miss Jacobs?"

Jeni shook her head when Caleb cut a huge piece of pancake and shoved it into his mouth.

Men!

Daniel refilled his cup and set the coffeepot aside. "Nothing in the telegram on that this time. He'll chase down every lead, though. That's just his way."

Caleb nodded, and both men tucked into their breakfast like they'd not eaten in weeks.

Jeni laughed. It was always like this with the Maxwell men, as if they were starving to death. No matter how much food she cooked, they devoured every bit.

"If you two don't slow down, you'll have indigestion."

They both laughed at her and continued to eat.

She sighed. "I hope Will writes soon. I wish we had more details. I want to know where he's staying and what he's doing. I hope he'll go over and see Denise and Sarah while he's in Boston."

"He's keeping an eye on them." Caleb said.

"I know, but I secretly hope he'll fall in love with Denise and bring her home with him." She giggled.

Jeni spun the letter on the table. She ate her breakfast and listened to chatter about breeding programs, harvesting crops, and the weather. Her mind drifted into a daydream as her baby became active inside her belly. She smiled and rubbed her stomach. The sugar in the syrup must've given him a bit of energy.

Caleb's hand covered hers, and he leaned over and kissed the side of her head.

They had two weeks of lovely peace on the ranch. With Mr. Benson in hiding, even the gunslingers and bounty hunters had given up their pursuit. The men who'd come in the winter had done an excellent job of spreading the truth of the story around as they'd traveled back to their homes or other jobs, and as far as they could tell, they were safe for the time being.

"Go sit down and read your letter. I'll clean up." Caleb kissed her, and with a hand to the small of her back, sent her towards the living room. When she turned, he was watching her. He mimicked her as she waddled across the room, but the smile on his face was full of love.

Jeni felt guilty for leaving him to clean, but she

left him to do the job. He didn't mind doing it, and he knew how much she enjoyed letters from home. Denise must be about ready to deliver her baby by now. Sarah should be done with her fancy finishing school, too.

With a contented sigh, she settled down and opened her envelope.

———

DANIEL SMILED AND HANDED CALEB A DISH TO RINSE. "It's good to see you two back on track."

When Jeni had settled into the armchair by the window, Caleb turned back to the kitchen and grinned, "You're telling me."

"What changed?" Daniel asked.

"We worked it out." How they worked it out would remain between husband and wife. He smiled over at her. He never could've imagined that he could be so happy.

"I'm happy to see it. It's weird, but I sort of missed you two together."

Caleb nodded in understanding. "I remember for a long time, after Amy died, how hard it was to see Caine without her. They were always together, always touching. I was jealous because I'd never had anything like that before. Now that I have it, I can't even think about what he went through when he lost her." He stared at Jeni again, rocking in her chair and smiling at the paper in her hand. "I don't think I'd survive."

"I remember feeling that too." Daniel admitted.

He didn't say anything about feeling jealousy for the relationship between Caleb and Jeni. Still, Caleb had seen the proof of it in his eyes from time to time. He'd seen a desire for a similar bond in the eyes of all his brothers over the last half a year. They wanted to love for themselves, even if some of them would rather fight a bear than admit it. Caleb wanted to see them find it, too.

"When Jeni and I started to connect like that, it changed everything. I really treasured it. I know how special it is, and I know it can be taken away. In an instant. I don't take it for granted."

Daniel scoffed. "Looked like you were going to throw it away for a while there."

"It was a rough patch. We worked our way through it. And I expect it won't be our last. She seems to perk right up for a fight sometimes."

Daniel picked up a towel, snapped Caleb with it, then picked up a mug to dry. Together, the two of them had the kitchen put back together in no time.

Caleb worked as he talked, glancing from time to time at his beautiful, pregnant wife reading her letter by the fire, and his heart was filled

He nodded at the bread on the counter, and Daniel wrapped a loaf in a towel and tucked it into the breadbox. "I was so angry when she put herself in danger on the train like that. The problem was that I had no outlet for the anger." He gave a little snort. "Will said it would have been easier if she were a man so I could punch her." He laughed and turned, leaning a hip on the counter and crossing his arms over his chest. "It's true, though. At least when

I'm pissed at you, I can dot your eye. With her, there is no acceptable way to vent the anger."

Caleb watched her rub her belly as she perused her letter. She was so content. Jeni smiled at something on the page, and it stole his breath. For a while, she frowned and furrowed her brows, but in the end, she looked happy. She still had the power to make his heart skip.

"Instead of pushing her away," he went on, "I needed to pull her close. When I did, everything mended itself."

"I don't think I've ever heard you string so many words together at once in your life. Especially so many sentimental ones." Daniel nudged his good friend with an elbow to the ribs. Shoulder to shoulder, they stood, leaning against the counter and watched Jeni read. "It's nice. I really am happy for you."

Daniel said goodbye and grabbed his hat on his way to the door. Settling it on his head, he said goodbye to Jeni and let himself out.

Caleb joined Jeni near the fire. She lowered the letter to her lap with a contented smile pasted on her face. "Things are well in Boston for the moment. What was Daniel so serious about earlier?"

I think he's a little lonely." Caleb slid the curtain to shield Jeni's eyes from the sun.

Jeni folded her letter and slid it into the pocket of her apron. "He should look a little more closely at Opal. They would be a perfect match, and they're already such good friends."

Don't start matchmaking. That never ends well.

If they're meant to be together, they will find their way to each other."

Jeni shook her head.

Caleb smiled. She had every intention of of getting involved with his brother's love lives, and nobody was going to stop her. He chuckled and got up to head out to the barn.

Jeni tried to rise, gave up, and laughed. "I'm not so sure I can get up on my own."

With enjoyment, Caleb gave her his hand..

"I CAN'T READ THE WHOLE LETTER TO YOU BUT LISTEN to this, that rascal, Dylan Johnson, who Denise was engaged to, turned her down. He was engaged to another woman the whole time and now he is refusing that the baby could be his. She should have waited until they were married, but she thought it would be ok since they were engaged. That's what he said, and she trusted him completely. What kind of man would treat a woman like that?" Jeni pounded her fist against the table. If she could go to Boston, she'd search that man out and give him a piece of her mind. She hoped he would run into Sarah, then he'd be sorry.

"I'm so mad I could spit nails," she went on. "I bet Sarah had to be restrained from hunting him down. I wish I could go to Boston and shoot him myself.

"Tell Daniel to send a telegram to Will. Tell him to go find Dylan Johnson and shoot him for me."

She aggressively wiped at a spot on the table with a rag. "Mr. Benson is either dead or in hiding. Nobody knows what's going on with him, but it's rumored that his enterprise is shut down. Denise said they heard that there was some sort of big criminal investigation going on. I guess it's in the papers and everything.

"Do we get copies of the Boston papers out here? Probably not. Well, maybe. Anyway… Nobody seems to know what is going on, but I think it's probably a far more pressing issue than his search for me. I'll sleep easier now." She tossed the rag toward the cleaning bucket and missed, sloshing water on the floor.

Caleb pressed her back down into her chair and cleaned it up himself. "We don't know for sure. I won't rest easy until I know he's dead."

She continued as if he hadn't spoken. "Sarah's found herself in some kind of trouble and is considering going over to see Mrs. Phillips at the Mail-Order Bride agency. When I was looking into it, she thought I was insane, but now that she's in need of a quick solution, it's not such a bad idea. Ha. We'll see how that goes for her.

"She witnessed a bank robbery or something, and now someone's following her. Her daddy won't let her come back to work on the ranch like she thought he would. He's always been a hard man, for all that she loves him still. He's forcing her to stay in town and wear fancy dresses and look for a fancy husband. She doesn't want any part of that. Actually, being a mail-order bride is perfect for her. She'd love the adventure of it all. Her poor husband, though…."

Jeni shrugged and continued to ramble on, grateful that Caleb would listen to her chatter about home and people he'd never met. She loved sharing news of people from home, and sometimes he said he felt like he knew them personally.

Caleb had once told her he found it charming, how she got all fired up over her friend's lives. She couldn't help it. Jeni adored Denise and Sarah. She missed them and hoped they would come to Hope. Sarah could marry Hank, and Denise could marry Will, and they could all live happily ever after.

She smiled to herself. She would write to Will again and insist that he visit her friends. Denise would charm him, and he'd fall in love with her, she was sure. Now that she was happily married, she could think of nothing but seeing her friends settled likewise.

Jeni watched Caleb as he did her work for her. He never stopped worrying or trying to accommodate. The summer of hard work on the ranch had done him good. He'd filled out and bulked up, and her handsome husband was more gorgeous than ever. The exaggerated emotions of pregnancy only seemed to fill her with more love for him. Her eyes turned moist as she studied him, scrubbing laundry and listening to her carry on.

The baby rolled, and she pressed down to get a heel out of her ribs. She thought about Scott. There were still so many things about how her relationship with Scott had gone that she regretted, but she would always think of him with love and gratitude. If she hadn't been so blind, she might have spared his life. Reverend Simon had told her so many times, *"All things happen for a reason, and God has a plan."*

She continued to press that pesky little foot into a more comfortable position, but her stubborn little angel persisted. She laughed; perhaps it was a sign that this was Scott's child after all.

JENI WAS CONSTANTLY NUDGING THE BABY AWAY FROM her ribs these days. That little one was going to be a handful, and Caleb couldn't wait to meet him. He watched the sweet smile on her face; she was thinking about Scott. Whenever the baby got up in her ribs like that, she'd think of his cousin, and that sweet expression would spread through her features.

He finished the chores and put things away. When he returned, she was still in the same position, lost in her thoughts. Caleb took the seat next to her and pulled her into his lap. He only had a little while before he had to head out to work, but he'd take every minute he could get with her in his arms.

Her body relaxed against his without hesitation, filling him with warmth and surrounding him with her rose scent. She tucked her head under his chin and breathed him in just the same as he did.

When her breathing evened out and her body went boneless, he kissed her head and smiled. He didn't put her down right away. He sat in the kitchen chair and said a prayer of thankfulness and hope. He prayed for their future and for the health of their baby.

Holding his family in his arms like this was like having the whole world in his arms. When he finally admitted to himself, he wouldn't get any work done, he stood with her in his arms and carried her to the bedroom.

JENI STRETCHED AND MOANED AS SHE TIPPED HER FACE up to the glorious colors of the Montana sunset. She'd nearly finished pulling the ripe tomatoes from her garden. The dirt and tomatoes released such rich perfume into the air that she spent as much time as her back would allow working in the soil.

She was living her dream, but it was nothing like she'd imagined. She had everything she'd ever wanted, and more.

She had love, a family, and a baby on the way, but also respect. Jeni filled her lungs with clean air, feeling secure and hopeful for a beautiful future.

She thought she needed love and safety, and she had those things. She'd needed so much more than she knew, though, and she would fight to keep what she had, and treasure it forever.

Looking up, she saw Caleb leaving the barn. He'd gone in with his chestnut gelding twenty minutes earlier, both looking hard-worked and ready for food. He hadn't seen her, so she could study him. He looked at the house and smiled, but diverted his steps to the pump in the yard. He always cleaned up before he came home to her.

Caleb stripped to the waist and then pumped water over his head.

When he stood, he caught sight of her in the garden, and his smile stretched all the way across his face. He transformed from handsome to gorgeous; and her breath hitched in her chest as her heartbeat sped. He turned to head in her direction, and she couldn't tear her eyes from him.

He was her husband.

She'd never get enough of him.

He pulled her into his arms and she knew he was everything that she would ever need.

Even as she had that thought, the baby kicked against his palm.

They were everything she'd ever need.

WHY WON'T ROGER BENSON LEAVE JENI ALONE? IF YOU want to know, you'll have to continue the series. Sarah Forbes is going to shake things up for Caine Maxwell in Sarah Finds Freedom!

AS I'VE MENTIONED BEFORE, REVIEWS ARE MORE valuable than gold. I'd be grateful if you'll take a moment to leave a few lines for the readers to come.

THE
MAXWELL
BRIDES
SERIES
BOOK 2

Sarah
finds
freedom

KRISSYANN
GRANGER

Chapter 1

J uly 1885

Of all the goddamn lowdown, harebrained ideas!

What the hell was she thinking?

Just keep breathing!

"Sarah Forbes, you're an idiot," she whispered as she rocked with the stagecoach and kicked herself. She longed to escape her father's control, but not like this. She wanted to scream, to cry, to shoot something, to run away—anything.

She was good and trapped..

She was going to be sick.

Sarah filled her lungs with as much air as she could manage and blew it out slowly. She was strong enough to get through anything if she could just keep breathing and take things one step at a time.

From the top of her deep peacock blue feathered hat to the bottom of her shiny black boots, she'd taken special care to look perfect. Her traveling suit, an exact match for her hat, was as neat as possible after nearly a week of travel. The warm brown hair under her too-fancy hat had been coiffed precisely. Her gloved hands rested primly in her lap. A good first impressions was everything.

She'd heard about first impressions a million times in finishing school.

Oh, how she hoped it was true.

Grateful that the coach had no other passengers watching her, she struggled to breathe through the bumping and rocking. She'd never stop cursing her damned corset. Her calm appearance boiled down to good training. Finishing school, while mostly torturous, had benefits.

Faking calm being one of them.

Sarah could handle herself under pressure. Point her at a wild horse and she'd break him. Heck, even in the middle of a bank robbery she'd been cool as a cucumber. That's why this anxiety was getting the best of her, it was an unfamiliar feeling, and it was not something she intended to get used to. The best she could do under the circumstances was to hold her head high and try to fool herself. It was too much to ask for more than that.

Her heart rate had been speeding out of control for nearly a week. The weight on her chest grew by the hour, and the urge to tear her hair out increased exponentially as she neared her destination. She clung to her training and practiced her best impression of calm.

She was pretty enough. Not as pretty as her

friends, but she didn't send children running in fear. Her father kept her outfitted in only the best clothes, and as much as she hated it, she had a talent for styling herself attractively. She was small, barely five feet tall, with a slim build. Her petite size stood in opposition to her enormous personality, and it often gave the wrong impression. Her looks and sass were a combination that either attracted people or turned them away. As much as she looked the part of a lady, she still struggled to manage herself as one. Her language and temper were mighty tough to wrangle sometimes.

Finishing school had its limits.

She smiled to herself; she needed to make a good impression, and she could manage that. At least for a little while.

The stagecoach hit a rough patch of road, and for the next two minutes, Sarah's brain drained as her lungs expelled all of their air. The bones of her corset dug in hard, and she clutched the side of the carriage, trying to keep her seat.

Thank God for a short stagecoach ride.

She steadied the basket rocking at her feet as she tried to avoid smashing into the walls. The inside of the coach was roasting hot, which did nothing to soothe her nerves. She didn't want to arrive with sweat dripping down her back, but that's how she would show up. It was hardly an impression she wanted to give, but stagecoach travel in the middle of a midwestern summer was a sweaty adventure, no matter how much of a lady one was trying to be.

She beat at the dust on her skirt, making sure not to brush any into the basket on the floor.

As the road leveled back out, she struggled to fill her lungs with air, choking instead on dust.

The scenery flew by the window, and Sarah enjoyed the rise of purple mountains in the distance. She rocked and watched as her mind wandered, and she imagined how her new friends and family would receive her. People generally either liked her right away, or they didn't; there never seemed to be any in-between. She would never be universally likable, as her dear friend Denise. The thought of Denise shook her heart. She missed her so much already.

Women either enjoyed her sarcasm and energy, or they found her crass. Men judged her as unlady-like and challenging, or they thought her funny.

How would they find her in Hope, Montana Territory?

Her delicate features gave the appearance of vulnerability and weakness, which masked the strength of her spirit and considerable skills. It caused people to misjudge her, which she'd learned to take advantage of. All it took was one look at her pouty lips, honey brown eyes, and pointed little chin, and people thought she was helpless. She didn't enjoy being patronized, but she was smart enough to use her fragile appearance as a weapon when she needed it.

Sarah was not a child.

Fancy finishing school in Boston didn't change

who she was at heart. She was still the cowboy her father raised her to be, and that would never change.

She just did it with excellent posture, and her pinky raised.

Sarah laughed at herself for that. She imagined breaking a horse with a delicate china teacup in her hand, pinky up. She sighed as deeply as her corset would allow. After faking perfect manners for three years, she was dying to shuck the corset and get back to work.

She'd been raised by cowboys, and they'd raised her rough. Sarah could out-shoot and out-ride almost all the boys she'd grown up with. She'd learned to fight smart, to use her intelligence, speed, and agility where she lacked physical strength. Sarah could throw a knife as competently as any man and always wore one strapped to her thigh. She slid one gloved pinky to the right and fondled the comforting hard edge beneath her skirt.

That's why she followed through with this stupid plan, and that's why she'd stick with it. It was this or a gilded cage. No matter what this was, it was better than the alternative.

As soon as she entered finishing school, her father expected her to be a different person. As if she could throw off who she was and become someone else. It filled her with resentment, and it ruined her reputation—the one that mattered.

Once the farmhands saw her as pretty, they stopped seeing her as capable, and losing their respect was a devastating blow. She'd tried to convince them she was the same girl she'd always been, but they couldn't see her passed the dresses and coiffed hair.

They thought her better suited to embroidering cushions than breaking horses. She'd show them.

There would be no gilded cage for her.

Sarah would find her own future, because, no matter what happened, she'd be free. So there she sat, primly, on the seat of the coach, taking her future into her own hands. Hope and prayers fueled her journey; they were all she had. She grinned down at the basket on the floor.

They were almost all she had.

Read the rest of Sarah's story here https://amzn.to/3O2QeNn

About the Author

When Krissyann Granger isn't writing historical romance novels or chasing children, you can find her learning a new skill or craft. A lifelong lover of fiber arts, Krissyann creates one of a kind items. Using her own hand dyed, and sometimes hand spun yarn, she designs and knits clothing for herself and her children. Between knitting, hiking the Adirondack High Peaks, and painting furniture, Krissyann keeps quite busy. Krissyann shares her struggles with ADHD and writing on her Facebook page.

Made in the USA
Monee, IL
27 June 2023

37488693R00203